Praise for The Morganville Vampire novels

'An electrifying, enthralling
coming-of-age supernatural tale'
The Best Reviews

'A solid, utterly compelling story that you will find
addictive and hypnotic. If Rachel Caine is not on
your auto-buy list, put her there immediately,
if not sooner'
The Eternal Night

'Rachel Caine brings her brilliant ability to blend
witty dialogue, engaging characters,
and an intriguing plot'
Romance Reviews Today

'A rousing horror thriller that adds a new
dimension to the vampire mythos'
Midwest Book Review

The Dead Girls' Dance

The Morganville Vampires

BOOK TWO

RACHEL CAINE

This edition first published in Great Britain in 2008 by
Allison & Busby Limited
13 Charlotte Mews
London, W1T 4EJ
www.allisonandbusby.com

A CIP catalogue record for this book is available from
the British Library.

First published in the USA in 2007 by NAL Jam,
an imprint of New American Library,
a division of Penguin Group (USA) Inc.

10 9 8 7 6 5

ISBN 978-0-7490-7986-4

Typeset in 10.5/14 pt Sabon by
Terry Shannon

Printed and bound in Great Britain by
CPI Bookmarque Ltd, Croydon, Surrey

RACHEL CAINE is the author of more than fifteen novels, including the Weather Warden series. She was born at White Sands Missile Range, which people who know her say explains a lot. She has been an accountant, a professional musician, and an insurance investigator, and still carries on a secret identity in the corporate world. She and her husband, fantasy artist R. Cat Conrad, live in Texas with their iguanas, Pop-eye and Darwin, a *mali uromastyx* named (appropriately) O'Malley, and a leopard tortoise named Shelley (for the poet, of course).

www.rachelcaine.com.

*For Ter, who helped lay
the cornerstone of Morganville.*

*For Katy, who helped me through
the plot jitters!*

Acknowledgments

Musical inspiration from Joe Bonamassa,
a genius at his art.

Editorial excellence from Liz Scheier,
truly a master.

And a special shout-out to my friends at
Mysterious Galaxy bookstore in San Diego!

CHAPTER ONE

It didn't happen, Claire told herself. *It's a bad dream, just another bad dream. You'll wake up and it'll be gone like fog…*

She had her eyes squeezed tight shut. Her mouth felt dry, shrivelled-up, and she was pressed against Shane's hot, solid side, curled up on the couch in the Glass House.

Terrified.

It's just a bad dream.

But when she opened her eyes, her friend Michael was still dead on the floor in front of her.

'Shut those girls up, Shane, or I will,' Shane's father snapped. He was pacing the wooden floor, back and forth, hands clasped behind him. He wasn't looking at Michael's body, shrouded under a thick, dusty velvet curtain, but it was *all* Claire could see, now that she'd opened her eyes again. It was as big as the world, and it wasn't a dream, and it wasn't going away. Shane's dad was here, and he was terrifying, and Michael—

Michael was dead. Only Michael had already been dead, hadn't he? Ghostly. Dead during the day...alive at night...

Claire realised she was crying only when Shane's dad turned on her, staring with red-rimmed eyes. She hadn't felt that scared when she'd stared into vampire eyes...well, maybe once or twice, because Morganville was a scary place, generally, and the vampires were pretty terrifying.

Shane's father – Mr Collins – was a tall, long-legged man, and his hair was wild and curly and going grey. Long enough to reach the collar of his leather jacket. He had dark eyes. Crazy eyes. A scruffy beard. And a huge scar running across his face, puckered and liver coloured.

Yeah, definitely scary. Not a vampire, just a man, and that made him scary in whole different ways.

She sniffled and wiped her eyes and quit crying. Something in her said, *Cry later; survive now.* She figured that voice had spoken inside of Shane, too, because Shane wasn't looking at the velvet-covered sprawl of his best friend's body. He was watching his father. His eyes were red, too, but there were no tears.

Now Shane was scaring her, too.

'Eve,' Shane said softly, and then, louder, 'Eve! Put a sock in it!'

Their fourth roommate, Eve, was collapsed in an awkward heap against the far wall by the bookcases, as far from Michael's body as she could get. Knees up, head down, she was crying hard and hopelessly. She looked up when Shane yelled her name, and her face was streaked with black from running mascara, half her Goth white make-up gone. She had on her death's-head Mary Jane shoes, Claire noticed. She didn't know why that seemed important.

Eve looked completely lost, and Claire slipped off the couch and went to sit beside her. They put their arms around each other. Eve smelt of tears and sweat and some kind of sweet vanilla perfume, and she couldn't seem to stop shaking. Shock. That was what they always said on TV, anyway. Her skin felt cold.

'Shhhh,' Claire whispered to her. 'Michael's OK. It's all going to be OK.' She didn't know why she said that – it was a lie; it had to be a lie; they'd all seen...what happened...but something told her it was the right thing to say. And sure enough, Eve's sobbing slowed, then stopped, and she covered her face with shaking hands.

Shane hadn't said anything else. He was still watching his dad, with the kind of intense stare most guys reserved for people they'd like to pound into hamburger. If his dad noticed, he clearly didn't care. He continued to pace, up and down. The guys he'd brought with him – walking slabs of muscle in black motorcycle leather, shaved heads and tattoos and everything – were standing in the corners, arms folded. The one who'd killed Michael looked bored as he flipped the knife in his fingers.

'Get up,' Shane's dad said. He'd stopped pacing, and was standing right in front of his son. 'Don't you dare give me any crap, Shane. I told you to stand up!'

'You didn't have to do that,' Shane said, and slowly stood, feet slightly apart. Ready to take (or give) a punch, Claire thought. 'Michael wasn't any threat to you.'

'He's one of them. Undead.'

'I said he wasn't a threat!'

'And *I* say that you just don't want to admit your friend's turned freak of nature on you.' Shane's dad reached out and awkwardly punched Shane on the shoulder. It was supposed to be a gesture of affection, Claire supposed. Shane just rode with the blow. 'Anyway, done is done. You know why we're here. Or do you need a reminder?'

When Shane didn't answer, his father reached into his leather jacket and took out a handful of photographs. He threw them at Shane. They bounced off of Shane's chest, and he reflexively tried to catch them, but some drifted free and fell to the wood floor. Some slid over towards Claire and Eve.

'Oh God,' Eve whispered.

They were pictures of Shane's family, Claire guessed – Shane as a cute little boy, arm around an even tinier little girl with a cloud of curly black hair. A pretty woman standing behind them, and a man she could barely recognise as Shane's dad. No scar, back then. Hair cut short. He looked...normal. Smiling and happy.

There were other pictures, too. Eve was staring at one of them, and Claire couldn't make any sense of it. Something black and twisted and—

Shane bent over and snatched it up, fumbling it back into the pile.

His house burnt. He got out. His sister wasn't so lucky.

Oh *God*, that twisted thing was Alyssa. That was Shane's sister. Claire's eyes filled up with tears, and she covered her mouth with both hands to hold in a scream, not because what was in the picture was gross – it was – but Shane's *own father* had made him look at it.

That was cruel. Really cruel. And she knew it wasn't the first time.

'Your mother and sister are both dead because of this place, because of the *vampires*. You didn't forget that, did you, Shane?'

'I didn't forget!' Shane shouted. He kept trying to make the pictures fit into a neat stack, but he didn't look at them at all. 'I dream about them every night, Dad. Every night!'

'Good. It was you got this started. You'd better remember that, too. Can't back out now.'

'I'm not backing out!'

'Then what's all this crap, *Things have changed, Dad?*' Shane's dad mimicked him, and Claire wanted to punch him, never mind that he was about four times her size and probably a whole lot meaner. 'You hook up with your old friends and next thing I know, you lose your nerve. That thing was Michael, right? The Glass kid?'

'Yes.' Shane's throat worked hard, and Claire saw tears glitter in his eyes. 'Yeah, it was Michael.'

'And these two?'

'Nobody.'

'That one looks like another vamp.' Shane's father fixed his red-rimmed glare on Eve, and took a step towards where Claire and Eve were huddled on the floor.

'You leave her alone!' Shane dropped the pictures into a pile on the couch and jumped into his father's path, fists clenched. His dad's eyebrows raised, and he gave Shane a scar-twisted grin. 'She's not a damn vampire. That's Eve Rosser, Dad. Remember Eve?'

'Huh,' his father said, and stared at Eve for a few seconds before shrugging. 'Turned into a wannabe, then, just about as bad in my book. What about the kid?'

He was talking about Claire.

'I'm not a kid, Mr Collins,' Claire said, and clambered to her feet. She felt awkward, all strings and wires, nothing working right. Her heart was hammering so hard, it hurt to breathe. 'I live here. My name is Claire Danvers. I'm a student at the university.'

'Are you.' He didn't make it a question. 'You look a little young.'

'Advanced placement, sir. I'm sixteen.'

'Sweet sixteen.' Mr Collins smiled again, or tried to – the scar pulled the right side of his mouth down. 'Never been kissed, I'll bet.'

She felt her face go red. Couldn't stop it, or keep herself from looking at Shane. Shane's jaw was set tight, muscles fluttering. He wasn't looking at anything in particular.

'Oho! So it's like that. Well, you watch yourself around the jailbait, my boy.' Still, Shane's dad looked weirdly pleased. 'My name's Frank Collins. Guess you figured out that I'm this one's father, eh? Used to live in Morganville. I've been gone a few years now.'

'Since the fire,' Claire said, and swallowed hard. 'Since Alyssa died. And…Shane's mom?' Because Shane had never said a word about her.

'Molly died later,' Mr Collins said. 'After we left. Murdered by the vamps.'

Eve spoke for the first time – a soft, tentative voice. 'How did you remember? About

Morganville, after you left town? I thought nobody did, once they left.'

'Molly remembered,' Mr Collins replied. 'Little bit at a time. She couldn't forget Lyssa, and that opened the door, inch by inch, until it was all there. So we knew what we had to do. We had to bring it down. Bring it all down. Right, boy?'

Shane nodded. It didn't look like agreement so much as a wish not to get smacked for disagreeing.

'So we spent time preparing, and then I sent Shane here back to Morganville to map the town for us, identify targets, do all the stuff we wouldn't have time to do once we rolled in. Couldn't wait any longer once he yelled for help, though. Came running.'

Shane looked sick. He wouldn't look at Eve, or Claire, or Michael's body. Or his father. He just – stared. There were tear tracks on his cheeks, but Claire couldn't remember seeing him cry, really.

'What are you going to do?' Claire asked faintly.

'First thing, I guess we bury that,' Mr Collins said, and nodded towards Michael's shrouded body. 'Shane, best you stay out of the way—'

'No! No, don't you touch him! I want to do it!'

Mr Collins gave him a long frowning look. 'You know what we're going to have to do' – he glanced at Eve and Claire – 'to make sure he doesn't come back.'

'That's folklore, Dad. You don't have to—'

'That's the way we're going to do things. The right way. I don't want your friend coming back at me next time the sun goes down.'

'What is he talking about?' Claire whispered to Eve. Sometime in the last few minutes, Eve had gotten up to stand next to her, and their hands were clasped. Claire's fingers felt cold, but Eve's were like ice.

'He's going to put a stake in his heart,' Eve said numbly. 'Right? And garlic in his mouth? And—'

'You don't need all the details,' Mr Collins interrupted. 'Let's get this done, then. And once we're finished, Shane's going to draw us a map of where to find the high-rolling vampires of Morganville.'

'Don't you know?' Claire asked. 'You lived here.'

'Doesn't work like that, little girl. Vamps don't trust us. They move around, they have all kinds of Protection to keep themselves safe from retribution. But my boy's found a way. Right, Shane?'

'Right,' Shane said. His voice sounded absolutely flat. 'Let's get this done.'

'But...Shane, you can't—'

'Eve, *shut up*. Don't you get it? There's nothing we can do for Michael now. And if he's dead, it won't matter what we do to him. Right?'

'You *can't*!' Eve yelled it. '*He isn't dead!*'

'Well,' Mr Collins said, 'I guess that'll be his

problem when we plant a stake in him and chop off his head.'

Eve screamed into her clenched fists, and collapsed to her knees. Claire tried to hold her up, but she was more solid than she looked. Shane instantly whirled and crouched next to her, hovering protectively and glaring at his father and the two motorcycle dudes standing guard over Michael's body.

'You're a bastard,' he said flatly. 'I told you, Michael was no threat to you before, and he's no threat now. You killed him already. Let it go.'

For answer, Shane's father nodded to his two friends – accomplices? – who then reached down, seized hold of Michael's body, and dragged him out and around the corner to the kitchen door. Shane bolted back to his feet.

His father stepped into his path and backhanded him across the face, hard enough to stagger him. Shane put up his palms – defence, not offence. Claire's heart sank.

'Don't,' Shane panted. 'Don't, Dad. Please don't.'

His father lowered the fist he'd raised for a second blow, looked down at his son, and turned away. Shane stood there, shaking, eyes cast down, until his father's footsteps moved away, towards the kitchen.

Then Shane spun around, lunged forward, and

grabbed Claire and Eve by the arms. 'Come on!' he hissed, and towed them both stumbling towards the stairs. 'Move!'

'But—,' Claire protested. She looked over her shoulder. Shane's father had gone to look out the window, presumably at whatever they were doing in the backyard (oh God) to Michael's body. 'Shane—'

'Upstairs,' he said. He didn't leave them much choice; Shane was a big guy, and this time he was using his muscle. By the time Claire got herself together, they were upstairs, in the hallway, and Shane was shoving open the door to Eve's room. 'Inside, girls. Lock the door. I mean it. Don't open it for anybody but me.'

'But...Shane!'

He turned to Claire, took hold of both of her shoulders in those big hands, and leant forward to plant a warm kiss on her forehead. 'You don't know these guys,' he said. 'You're not safe. Just...stay in there until I get back.'

Eve, looking dazed, murmured, 'You have to stop them. You can't let them hurt Michael!'

Shane locked eyes with Claire, and she saw the grim sadness. 'Yeah,' he said. 'Well, that's pretty much done. Just – I have to look out for you now. It's what Michael wants.'

Before Claire could summon up anything else in protest, he pushed her back over the threshold and slammed the door. He banged on it once with his fist. 'Lock it!'

She reached up and flipped the dead bolt, then turned the old-fashioned key, as well. She stayed where she was, because she could feel, somehow, that Shane hadn't moved away.

'Shane?' Claire pressed herself against the door, listening. She thought she could hear his uneven breathing. 'Shane, don't let him hurt you again. *Don't.*'

She heard a breathless sound that was more like a sob than a laugh. 'Yeah,' Shane agreed faintly. 'Right.'

And then she heard his footsteps moving away, down the hall to the stairs.

Eve was sitting on her bed, staring into space. The room smelt like a fireplace, thanks to the fire that had raged next door, in Claire's room, but there was only some smoke damage, nothing really serious. And besides, with all the black Goth stuff everywhere, you couldn't even really tell.

Claire sat down on the bed beside Eve. 'Are you OK?'

'No,' Eve said. 'I want to go look out the window. But I shouldn't, right? I shouldn't see what they're doing.'

'No,' Claire agreed, and swallowed hard. 'Probably not a good idea.' She rubbed Eve's back gently and thought about what to do...and that wasn't much. It wasn't like allies were exactly falling off the trees around here... Besides Shane, they had nobody else. Their second-best choice was a vampire.

How scary was *that*?

Still, she *could* call Amelie. But that was a little like arming a nuclear weapon to take care of an ant problem. Amelie was so badass, the other badass vampires backed down without a fight. She'd said, *I will make it known that you are not to be troubled. However, you must not further disturb the peace. If you do, and it is your fault, I will be forced to reconsider my decision. And that would be...*

'Unfortunate,' Claire finished aloud, in a whisper. Yeah. Pretty unfortunate. And there was no way that this didn't constitute disturbing the peace – or wouldn't, as soon as Shane's dad got rolling. He'd come to kill vampires, and he wasn't going to be stopped by any little considerations like, oh, his son's life and safety.

No, not a good idea to call Amelie.

Who else? Oliver? Oliver wasn't exactly at the top of Claire's Best Friends Forever list, although in the beginning she'd thought he was pretty cool, for an old guy. But he'd been playing her, and he was the second-most badass vamp in town. Who'd use them, and this situation, against Amelie if he could.

So no. Not Oliver, either. The police were

bought and paid for by the vampires. Her teachers at school...no. None of them had impressed her as being willing to stand up to pressure.

Mom and Dad? She shuddered to think what would happen if she put in a frantic yell to them... For one thing, they'd already had their memories altered by Morganville's strange psychic field, or so she assumed, since they'd forgotten all about ordering her home for living off campus. With boys. Mom and Dad weren't exactly the kind of backup she needed, not up against Shane's dad and his bikers.

Her cousin Rex...now, there was an idea. No, Rex had been sent to jail three months ago. She remembered Mom saying so.

Face facts, Danvers. There's nobody. Nobody coming riding to the rescue.

It was her, Eve, and Shane against the world.

So the odds were about three billion to one.

CHAPTER TWO

It was a long, long day. Claire eventually stretched out on one side of the bed, Eve on the other, each wrapped in her own separate cocoon of misery and heartache.

They didn't talk much. There didn't seem to be a lot to talk about.

It was almost dark when the doorknob rattled, sending Claire into a heart-pounding terror seizure; she advanced slowly, and whispered, 'Who is it?'

'Shane.'

She unlocked fast and opened up. Shane came in, head down, carrying a tray on which sat two bowls of chilli – which made sense, because it was nearly the only thing Shane knew how to fix. He set it down on the edge of the bed, next to Eve, who was sitting like an unstuffed rag doll, limp with grief and dejection.

'Eat something,' he said. Eve shook her head.

Shane picked up a bowl and shoved it in her direction; she took it just to avoid wearing it, and glared at him.

Claire saw her expression change into something else. Blank at first, then horrified.

'It's nothing,' Shane said as Claire came around to see. It wasn't nothing. It was bruises, dark ones, spilling over his cheek and jaw. Shane avoided looking at her. 'My fault.'

'Jesus,' Eve whispered. 'Your dad—'

'My fault,' Shane snapped back, got up, and headed for the door. 'Look, you don't understand. He's right, OK? I was wrong.'

'No, I don't understand,' Claire said, and grabbed his arm. He pulled free without any effort at all and kept walking. 'Shane!'

He paused in the doorway and looked back at her. He looked bruised, beaten, and sullen, but it was the desperation in his eyes that scared her. Shane was always strong, wasn't he? He had to be. She needed him to be.

'Dad's right,' he said. 'This town is sick, it's poisoned, and it's poisoning us, too. We can't let it beat us. We have to take them out.'

'The vampires? Shane, that's stupid! You can't! You know what'll happen!' Eve said. She put the bowl of chilli back on the tray and got off the bed, looking tear-streaked and forlorn but more like herself. 'Your dad's crazy. I'm sorry, but he is. And you can't let him drag you down with him. He's going to get you killed, and Claire and me, too. He already—' She caught her breath and gulped. 'He already got Michael. We can't let him do this. Who knows how many people are going to get hurt?'

'Like Lyssa got hurt?' Shane asked. 'Like my mom? *They killed my mom, Eve!* They were willing to burn us up in this house yesterday, don't forget, and that included Michael.'

'But—'

'This town is bad,' Shane said, and looked at Claire, almost pleading. 'You understand, right? You understand that there's a whole world out there, a whole world that isn't like this?'

'Yes,' she said faintly. 'I understand that. But—'

'We're doing this. And then we're getting out of this place.'

'With your father?' Eve managed to put a whole dictionary of contempt into that. 'I don't think so. I look good in black, but not so great in black and blue.'

Shane flinched. 'I didn't say... Look, just the three of us. We get out of town while my dad and the others—'

'We run?' Eve shook her head. 'Brilliant. And when the vamps have a big party and roast your dad and his buddies, what then? Because they're definitely going to come looking for us. Nobody escapes who had any part in killing a vampire, you know that. Unless you really believe that your dad and his idiot muscle are going to be able to take down hundreds of vamps, all their human allies, the cops, and, for all I know, the U.S. Marines.'

'Eat your damn chilli,' Shane said.

'Not without something to drink. I know your chilli.'

'Fine! I'll get you Cokes!' He slammed the door behind him. 'Lock it!'

Claire did. This time, Shane didn't linger in the hall; she heard the hard thump of his boots as he went downstairs.

'Did you have to do that?' she asked Eve. She leant against the door and folded her arms.

'Do what, exactly?'

'He's confused. He lost Michael, his dad's got him—'

'Say it, Claire: his dad's got him brainwashed. Worse. I think his dad's beaten the fight out of him. He's certainly beaten the brains out of him.' Eve wiped at her face impatiently; there were more tears streaming down her cheeks, but it was more like water escaping under pressure than real sobs. 'His dad wasn't always like this. He used to be...well, not nice, because he was kind of a drunk, but better. Way better than this. After Lyssa he just went...crazy. I didn't know about Shane's mom. I thought she just, you know...killed herself. Shane never really said.'

Claire hadn't heard any footsteps on the stairs, but she heard and felt a soft knock through the door, and then a rattle of the doorknob. She unlocked and swung it open, holding out her hands for the Cokes she expected Shane to thrust at her...

...and there was a grinning, smelly mountain of a man in the doorway. The one who'd stabbed Michael.

Claire let go of the door and stumbled back, thinking only an instant later, *Stupid, that was stupid – you should have slammed it*...but it was too late; he was already inside, closing the door behind him.

And locking it.

She looked in terror at Eve. Eve lunged forward, grabbed Claire, and hustled her around to the far side of the bed...and stepped in front of her. Claire looked frantically around for a weapon. Anything. She picked up a heavy-looking skull, but it was plastic, light and utterly useless.

Eve yanked a field hockey stick from under her bed.

'Let's do this nice,' the man said. 'That little stick isn't going to do you any good, and it's only going to piss me off.' His lips widened in a grin, revealing big, square, yellow teeth. 'Or get me all excited.'

Claire felt sick and faint. This wasn't like Shane coming into her room the other night, not at all. This was the flip side of men, and although she'd heard about it – you couldn't grow up without that – she'd never really *seen* it. Some jerks, sure, but there was something horrible about this guy. Something that looked at her and Eve like pieces of meat he was about to devour.

'You're not touching us,' Eve said, and raised her voice. 'Shane! Shane, get your ass up here *now*!'

There was a touch of panic in her voice, although she was putting on a good front. Her hands were shaking where they gripped the hockey stick.

The man glided around the end of the bed, prowling like a cat. Six feet tall, at least, and as broad as two of Eve, maybe bigger. His bare arms were ripped with muscle. His blue eyes looked shallow and hungry.

Claire heard the thump of footsteps outside, and then a *bang* as Shane fetched up against the locked door. He rattled the knob and pounded hard. 'Eve! Eve, open up!'

'She's busy!' the biker yelled, and laughed. 'Oh yeah, gonna be *real* busy.'

'No!' Shane screamed it, and the door shook with the strength of the blows he put into it. 'Stay away from them!'

Eve backed Claire up, all the way to the window. She took a swipe at the biker, who just stepped back out of range, still laughing.

'Get your dad!' she yelled at Shane. 'Make him do something!'

'I'm not leaving you!'

'Do it, Shane, *now*!'

Footsteps pounded down the hall. Claire swallowed, feeling suddenly even more alone and vulnerable. 'Do you think his dad will come?' she whispered. Eve didn't answer.

'Swear to God, you come near us and—'

'Like this?' The biker sidestepped a slash from the hockey stick, grabbed it on the way, and yanked it out of Eve's hands. He tossed it over his shoulder to land on the floor with a clatter. 'This near enough? Whatcha gonna do, doll girl? Cry all over me?'

Claire hid her eyes as the biker reached out for Eve with one tattooed hand.

'No,' Eve said breathlessly. 'I'm going to let my boyfriend beat the crap out of you.'

There was a dull *thunk* of wood meeting flesh, and a howl. Then another, harder *thunk*, and a crash as a body hit the floor.

The biker was down. Claire stared at him in disbelief, then looked past him, to the figure standing there with the field hockey stick in both hands.

Michael Glass. Back from the dead, again, a gorgeous blond avenging angel, breathing hard. Flushed with anger, blue eyes flashing. He glanced at the two girls, making sure they were OK, and then put the blade of the hockey stick on the biker's throat. The biker's eyes fluttered and tried to open, but didn't make it. He relaxed into unconsciousness.

Eve flew towards Michael, leapt over the biker's body, and fastened herself around Michael like she was trying to be sure he was all there. He must have been; he winced from the force of the impact, then kissed her on the top of her head without looking away from the man lying limp at their feet.

'Eve,' he said, and then glanced at her and gentled his tone. 'Eve, honey, go open the door.'

She nodded, stepped away, and followed instructions. Michael handed her the hockey stick, grabbed the biker by the shoulders, and towed him quickly out into the hallway. He closed the door again, locked it, and said, 'Right, here's the story. Eve, you knocked him out with the hockey stick and—'

He didn't finish, because Eve grabbed him and pushed him back against the door, wrapping herself around him like a Goth-girl coat. She was crying again, but silently; Claire could see her shoulders shaking. Michael sighed, put his arms around her, and bent his blond head to rest against her dark one.

'It's OK,' he murmured. 'You're OK, Eve. We're all OK.'

'You were *dead*!' she wailed, muffled by the fact that her face was still pressed against his chest. 'Damn you, Michael, you were *dead*, I saw them kill you, and…they—'

'Yeah, it wasn't too pleasant.' Something passed fast and hot across Michael's eyes, the reflection of a horror that Claire thought he didn't want to remember or share. 'But I'm not a vampire, and they can't kill me like a vampire. Not while the house owns my soul. They can do pretty much anything to my body, but it just…gets fixed.'

The prospects of that made Claire sick, like standing on the edge of a huge and unexpected drop. She stared at Michael, wide-eyed, and saw he understood the same things she did: that if Shane's father and his merry band of thugs found out, they might decide to test that out. Just for fun.

'That's why I'm not here,' Michael said. 'You can't tell them. Or Shane.'

'Not tell Shane?' Eve pulled back. 'Why not?'

'I've been watching,' he said. 'Listening. I can do that when I'm, you know—'

'A ghost?' Claire supplied.

'Exactly. I saw—' Michael didn't go on, but Claire thought she knew what he'd been about to say.

'You saw Shane's dad hit him,' she said. 'Right?'

'I don't want to make him keep secrets from his dad. Not now.'

Footsteps pounding up the stairs, then slowing when they hit the hallway. Michael touched his finger to his lips and eased out from Eve's frantic grip. He pressed his lips silently to hers.

'Hide!' Claire whispered. He nodded and opened the closet, rolled his eyes at the mess inside, and forced his way in. Burying himself in piles of clothes, Claire hoped.

Miranda had been trapped in that closet after trying to knife Eve, before the house had caught fire; she'd really done a job of messing things up. Eve was going to be furious.

Both girls jumped at a hard blow on the door. Eve hastily unlocked the door and stepped back as it flew open, and Shane charged through.

'How—?' He was breathing hard, and he had a crowbar in his hand. He'd have broken through the locks, Claire realised, if he'd had to. She came towards him slowly, trying to figure out what he was feeling, and he dropped the crowbar and wrapped his arms around her, lifting her up off the ground. His face was buried in the crook of her neck, and the warm, fast pump of his breath on her skin made her shiver in raw delight. 'Oh Christ, Claire. I'm sorry. I'm so sorry.'

'Not your fault,' Eve said. She held out the field hockey stick. 'Look! I hit him. Um, twice.'

'Good.' Shane kissed Claire's cheek and let her slide back down to the floor, but he kept hold of her arms. His eyes, bright under the bruises and swelling, surveyed her carefully. 'He didn't hurt you? Either of you?'

'I hit him!' Eve repeated brightly, and brandished the stick again for emphasis. 'So, no, he didn't hurt us. We hurt him. You know, all alone. Without any help. Um, so...where's your dad? He charges to the rescue pretty slow.'

Shane closed the door and locked it again as the biker in the hall groaned and rolled over on his side. He didn't answer, which was answer enough. Shane's dad needed his bikers more than he needed Eve or Claire. They were expendable. Worse, they'd probably just become rewards.

'We can't stay here,' Eve said. 'It isn't safe. You know that.'

Shane nodded, but he looked bleak. 'I can't come with you.'

'Yes, you can! Shane—'

'He's my dad, Eve. He's all I've got.'

Eve snorted. 'Yeah, well, what you've got I'd give back.'

'Sure, you just walked away from your folks—'

'Hey!'

'Didn't even care what happened to them—'

'*They* didn't care what happened to *me*!' Eve almost shouted it. Suddenly, the hockey stick in her hands wasn't so much for display. 'Leave my family out of this, Shane – you don't have a clue. Not a *clue*.'

'I've met your brother,' Shane shot back.

They both went quiet. Dangerously quiet. Claire cleared her throat. 'Brother?'

'Leave it alone, Claire,' Eve said. She sounded dead calm, not at all like herself. 'You *really* don't want to get into it.'

'Bones in every family closet in Morganville,' Shane said. 'Yours rattle pretty loud, Eve. So don't judge me.'

'Here's a thought: why don't you *get the hell out of my room, you asshole!*'

Shane picked up his crowbar, opened the door, and stepped outside. He reached down and hauled the biker to his feet, and shoved him towards the stairs. The biker went, still groaning and weaving.

Claire peeked through the gap in the door until she was sure they were gone, then nodded to Eve, who dumped the hockey stick and opened the closet door. 'Oh, crap,' she sighed. 'I hope nothing's torn in there. It is *not* easy to get clothes in this town. Michael?'

Claire looked over her shoulder. A pile of black and red netting stirred, and Michael's blond head appeared. He sat up, brushing off Goth, and silently held up a pair of black lace panties. Thong.

'Hey!' Eve yelped, and grabbed them from his fingers. 'Personal! And...laundry!'

Michael just smiled. For a guy who'd been stabbed, hacked up, and buried less than twenty-four hours ago, he looked remarkably composed. 'I'm not even going to ask what you wore them with,' he said. 'It's more fun to imagine.'

Eve snorted and gave him a hand up. 'Shane's taken our new boyfriend downstairs. What now? We can't exactly shimmy down a drainpipe.'

'Not in fishnets, you can't,' he agreed, straight-faced. 'Get changed. The less attention you attract from these guys, the better.'

Eve grabbed a pair of blue jeans from the floor of the closet, and a baby-doll T that must have been a gift; it was aqua blue, with a sparkle rainbow over the chest. Very *not* Eve. She glared at Michael and tapped her foot.

'What?' he asked.

'Gentlemen turn around. Or so I've heard.'

He faced the corner. Eve stripped off her spiderweb-lace shirt and the red top beneath, and stepped out of the red and black tartan skirt. The fishnets were garters – *totally* sexy. 'Not a word,' she warned Claire, and rolled them down. She didn't take her eyes off of Michael. There was red burning hot in her cheeks.

Dressing took thirty seconds, and then Eve grabbed up the scattered clothes, the garter belt, and the fishnets, and stuffed them into the closet before saying, 'OK, you can turn around.'

Michael did, leaning against the wall with his arms folded. He was smiling slightly, eyes half-closed.

'What?' Eve demanded. She was still blushing. 'Don't I look stupid enough now?'

'You look great,' he said, and crossed to kiss her lightly on the lips. 'Go wash your face.'

Eve went to the bathroom and shut the door. Claire said, 'You've got some kind of a plan, right? Because we don't. Well, Shane thinks we should let his dad do whatever, and run, but Eve doesn't think it's a good idea—'

'It's suicide,' Michael said flatly. 'Shane's dad is an idiot, and he's going to get Shane killed. You, too.'

'But you've got a plan.'

'Yeah,' Michael said. 'I have a plan.'

When Eve came back from the bathroom, Michael put his finger to his lips again, unlocked the door, and walked them across the hall. He reached behind the picture frame and pushed the hidden button, and the panelling creaked open to reveal one of the secret rooms of the Glass House. Amelie's room, Claire remembered. The one the vampire liked the best, probably because there were no windows and the only exit was from a concealed button. How weird was it to be living in a house built – and, really, owned – by a vampire?

'Inside,' Michael whispered. 'Eve. Cell phone?'

She patted her pockets, held up a finger, and dashed back to her room. She came back holding it up. Michael hustled them up the narrow staircase, and the door hissed shut behind them. No knob on this side, either.

Upstairs, the room was just as Claire had last seen it – elegant Victorian splendour, a little dusty. This room, like all of the house, seemed to have a sense of something present in it, something just out of sight. *Ghosts*, she thought. But Michael seemed to be the only ghost, and he was as normal as could be.

Then again, the house was alive, kind of, and it was keeping Michael alive, too. So maybe not so normal.

'Phone,' Michael said, and held out his hand as he sat down on the couch. Eve handed it over, frowning.

'Just who are you planning to call?' she asked. 'Ghostbusters? It's not like we have a lot of options...'

Michael grinned at her and pressed three keys, then activated the call. The response was nearly immediate. 'Hello, 911? This is Michael Glass, 716 Lot Street. I have intruders in my house. No, I don't know who they are, but there are at least three of them.'

Eve's mouth flopped open in surprise, and Claire blinked, too. Calling the police seemed so...*normal*. And so wrong.

'You might want to tell the officers that this house and its occupants are under the Founder's

Protection,' he said. 'They can verify that, I guess.'

He smiled and hung up a moment later, handed the phone back, and looked *very* smug.

'And Shane?' Claire asked. 'What about Shane?'

Michael's self-assurance faded. 'He's making his own choices,' he said. 'He'd want me to look out for the two of you first. And the only way I can do that is to get these guys out of my house. I can't protect you twenty-four/seven – in the daytime, you're vulnerable. And I'm not going to float around and watch while you get—' He didn't finish, but Claire – and Eve – knew where that was going. They both nodded. 'Once they're out of the house, I can keep them from coming back, unless Shane lets them in. Or one of you, though I can't see that happening.'

More headshakes, this time more violent. Michael kissed Eve's forehead with obvious affection, and ruffled Claire's hair. 'Then this is the best way,' he said. 'It'll shake them up, anyway.'

'I'm sorry,' Eve said in a small voice. 'I didn't think. I'm so used to thinking of the cops as enemies, and besides, they were just trying to kill us. Right?'

'Things change. We have to adapt.'

Michael was pretty much the king of that, Claire thought. He'd gone from a serious musician with his whole focus on making a name for himself, to a part-time ghost trapped in a house, to a part-time ghost trapped in a house forced to take in roommates to make the bills. And now he was trying to save their lives, and he still couldn't escape himself.

Michael was just so...responsible. Claire couldn't even imagine how someone got that way. Maturity, she guessed, but that was a lot like a road through fog to her. She had no idea how she was supposed to get there. Then again, she supposed nobody really did know, and you just stumbled through it.

They waited.

After about five minutes there was a wail of sirens in the distance – very faint, because the room was well soundproofed. That meant the sirens were close. Maybe even by the house already. Claire rose and pressed the button concealed in the lion's-head arm of the couch, and the sirens immediately increased in volume as the secret door opened. She hurried down the steps and peered out. No one in the hallway, but from downstairs she heard angry shouting, and then the sound of a door banging open. Motorcycle engines roaring, tyres squealing.

'They're going,' she yelled up, and pelted out into the hallway, down the stairs, breathless to find Shane.

Shane was up against the wall, and his father was holding him by the throat. Outside, police sirens suddenly cut off.

'Traitor,' Shane's dad said. He had a knife in his hand. 'You're a traitor. You're *dead* to me.'

Claire skidded to a stop, found her voice, and said, 'Sir, you'd better get out of here unless you want to end up talking to the vampires.'

Shane's father turned his face towards her, and his expression was twisted with fury. 'You little *bitch*,' he said. 'Turning my son against me.'

'No—' Shane grabbed at his father's hand, trying to pry it free. 'Don't—'

Claire backed up. For a second, neither Shane nor his dad moved, and then Shane's father let him go, and raced for the kitchen door. Shane dropped to his knees, choking, and Claire went to him...

...just as the front door banged open, splintering around the lock, and the police charged in.

'Oh man,' Shane whispered, 'that *sucks*. We just fixed that door.'

Claire clung to him, terrified, as the police swarmed through the house.

CHAPTER THREE

Shane wasn't talking to the cops. Not about his dad, and not about anything. He just sat like a lump, eyes down, and refused to answer any questions from the human patrol officers; Claire didn't know *what* to say – or, more importantly, what not to – and stammered out a lot of 'I don't know' and 'I was in my room' sort of answers. Eve – more self-possessed than Claire had ever seen her – stepped in to say that she'd heard the intruders downstairs breaking things, and she'd pulled Claire into her room and locked the door for protection. It sounded good. Claire supported it with a lot of nodding.

'Is that so?' A new voice, from behind the cops, and they parted ranks to admit two strangers. Detectives, it looked like, in sport jackets and slacks. One was a woman, frost pale, with eyes like mirrors. The other one was a tall man with grey close-cropped hair.

They were wearing gold badges on their belts. So. Detectives.

Vampire detectives.

Eve had gone very still, hands folded in her lap. She looked carefully friendly. 'Yes, ma'am,' she said. 'That's what happened.'

'And you have no idea who these mysterious intruders might have been,' said the male vamp. He looked – scary. Cold and hard and scary. 'Never saw them before.'

'We didn't see them at all, sir.'

'Because you were…locked in your room.' He smiled, and flashed fang. Clear warning. 'I can smell fear. You give it off like the stench of your sweat. Delicious.'

Claire fought back an urge to whimper. The human cops had backed up a step; one or two looked uncomfortable, but they weren't about to interfere with whatever was about to happen. Which was nothing, right? There were rules and stuff. And they were the victims!

Then again, she didn't suppose the vamps cared all that much for victims.

'Leave them alone,' Shane said.

'It speaks!' the woman said, and laughed. She sank down into a crouch, elegant and perfectly balanced, and tried to peer into Shane's face. 'A knight-errant, defending the helpless. Charming.' She had an old-world accent, sort of like blurred

German. 'Do you not trust us, little knight? Are we not your friends?'

'That depends,' Shane said, and looked right at her. 'You take your orders from Oliver, or the Founder? Because if you touch us – any of us – you have to take it up with her. You know who I mean.'

She lost her amused expression.

Her partner made a noise, halfway between a bark of laughter and a growl. 'Careful, Gretchen, he snaps. Just like a half-grown puppy. Boy, you don't know what you're saying. The Founder's mark is on the house, yes, but I see no bands on your wrists. Don't be stupid and make bold claims you can't back up.'

'Bite me, Dracula,' Shane snapped.

Gretchen laughed. 'A wolf pup,' she said. 'Oh, I like him, Hans. May I have him, since he's a stray?'

One of the uniformed cops cleared his throat. 'Ma'am? Sorry, but I can't allow that. You want to file the paperwork, I'll see what I can do, but—'

Gretchen made a frustrated noise and came back to her feet. 'Paperwork. Fah. In the old days we would have run him down like a deer for insolence.'

'In the old days, Gretchen, we were starving,' Hans said. 'Remember? The winters in Bavaria? Let him howl.' He shrugged and gave Eve and Claire a smile that looked a little less terrifying than before. 'Sorry. Gretchen gets carried away. Now, you're sure none of you knew these intruders?

Morganville's not that big a town. We're all pretty close-knit, especially the human community.'

'Strangers,' Eve said. 'I think they might have been strangers. Maybe just...passing through.'

'Passing through,' Hans repeated. 'We don't get a lot of casual visitors. Even biker gangs.' He studied them each in turn, and while his eyes were on her Claire felt as if she were being x-rayed. Surely he couldn't really see her thoughts, right? Hans finished with his gaze on Shane, fixed and dark. 'Your name.'

'Shane,' he said. 'Shane Collins.'

'You left Morganville with your family a few years ago, yes? What brought you back?'

'My friend Michael needed a roommate.' Shane's eyes flickered, and Claire realised that he'd just made a mistake. A big one.

'Michael Glass. Ah, yes, the mysterious Michael. Never around when anyone comes calling during the day, but always present at night. Tell me, is Michael a vampire?'

'Wouldn't you know?' Shane shot back. 'Last I heard, nobody had made a new vampire in fifty years or more.'

'True.' Hans nodded. 'Yet it's curious, isn't it? That your friend seems so hard to keep around?'

They knew. They knew *something*, anyway; Claire supposed Oliver would have no reason to keep secrets, especially Michael's secrets. He'd probably blabbed it to all of his minions that Michael was a ghost, caught between worlds – not quite vampire, not quite human, not quite anything.

'It's night,' Gretchen pointed out. 'So where is he? Your friend?'

Shane swallowed, and it was hard to miss the wave of misery that went through him. 'He's around.'

'Around where, exactly?'

Claire exchanged a look of dread with Eve. Shane still thought Michael was dead, buried in the backyard...and Michael had been pretty firm on the idea that Shane shouldn't know...

'I don't know,' Shane said. The tips of his ears were turning red.

Hans the Detective smiled slowly. 'You don't know much, son. And yet you look like you're not completely stupid, so how exactly does that work? Did you hide in the room with the girls?' He leant on the last word, and his vampire partner laughed.

Shane got up. There was something insane in his eyes, and Claire felt her heart stop beating because this was bad, very bad, and Shane was going to do something horribly unwise, and there was no way they could stop him...

'You're looking for me?'

They all turned.

Michael was standing at the top of the stairs. He was pulling on a plain black T-shirt with blue jeans, and he looked like he'd just rolled out of bed. His feet, Claire saw, were bare as usual.

Shane sat down. Fast and hard. Michael took his time coming down the stairs, making sure they were all focused on him instead of Shane, to give Shane time to get through what he was feeling – which was, Claire thought, a lot to pack into less than thirty seconds. Relief, of course, which brought a sheen of tears to his eyes. And then, predictably, he got pissed, because, well, he was a guy, he was Shane, and that was how he handled being scared.

So, really, by the time Michael padded down the last step to the wooden floor and crossed over to the couch through the circle of police, things were pretty much just as they'd been, except that Shane wasn't about to push the button on his nuclear temper.

'Hey,' Michael said to him. Shane moved over on the couch to make room. Guy room, which left plenty of empty space. 'What's up?'

Shane looked at him like he might be crazy, not just nearly dead part-time. 'Cops, man.'

'Yeah, man, I can see that. How come?'

'You're telling me you actually slept through all that? Dude, you need to see a doctor or something. Maybe you have a disease.'

'Hey, I need the sleep. Lisa, you know.' Michael grinned. They were good at this, Claire realised – good at playing normal, even if there wasn't a normal thing in the world about their situation. 'So what happened?'

'You weren't aware of intruders in your home?' asked Gretchen, who'd been watching the exchange – and the correspondingly shrinking chance of bloodshed – with disappointment. 'The others described it as quite loud.'

'He can sleep through World War Three,' Shane said. 'I told you, it's some kind of sickness or something.'

'I thought you said you didn't know where he was,' Hans said. 'Wasn't he in his room?'

Shane shrugged. 'I'm not his keeper.'

'Ah,' Gretchen said, and smiled. 'That is where you are wrong, little knight. You are all your brothers' keepers here in Morganville, and you can all suffer for their crimes. Which you should know and remember.'

Hans looked bored now. 'Sergeant,' he said, and the most senior uniformed cop stepped out of the ranks. 'I leave this in your hands. If you find anything out of the ordinary, let us know.'

Just like that, the vamps were gone. They moved fast, and silently; they didn't seem to want to blend in much, Claire thought, and tried not to tremble. She sank down on the couch beside Shane, nearly crawling into his lap. Eve crowded in between the two boys.

'Right.' The sergeant didn't look happy with having the whole thing dumped in his lap again, but he also looked resigned. Couldn't be the easiest thing, Claire thought, having vamps for bosses. They didn't seem to have a long attention span. 'Glass, right? Occupation?'

'Musician, sir,' Michael said.

'Play around town, do you?'

'I'm rehearsing for some upcoming gigs.'

The cop nodded and flipped pages in a black leather book. He ran a thick finger down a list, frowned, and said, 'You're behind on your donations, Glass. About a month.'

Michael threw a lightning-fast glance at Shane. 'Sorry, sir. I'll get out there tomorrow.'

'Better, or you know what happens.' The cop ran down the roster. 'You. Collins. You still unemployed?' He gave him a stare. A long one. Shane shrugged, looking – Claire thought – as dumb as possible. 'Try harder.'

'Common Grounds,' Eve volunteered before he could start in on her. 'Eve Rosser, sir, thank you.' She was vibrating all over – she was so nervous – which was funny; when she'd been on her own, she'd been cool and calm. She had hold of both Michael's and Shane's hands. 'Although, um, I'm thinking of making a change.'

The cop seemed bored now. 'Yeah, OK. You, the kid. Name?'

'Claire,' she said faintly. 'Um...Danvers. I'm a student.'

He looked at her again, and kept looking. 'Shouldn't you be in the dorm?'

'I have permission to live off campus.' She didn't say from whom, because it was primarily herself.

He watched her for another few seconds, then shrugged. 'You live off campus, you follow the town rules. Your friends here'll tell you what they are. Watch on campus about how much you pass along – we got enough problems without panicking students. And we're real good at finding blabbermouths.'

She nodded.

That wasn't the end of it, but it was the end of her discussions with them; the police poked around a little, took some pictures, and left the house a few minutes later without another word to any of them.

For a good ten seconds after the police closed the front door – or closed it as much as was possible with a busted lock – there was silence, and then Shane turned to Michael and said, 'You fucking bastard.' Claire swallowed hard at the tight fury in his voice.

'You want to take this outside?' Michael asked. *He* sounded neutral, almost calm. His eyes were anything but.

'What, you can leave the house now?'

'No, I meant another room, Shane.'

'Hey,' Eve said, 'don't—'

'Shut up, Eve!' Shane snapped.

Michael came off the couch like somebody had pushed him; he reached down, grabbed Shane by the T-shirt, and yanked him upright. 'Don't,' he said, and gave him one hard shake. 'Your father's an asshole. It's not a disease. You don't have to catch it.'

Shane grabbed him in a hug. Michael rocked back a little from the impact, but he closed his eyes and hung on for a moment, then slapped Shane's back. And of *course* Shane slapped his back, too, and they stepped way apart. Manly. Claire rolled her eyes.

'I thought you were dead,' Shane said. His eyes looked suspiciously bright and wet. 'I saw you die, man.'

'I die all the time. It doesn't really take.' Michael gave him a half smile that looked more grim than amused. 'I figured it was better to let your dad think he'd taken me out. Maybe he wouldn't be so hard on the rest of you.' His gaze swept over the bruises on Shane's face. 'Brilliant plan. I'm sorry, man. Once I was dead, I couldn't do much until night came around again.'

He said it so matter-of-factly that Claire felt a shiver. 'Do you remember...you know, what they did to you?'

Michael glanced at her. 'Yeah,' he said. 'I remember.'

'Oh hell.' Shane collapsed back on the sofa and

put his head in his hands. 'God, man, I'm sorry. I'm so sorry.'

'Not your fault.'

'I called him.'

'You called him because it looked like we were all pulling an Alamo. You didn't know—'

'I know my dad,' Shane said grimly. 'Michael, I want you to know, I wasn't... I didn't come here to do his dirty work. Not...not after the first week or so.'

Michael didn't answer him. Maybe there was no answer to that, Claire thought. She scooted closer to Shane and stroked his ragged, shoulder-length fine hair. 'Hey,' she said. 'It's OK. We're all OK.'

'No, we're not.' Shane's voice was muffled by his hands. 'We're totally screwed. Right, Mike?'

'Pretty much,' Michael sighed. 'Yeah.'

'The cops will find them,' Eve said in an undertone to Claire as both girls stood in the kitchen making pasta. Pasta, apparently, was a new thing that Eve wanted to try. She frowned down at the package of spaghetti, then at the not-yet-bubbling pot of water. 'Shane's dad and his merry band of assholes, I mean.'

'Yeah,' Claire agreed, not because she thought they would, but because, well, it seemed like the thing to say. 'Want me to warm up the sauce?'

'Do we do that? I mean, it's in a jar, right? Can't you just dump it over the pasta?'

'Well, you *can*, but it tastes better if you warm it up.'

'Oh.' Eve sighed. 'This is complicated. No wonder I never cook.'

'You make breakfast!'

'I make two things: bacon and eggs. And sometimes sandwiches. I hate cooking. Cooking reminds me of my mother.' Eve took another pot from the rack and banged it down onto the massive stove. 'Here.'

Claire struggled with the top on the spaghetti sauce jar, and finally got it to release with a *pop*. 'You think they're going to stay mad at each other?' she asked.

'Michael and Shane?'

'Mmm-hmmm.' The sauce plopped into the pot, chunky and wet and vaguely nauseating. Claire considered the second jar, decided that if two of the four of them were boys, more was better. She got it opened and in the pot, as well, then turned on the burner and set it to simmer.

'Who knows?' Eve shrugged. 'Boys are idiots. You'd think Shane could just say, "Oh man, I'm glad you're alive," but no. It's either guilt or amateur night at the Drama Queen Theatre.' She blew out a frustrated breath. '*Boys*. I'd turn gay if they weren't so sexy.'

Claire tried not to laugh, but she couldn't help it, and after a second Eve smiled and chuckled, too.

The water started boiling. In went the pasta.

'Um…Eve…can I ask…?'

'About what?' Eve was still frowning at the pasta like she suspected it was going to do something clever, like try to escape from the pot.

'You and Michael.'

'Oh.' A surge of pink to Eve's cheeks. Between that and the fact that she was wearing colours outside of the Goth red and black rainbow, she looked young and very cute. 'Well. I don't know if it's…God, he's just so—'

'Hot?' Claire asked.

'Hot,' Eve admitted. 'Nuclear hot. Surface of the sun hot. And—'

She stopped, the flush in her cheeks getting darker. Claire picked up a wooden spoon and poked the pasta, which was beginning to loosen up. 'And?'

'And I was planning on putting the moves on him before all this happened. That's why I had on the garters and stuff. Planning ahead.'

'Oh, wow.'

'Yeah, embarrassing. Did he peek?'

'When you were changing?' Claire asked. 'I don't think so. But I think he wanted to.'

'That's OK, then.' Eve blinked down at the pasta, which had formed a thick white foam on top. 'Is it supposed to be doing that?'

Claire hadn't ever seen it happen at her parents'

house. But then again, they hadn't made spaghetti much.

'I don't know.'

'Oh crap!' The white foam kept growing, like in one of those cheesy science fiction movies. The foam that ate the Glass House...it mushroomed up over the top of the pot and down over the sides, and both girls yelped as it hit the burners and began to sizzle and pop. Claire grabbed the pot and moved it. Eve turned down the burner. 'Right, pasta makes foam, good to know. Too hot. Way too hot.'

'Who? Michael?' Claire asked, and they dissolved in giggles.

Which only got worse when Michael walked in, went to the refrigerator, and retrieved the last two beers from his birthday pack. 'Ladies,' he said. 'Did I miss something?'

'Pasta boiled over,' Claire gulped, trying not to giggle even harder. Michael looked at them for a second, curious, and then shrugged and left again. 'Do you think he's telling Shane right now that we're insane?'

'Probably.' Eve managed to control herself, and put the pasta back on the burner. 'Is this shock? Are we in shock right now?'

'I don't know,' Claire said. 'Let's see, we've been barricaded in the house, attacked, nearly burnt to death. Michael was murdered right in front of us, then came back, and we got interrogated by the big, scary vampire cops? Yeah, maybe shock.'

Eve choked on another snort/giggle. 'Maybe that's why I decided to cook.'

They watched the pasta bubble in silence. The whole room was starting to smell warm with spices and tomato sauce, a comforting and homey sort of smell. Claire stirred the spaghetti sauce, which was looking delicious now that it was simmering.

The kitchen door banged open again. Shane, this time, a beer in one hand. 'What's burning?'

'Your brain. So, did you two girls kiss and make up?' Eve asked, stirring the pasta.

He glowered at her, then turned to Claire. 'What the hell is she making?'

'Spaghetti.' And technically, it was Claire mostly, but she decided not to mention it. 'Um, about your dad – do you think they're going to catch him?'

'No.' Shane hip-bumped Eve out of the way at the stove and did some spaghetti maintenance. 'Morganville's got a lot of hiding places. That's mostly for the vamps' benefit, but it'll work for him, too. He'll go to ground. I've been sending him maps. He'll know where to go.'

'Maybe he'll just leave?' Eve sounded hopeful. Shane dragged a piece of spaghetti out of the tangle in the pot and pressed it against the metal with the spoon. It sliced cleanly.

'No,' Shane said again. 'He definitely won't leave. He's got no place else to go. He always said that if he crossed the border into Morganville again, he was here until it was done.'

'You mean until *he's* done.' Eve crossed her arms, not as if she was angry, more like she was cold. 'Shane, if he goes after even one vampire, we are dead. You know that, right?'

He picked up the beer bottle and drank, avoiding an answer. He flipped off the burner under the spaghetti, took the pot to the sink, and drained it with the edge of a lid. Like a real chef or something.

Which, Claire had to admit, was pretty much totally hot, the way he moved so confidently. She liked to cook, but he had *authority*. In fact, she was paying a lot more attention to what Shane did today – the way he moved, the way his clothes fit – or didn't, in his case, because Shane was wearing his jeans loose and just baggy enough to give her fantasies about them sliding down. Which made her blush.

She concentrated on getting down the bowls from the cupboard. Mismatched bowls, two out of four of them chipped. She put them out on the counter as Shane returned with the spaghetti and began portioning it out. Eve grabbed the sauce and followed him down the line, ladling.

It looked pretty tasty, actually. Claire picked up two bowls and carried them into the living room, where Michael was tuning his guitar as if nothing had happened, as if he hadn't been stabbed through the heart and dragged outside and – oh my God, she didn't want to finish that thought at all.

She handed him the bowl. He set the guitar carefully back in its case – somehow, with all the mayhem that had gone on in the past two days, it had escaped damage – and dug in as Eve and Shane trailed in with their own dinner. Eve had two chilled bottles of water under one arm. She tossed one to Claire as she sat down cross-legged on the floor, next to Michael's knee.

Shane settled on the couch, and Claire joined him. For a few minutes nobody said anything. Claire hadn't realised that she was hungry, not really, but the second the sauce hit her tongue and exploded into flavours, she was *starving*. She couldn't gobble it fast enough.

'Hell's put in a skating rink,' Shane said. 'This is actually edible, Eve.'

Again, Claire had the impulse to claim credit...and managed not to, mostly because that would have required her to stop shovelling pasta into her mouth.

'Claire,' Eve said. 'She's the cook, not me. I just, you know, supervised.' Which gave Claire a pleasant little spurt of gratitude and surprise.

'See? I knew that.'

Eve flipped him off and noisily sucked some spaghetti into her mouth.

Claire got to the bottom of the bowl first – even before Michael or Shane – and sat back with a sigh of utter contentment. *Nap*, she thought. *I could take a nap.*

'Guys,' Michael said. 'We're still in trouble. You know that, right?'

'Yeah,' Eve said. 'But now we have *catered* trouble.'

He ignored her, except for a brief little quirk of a smile, and focused on Shane. 'You need to tell me everything,' Michael said. 'No bullshit, man. Every last thing, from the time you left Morganville.'

Shane seemed to lose his appetite.

Which, for Shane, was not a good sign *at all*.

The vampires had offered them money. Cash compensation. It was Morganville's version of Allstate, only it wasn't insurance – it was blood money for a dead child.

And the Collins family – Dad, Mom, and Shane – had packed up whatever had survived the fire that had taken Alyssa, and left town in the middle of the night. Running. That probably would have been that, Shane explained; people did leave town from time to time, and it was rarely any trouble. Michael's own parents had taken off. But...something went wrong with Molly Collins.

'At first, she'd just space,' Shane said. He'd drained his beer, and now he was just rolling the bottle between his palms. 'Stare at things, like she was trying to remember something. Dad didn't notice. He was drinking a lot. We ended up in Odessa, and Dad got a job at the recycling plant. He wasn't home much.'

'That must have been an improvement,' Eve muttered.

'Hey, let me get through it, OK?'

'Sorry.'

Shane took another deep breath. 'Mom...she kept talking about Alyssa. You have to understand, we didn't... I couldn't remember anything, except that she'd died. It was all just sort of a blur, but not the kind of blur you worry about, if you know what I mean...?'

Claire was fairly certain nobody did, but she remembered her conversation with her own parents. They'd forgotten things, and somehow, they hadn't really cared. So maybe she did understand.

'I started working, too. Mom...she just stayed in the motel. Wouldn't do anything except eat, sleep, sometimes take a bath if we yelled at her long enough. I figured, you know, depression...but it was more than that. One day, out of nowhere, she grabs me by the arm and she says, "Shane, do you remember your sister?" So I go, "Yeah, Mom, of course I do." And she says the weirdest thing. She says, "Do you remember the vampires?" I didn't remember, but it felt...like something in me was trying to. I got a bad headache, and I felt sick. And Mom...she just kept on talking, about how there was something wrong with us, something going wrong in our heads. About the vampires. About Lyssa dying in the fire.'

He fell silent, still rolling the beer bottle like some kind of magic talisman. Nobody moved.

'And I remembered.'

Shane's whisper sounded raw, somehow, vulnerable and exposed. Michael wasn't looking at him. He was looking down, at his own beer bottle, and the label he was peeling off in strips.

'It was like some wall coming down, and then it all just flooded in. I mean, it's bad enough to live through it and sort of cope with it, but when it comes back like that...' Shane visibly shuddered. 'It was like I'd just watched Lyss die all over again.'

'Oh,' Eve said faintly. 'Oh God.'

'Mom—' He shook his head. 'I couldn't handle it. I left her. I had to get away, I couldn't just... I had to *go*. You know? So I left. I ran.' A hollow rattle of a laugh.

'Saved my life.'

'Shane—' Michael cleared his throat. 'I was wrong. You don't have to—'

'Shut up, man. Just shut up.' Shane tipped the bottle to his lips for the last few drops, then swallowed hard. Claire didn't know what was coming, but she could see from the look on Michael's face that he did, and it twisted her stomach into a knot. 'So anyway, I came back a few hours later and she was in the tub, just floating there, and the water was red...razor blades on the floor—'

'Oh, honey.' Eve got up and stood there, hovering next to him, reaching out to touch him and then pulling back in jerky motions without making contact, like he had some force field of grief shielding him. 'It wasn't your fault. You said she was depressed.'

'Don't you get it?' He glared up at her, then at Michael. 'She didn't do it. She wouldn't. It was *them*. You know how they work: they close in; they kill; they cover it up. They must have gotten there right after I left. I don't know—'

'Shane.'

'—I don't know how they got her in the tub. There weren't any bruises, but the cuts were—'

'*Shane!* Christ, man!' Michael looked outright horrified this time, and Shane stopped. The two of them looked at each other for a long, wordless moment, and then Michael – visibly tense – eased back into his chair. 'Shit. I don't even know what to say.'

Shane shook his head and looked away. 'Nothing to say. It is what it is. I couldn't... Shit. Let me just finish, OK?'

As if they could stop him. Claire felt cold. She could feel Shane's body shaking next to her, and if *she* felt cold, how must he be feeling? Frozen. Numb. She reached out to touch him and, like Eve, just...stopped. There was something about Shane right now that didn't want to be touched.

'Anyway, my dad came home, eventually. Cops said it was a suicide, but after they were gone I told him. He didn't exactly want to hear it. Things got...ugly.' Claire couldn't imagine how ugly that had been, for Shane to actually admit it. 'But I made him remember.'

Eve sat on the floor, hugging her knees close to her chest. She looked at him with anime-wide eyes. 'And?'

'He got drunk. A lot.' Bitterness ran black through Shane's voice, and all of a sudden the beer bottle in his hand seemed to get a whole lot of significance for him, beyond just something to occupy his nervous hands. He set it down on the floor and wiped his palms on his blue jeans. 'He started hooking up with these bikers and stuff. I...wasn't in a real good place; I don't remember some of that. Couple of weeks later we got a visit from these guys in suits. Not vamps, lawyers. They gave us money, lots of it. Insurance. Except we both knew who it was from, and the point was, they were trying to figure out what we knew and remembered. I was too drugged out to know what was going on, and Dad was drunk, so I guess that saved our lives. They decided we were no threat.' He wiped his forehead with the heel of his hand and laughed – a bitter, broken sound like glass in a blender.

Shane on drugs. Claire saw that Michael had caught it, too. She wondered if he was going to say something, but maybe it wasn't the best time to say, *Hey, man, you using now?* Or something like that.

He didn't need to ask, as it turned out. Shane answered anyway. 'But I kicked it, and Dad sobered up, and we planned this out. Thing is, even though we remembered a lot of stuff, the personal stuff, we couldn't remember things about how to find vamps, or the layout of the town, or even who we were looking for. So that was my job. Come back, scout it out, find out where the vamps hide during the day. Report back. It wasn't supposed to take this long, and I wasn't supposed to…get tangled up.'

'With us,' Eve supplied softly. 'Right? He didn't want you to have any friends.'

'Friends get you killed in Morganville.'

'No.' Eve put a pale hand on his knee. 'Shane, honey, in Morganville, friends are the only things that keep you alive.'

CHAPTER FOUR

Claire couldn't believe how much had poured out of Shane – all that grief and horror and bitterness and anger. He'd always seemed sort of, well, *normal*, and it was a shock to see all the emotional bloodshed...and a shock to hear him talk so much, about things so personal. Shane wasn't a talker.

She collected the dishes and did them alone, comforted by hot water and the fizz of soap on her hands; she cleaned up pots and pans and splashes of red sauce, and thought about Shane finding his mom dead in a bloody bathtub. *I wasn't in a real good place*, Shane had said. The master of understatement. Claire wasn't so sure that she'd ever have been able to smile again, laugh again, function again, if that had happened to her, especially after losing a sister and winning the Drunk-Asshole Lottery with Dad. How did he do it? How did he keep it together, and stay so...brave?

She wanted to cry for him, but she was almost sure that he'd have been embarrassed, so she kept the misery inside, and scrubbed dishes clean. *He doesn't deserve this. Why don't they all just leave him alone? Why does he have to be the one everybody beats on?*

Maybe just because he'd shown he could take it, and make himself stronger for it.

The kitchen door swung open, and she jumped, expected Shane, but it was Michael. He walked over to the sink, ran some cold water in his hands, and splashed it over his face and the back of his neck.

'Bad night,' Claire said.

'Tell me about it.' He cut a sideways look towards her.

'Do you think he's right? About them, you know, killing his mother?'

'I think Shane's carrying around a load of guilt the size of Trump Tower. And I think it helps him to be angry.' Michael shrugged. 'I don't know. It's possible. But I don't think we can know one way or the other.'

That felt...sick, somehow. No wonder Shane was so reluctant to talk about it. She tried to imagine living with that kind of uncertainty, those memories, and failed.

She was glad she did.

'So,' Michael said. 'I've got about three hours

until morning. We need to make some plans about what we're going to do, and what we're *not* going to do.'

Claire nodded and set a plate aside to dry.

'First thing is, none of you leave the house,' Michael said. 'Got it? No school, no work. You stay indoors. I can't protect you if you go outside.'

'We can't just hide!'

'We can for a while, and we will. Look, Shane's dad can't run around out there forever. It's a temporary problem. Someone's going to find him.' The unspoken subject of what would happen to Shane's dad after he was caught was a whole other issue. 'As long as we don't do anything directly that ties us to whatever his dad does, we're OK. Amelie's word is good for that.'

'You're putting a lot of trust in—'

'A vampire, yeah, I know.' Michael shrugged and leant a hip against the counter, looking down on her. 'What choices do we have?'

'Not too many, I guess.' Claire studied him more closely. He looked tired. 'Michael? Are you OK?'

Now he looked surprised. 'Sure. Shane's the one who's got issues. Not me.'

No, Michael was all good. Killed, dismembered, buried, reborn…yeah, just another day in the life. Claire sighed. 'Guys,' she said mournfully. 'Michael, I'll stay home today, but I really do have to go to school, you know. Really.' Because her missing school was like a caffeine addict going without a daily jolt.

'Your education or your life, Claire. I'd rather you be alive and a little bit dumber.'

She met his eyes squarely. 'Well, I wouldn't. I'll stay home today. I don't promise about tomorrow.'

He smiled, leant forward, and put a warm sloppy kiss on her forehead. 'That's my girl,' he said, and left. She sighed again, this time happily, and found herself grinning. Michael might be Eve's new main crush, but he was still available as an oh-my-God-how-cute-is-*he* thrill.

Claire finished the dishes and went back to the living room. The TV was on, tuned to some forensics show, and Shane was slumped on the couch staring at it. No sign of Eve or Michael. Claire hesitated, thinking longingly about bed and forgetting about all this for a while, but Shane just looked so...alone.

She went and settled in next to him. She didn't say anything, and neither did he, and after a while his arm went around her and that was all right.

She fell asleep there, braced against his warm body.

It was nice.

Claire supposed that she should have known Shane might have nightmares – bad ones – but she'd never really thought about it. When Shane jerked and rolled off the couch, she thumped flat onto the cushions. The TV was still on – a flickering confusion of colour – and Claire flailed and scrambled for some grasp of what was going on through the fog of interrupted sleep.

'Shane?'

He was on his side on the floor, shuddering, curled up into a ball. Claire slid down next to him and put her hands on his broad back. Under the thin T-shirt his skin was clammy, and his muscles were as tense as steel cable. He was making these *sounds*, agonising gasps that weren't quite sobs but weren't quite not, either.

She didn't know what to do. She'd felt helpless a lot in the past few hours, but this was worse, somehow, because Michael and Eve were nowhere to be seen, and she wasn't sure if Shane would have wanted them to see him like this. Or if he wanted *her* to see him like this. Shane was all about the pride.

'I'm OK,' he gasped out. 'I'm OK. I'm OK.' He didn't sound OK. He sounded scared, and he sounded like a little boy.

He managed to sit up. Claire wrapped her arms around him, hugging him tight, and after a few seconds of resistance she felt him sag against her, and hug her back. His hand stroked her hair as if she might break. 'Shhh,' she whispered to him, the way her mother had whispered it to her when things got bad. 'You're here. You're safe. You're

OK.' Because wherever he'd been in his dreams, he hadn't been any of those three things.

If she expected him to talk about it, she was disappointed. He pulled back, avoided looking at her, and said, 'You should go to bed.'

'Yeah,' she agreed. 'You first.'

'Can't sleep.' Didn't want to, more likely; his eyes were red and blurred with exhaustion. 'I just need some coffee or something.'

'Coke?'

'Whatever.'

She fetched it for him, and Shane downed it like a frat boy at a mixer, belched, and shrugged an apology. 'Where's Michael?' She spread her hands. 'Eve?' She did another silent pantomime of ignorance. 'Well, at least somebody's getting a good night's sleep. They together?'

Claire blinked. 'I...don't know.' She hadn't thought about it, actually. She hadn't seen them go, didn't know if they'd gone to separate rooms or if Eve had finally worked up the courage to proposition Michael. 'Cause he'd never make the first move. That just wasn't Michael, somehow.

'Christ, I hope so,' Shane said. 'They deserve a little fun, even in hell.' He was kidding, but not. He *did* see Morganville as hell. Claire had to admit, he had a point.

It was hell, and they were the lost souls, and it was coming on towards morning and she'd been scared for what felt like a very, very long time…

He was watching her closely, in a way that made her feel warmth all over her skin, like a light sunburn.

'How about us?' she heard herself ask. 'Don't we deserve a little fun?'

I did not just say that.

Only she had.

He smiled. She wondered if the shadows were ever going to leave his eyes again. 'I could do something fun.'

'Ummm…' She licked her lips. 'Define fun.'

'Quit doing that, jailbait. It's distracting.'

The whole idea that somebody would even *think* of her as jailbait was tremendously exciting. Especially Shane. She tried to hide that, and act like she wasn't quaking on the inside like a Jell-O fruit salad. 'So now you want me to stay up? I thought you said I should go to bed.'

'You should.' He didn't put any particular emphasis on it. ''Cause if you stay down here, there's going to be fun. I'm just saying.'

'Video game fun?'

His eyes widened. 'You want to play video games?'

'Do you?'

'You are the weirdest girl.'

'Please. You live with *Eve*.' She was *not* doing this right. How did girls seduce boys? What did they say? Because she was pretty sure that talking about video games and bringing up roommates wasn't in the have-fun game plan. She was hyperaware of her body, too. How was she supposed to move? She felt awkward, all angles, and she wanted to be one of those graceful girls, all delicacy and elegance. Like in the movies.

Eve would know. She'd had those garter hose on, and those thong panties, and Claire didn't even own those things, or have any idea how to get them. And Eve had worn them for Michael, or maybe just as a secret little excitement for herself around Michael. Yeah, Eve would know what to say.

Say something sexy, she commanded herself, and in a blind panic, she opened her mouth and blurted, 'Do you think they're doing it?' She was so appalled that she clapped both hands over her mouth. She'd never in her life wanted to take back words so much, and so fast...and for a second, Shane just looked at her, like he couldn't figure out what she was talking about.

And then he laughed. 'Man, I hope. Those two could use a good...uh—' He blinked and she saw her age flash in front of his eyes. 'Hell. Never mind.'

Words weren't working for her. She leant forward and kissed him. It felt weird, and awkward, and he didn't immediately respond – maybe he was too surprised. Maybe she was doing it wrong, or she'd been wrong to make the move on him...

His lips parted under hers, damp and soft and warm, and she forgot all of that. Her entire life focused in on the sensations, the gentle pressure that grew more intense the longer the kiss went on.

Chaste kisses, then dirtier ones, and man, those tasted good. They tasted better the wider her mouth opened, and especially after his tongue touched hers.

She could have done a whole semester of kissing with Shane. Intense personal study. With lab classes.

Time really wasn't happening for her, but eventually Claire realised that there was a soft glow coming from the windows, and she was numb and sore from sitting on the floor. She winced as a muscle in her back protested, and Shane reached out, pulled her up, and settled himself on the couch.

He stretched out, and extended a hand to her. She stared, tingling and confused. 'There's no room.'

'Plenty of room,' he said.

She felt breathless and kind of wild, stretching out on the tiny area of sofa cushion available next to him, and then smothered a yelp as Shane picked her up and draped her over his chest and, *oh my God*, over all the rest of him, too.

'Better?' he asked, and raised his eyebrows. It was a real question, and he was looking for a real answer. Claire felt a blush building a fire in her cheeks, but she didn't look away from his gaze.

'Perfect,' she said.

It felt like being naked, except for all the clothes. The kisses this time were wet and urgent and deep, and the feeling of Shane's muscles tensing and relaxing under her was incredibly exciting. *This should be illegal*, she thought. Well, it was kind of illegal. Or would be, if any clothes came off.

Shane might not have been Michael, with all the responsibility, but he definitely wasn't that impulsive. At least, not with her. His hands roamed, but never to places where she wanted them to – badly – and some of the places they roamed made her wonder why she'd never wanted someone to touch her there before. Like the small of her back, where the skin dipped into a shallow valley. Or the back of her neck. Or the inside of her arms. Or...

As he was bringing his hands up her sides, his fingers just *barely* brushed the outer curve of her breasts, and she gasped into his mouth.

Shane immediately sat her upright, and moved to the other end of the couch. His face was flushed; his eyes were bright and no longer looked even a little bit tired. 'No,' he said, and held out his hand like a traffic cop when she tried to scoot closer. 'Red flag. If you make that sound again, we are in trouble. Or I am, anyway.'

'But—' Claire felt that blush creeping in again, and had no idea what it was going to be like to put

this into words. 'What about you? You know—'
She made a vague gesture that could have been
anything. Or nothing. Or anything.

'Don't worry about me. I needed this.' He was
still breathing deeply, but he did look better.
Steadier. More like…Shane, instead of that lost and
hurt little boy terrified of his nightmares. 'So? Did
we have fun?'

'Fun,' she agreed faintly. So much fun she felt
like a fizzed-up soda, ready to burst. 'Um, I need
to—'

'Yeah, me, too.' But Shane made no move to go.
Claire swallowed hard and took the course of the
better part of valour, up the stairs to her room. She
shut the door and locked it, threw herself on her
brand-new mattress – she hadn't even put sheets on
it yet, and they were a little light on blankets after
using most of them to fight the fire – and bounced.
The room smelt like a wet smoky dog, but she
didn't care.

Not at all.

Fun.

Oh yes.

Around noon, Claire heard the doorbell, and ran
downstairs. Shane was lying on the couch, sound
asleep. Still no sign of Eve, and she didn't expect to
have any Michael sightings, given the daylight
hours. She raced down the hall to the door, which

was braced with a wooden chair as a temporary lock, and hesitated.

'Michael? You there?' A chilly breeze swept across her, ruffling her hair. Wow. He was strong today. 'Can I open the door? One for yes, two for no.'

Apparently, yes. She pulled the chair away and peered outside. There were two men standing on the porch, both tall; one was lean and hard-looking, with black hair; the other one was a little pale (but not vamp pale) and heavyset, and where he wasn't balding, his very short hair looked brown.

They both displayed badges. Police.

'You're Claire, right?' the lean one said, and extended his hand. 'Joe Hess. This is my partner, Travis Lowe. How you doing?'

'Um...' She fumbled for the handshake. 'Fine, I guess.' Lowe also shook her hand. 'Is something... I mean, did you find—?' Because she both hoped that Shane's dad was in a holding cell, and was afraid of what that would mean for Shane. She rocked nervously back and forth on her heels, her eyes darting from one of them to the other.

Joe Hess smiled. Unlike most smiles she'd seen since coming to Morganville, this one seemed...uncomplicated. Clean, sort of. Not happy, because that would have been weird, but comforting. 'It's OK,' he said. 'No, we haven't found them, but you've got nothing to be afraid of. May we come inside?'

She heard shuffling footsteps behind her. Shane had woken up, and was standing in the hallway, barefoot and rumpled, with a fierce bed-head that got worse as he yawned and ran fingers through his hair, standing part of it on end.

How sick was it that she found that sexy?

Claire collected herself and pointed at the cops on the doorstep. Shane's eyes focused fast.

'Officers,' he said, and came towards the door. 'Anything you need?'

'I was just asking if we can come in and talk,' Detective Hess said. He'd stopped smiling, but he still looked kind. 'Informally.'

A chill moved softly over Claire's skin. A single wave of chill. *Yes*. Michael was OK with it.

'Sure,' Claire said, and stepped back to swing the door wider. The cops stepped over the threshold, Hess first, then Lowe, and Shane shot Claire a look she couldn't quite figure out and led the men back to the living room.

Lowe studied the place more than the two of them; he seemed to really appreciate it. 'Nice,' he murmured, which was the first thing he'd said. 'Great use of wood in here. Real organic.'

She couldn't really say *thank you*, because, hey, she didn't build it. She didn't even own it. But on Michael's behalf she said, 'We think so, too, sir.'

Claire settled nervously back on the sofa, perched on the edge. Shane remained standing, and Hess and Lowe moved around, not exactly searching, but cataloguing everything. Hess stayed focused on the two of them, and after a moment, he bent his knees and sat down in the chair that Michael had occupied last night. Déja vu, Claire thought. Hess seemed to shiver a little, and he looked up, maybe trying to locate the source of the draft that had just brushed past him.

Michael liked that chair.

'You had some trouble here last night,' Hess said. 'I know you had a talk with our colleagues Gretchen and Hans. I read the report this morning.'

No harm in admitting to that. Both Shane and Claire nodded.

'A little scary, huh?'

Claire nodded. Shane didn't. He gave the detective a narrow little smile. 'I'm a Morganville lifer. Define scary,' he said. 'Anyway, if you're playing good cop, bad cop—'

'I'm not,' Hess said. 'Trust me, you'd know if I was, because I'd be the bad cop.' And there was something in his eyes that – oddly – made Claire believe it. 'Look, I won't lie to you. Gretchen and Hans, they've got their own agendas. But so do we. We want to make sure you're protected, understand me? That's our job. We serve and protect, and Travis and I believe in that.'

Lowe paused in his slow amble to nod.

'We're neutral. There's a few of us in town who did enough good for each side to earn a little freedom, as long as we're careful.'

'What Joe means,' Detective Lowe said, 'is that they ignore us as long as we keep it on our side of the tracks. Humans are the slave race here; forget about skin colour. So we have to take care of our own when we can.'

'And when we *can't*,' Hess said, as smoothly as if they'd rehearsed all this, 'things get ugly. It ain't like the two of us are free agents. We're Switzerland. If you cross the line, you're on your own.'

Shane frowned at him. 'What can you do for us, if you're Switzerland?'

'I can make sure that Gretchen and Hans don't make any follow-up visits,' Hess said. 'I can keep most of the cops away from you, maybe not all. I can put out the word widely that you're not just under a Founder's seal; Travis and I are keeping an eye on you. That'll keep anybody else from trying to win friends by smacking you around.'

'Anybody human, he means,' Lowe amended. 'The vamps, they'll scare the shit out of you if they can, but they won't hurt you. Not unless you screw up and that Founder's seal goes away. Got me?'

Which had already happened, really. The screwing-up part. Well, technically, she supposed

Shane's dad hadn't broken any laws – yet – because Michael hadn't really died.

Except that he had.

God, Morganville made her head hurt.

A door slammed upstairs, and Eve came clattering down the stairs, fully dressed in Goth finery: a purple sheer shirt over a black corset thingy, a skirt that looked like it had gotten caught in a shredder, hose with skulls woven in, and her black Mary Janes. Very fierce. Her make-up was back in full force, ice white face, black-rimmed eyes, lips like three-day-old bruises.

'Officer Joe!' Eve practically flew across the room to hug him. Shane and Claire exchanged a look. Yeah, this wasn't something they were going to see every day. 'Joe Joe Joe! I've been wondering where you were!'

'Hi, Skippy. You remember Travis, right?'

'Big T!' Another hug. This, Claire thought, had tipped over the edge into the surreal, even for Morganville. 'I'm so glad to see you guys!'

'Ditto, kid,' Lowe said. He was smiling, and it transformed his face into something that was almost angelic. 'You've still got the numbers, right?'

Eve slapped her hand on the mobile phone strapped to her belt in a coffin-shaped holder. 'Oh yeah. Speed dial. But there hasn't been...um—'

Claire had the sudden weird feeling that Eve had something she couldn't talk about in front of them.

The cops seemed to think so, too, because their eyes met briefly, and then Hess said, 'You want an update? How about showing us to your coffee pot?'

'Sure!' Eve said brightly, and led them off into the kitchen.

'Well,' Shane said as the door shut behind them, 'that's bizarre.'

'Did I miss a chapter?' Claire asked. 'And are there Cliff's Notes?'

'No idea.'

The sound of conversation drifted in from the kitchen, music without words. Claire fidgeted, then got up and tiptoed over.

'Hey!' Shane protested, but he followed.

Hess was talking about somebody named Jason. Shane reacted, putting his hand on Claire's shoulder and lifting his finger to his lips.

What? she mouthed silently.

I want to hear.

Detective Lowe was talking. '—you probably would want to know that he's getting out today. Now, before you say anything, he's been warned. He's not about to go near you or your parents. He'll be monitored.'

'Monitored.' Eve sounded shaken. 'But...I thought he was going to be in jail for a long time! What about that girl...?'

'She withdrew the complaint,' Hess said. 'We couldn't keep him locked up forever, honey. I'm sorry.'

'But he's *guilty*!'

'I know. But now it's your word against his, and you know how that gets decided. You're not sworn to anybody, Eve. He is.'

Eve cursed. It sounded like she was trying not to cry. 'Does he know where I am?'

'He'll find out,' Hess said. 'But like I said, he's being monitored, and we'll keep an eye on all of you kids here. You leave Jason alone, he'll leave you alone. OK?'

If Eve agreed, she did it silently. Claire nearly tipped backward as Shane tugged on her shoulder; then she caught her balance and followed him back to the couch.

'Who's Jason?' She couldn't even wait until they were seated to ask.

'Crap,' he sighed. 'Jason's her brother. Last I heard, he was in jail for stabbing somebody. He's kind of a psycho, and Eve turned him in. No wonder she's freaked.'

'Her older brother?' Because Claire was picturing some Gothed-out muscular football type about ten feet tall, with a steroid habit.

'Younger,' Shane said. 'Seventeen, I guess. Skinny, creepy kid. I never liked him.'

'Do you think—?'

'What?'

'Do you think he'll come *here*? Try to hurt Eve?'

Shane shrugged. 'If he does, he'll be regretting it

all the way to the hospital.' He said it in a matter-of-fact kind of way that made Claire feel strangely warm. She fought to catch her breath. If Shane noticed, he didn't show it. 'As long as we stay here, we're safe.' He looked up at the blank ceiling. 'Right, Michael?'

A chill drifted over Claire's skin. 'Right,' she said, on Michael's behalf.

But she wondered.

CHAPTER FIVE

The cops left, Shane played some video games, and Claire studied. It was a normal kind of day, all things considered. Shane had the TV on, looking for any news that might show a clue as to what his dad was up to, but Morganville's local station (it had only one) seemed bland, vanilla, and content-free even on the newscast.

The night came; Michael drifted back into human form; they had dinner.

Normal life, such as it passed for in a place like Morganville. In the Glass House.

It was only at midnight, when Claire was drifting off to sleep to the distant, sweet sound of Michael's guitar, that she started wondering about what she was going to do in the morning. She couldn't just *hide*, no matter what Michael thought. She had a life – sort of – and she'd already missed enough classes this semester. It was go or withdraw, and withdrawing would make things worse. She'd never get her academic life together and go on to the Ivy League schools she was dreaming about.

She fell asleep thinking of vampires, fangs, pretty girls with mean smiles and cigarette lighters. Of fires and screaming. Of Shane's mom floating in the bathtub.

Of Shane, huddled in a corner, crying.

Not a great night. She woke up at first light, wondering if Michael was already gone again, and yawned and struggled her way out of bed and to the bathroom. Nobody else was up, of course. The shower felt good, and by the time she'd dried her hair and pulled on a plain white shirt and blue jeans and sneakers, and loaded up her backpack with the daily essentials, she felt ready to face the outside world.

Shane was asleep on the couch downstairs. She tiptoed past him, but a squeaky floorboard made it a useless exercise; he came bolt upright and stared at her with wild, uncomprehending eyes for a few seconds before he blinked and sighed. 'Claire.' He swung his legs off, sat up, and rested his head on the palms of his hands. 'Ow. Man, remind me that two hours of sleep doesn't really cut it.'

'I think you just reminded yourself. What were you doing up?'

'Talking,' he said. 'Michael needed to talk.'

Oh. Guy stuff. Stuff Michael hadn't wanted to

share with the girls. OK, fine, not her business. Claire hitched up her backpack and edged towards the hallway.

'Where are you going?' Shane asked without lifting his head.

'You know where I'm going.'

'Oh no, you're not!'

'Shane, I'm *going*. Sorry, but you don't get to tell me what to do.' Technically, she supposed he could; he was older, and in Michael's absence he was sort of the owner and operator of the house. But...no. Not even then. Once she started letting that happen – or happen again – she'd lose whatever independence she'd earned. 'I have to go to class. Look, I'll be fine. Amelie's Protection's still good, and the campus is neutral ground, you know that. Unless I screw up, I'll be OK.'

'It's not neutral ground for Monica,' he said, and looked up. 'She tried to kill you, Claire.'

True. Claire gulped down a hard little bubble of fear. 'I can handle Monica.' She didn't think she could, but at least she could avoid her. Running was always an option.

Shane stared at her with bloodshot, tired eyes for a few long seconds, then shook his head and flopped back against the couch cushions, arms spread wide. 'Whatever,' he said. 'Call if you get into trouble.'

Something in his tone made Claire want to shed

the backpack and crawl up on the couch next to him, cuddling close, but she straightened her spine and said, 'I will,' and marched to the door.

Two hard, fast chills swept over her. Michael, telling her a firm *no*.

'Bite me,' she said, shot the brand-new locks that Shane had installed, and exited into the warm Texas morning sun.

English class was boring, and she'd already read through everything in the curriculum, so Claire spent her time writing out her thoughts in the back of her journal. A lot of them centred on Shane, and Shane's lips, and Shane's hands. And curses, on the fact that she wasn't eighteen yet, and that it was a stupid rule anyway.

She was still thinking about the injustice of all that after class, when she ran into trouble.

Literally.

Claire turned the corner, head down, and collided with a tall, firm body that instantly grabbed her by the shoulders and shoved her, *hard*, backward. Claire nearly lost her balance, but skidded to a shaky and upright halt, bracing herself against the wall. 'Hey!' she yelled, more in shock than anger, and then her brain caught up with her eyes and she thought, *Oh, crap*.

It was Monica.

Monica Morrell looked polished and perfect,

from her shining straight hair to her flawless make-up to the cute, trendy sheer top over baby doll T she was wearing. No backpack for Monica. She had a designer bag, and she looked Claire up and down, glossed lips twisting in disdain. Of course, she wasn't alone. Monica never went anywhere without an entourage, and today it was her usual wing girls, Jennifer and Gina, as well as a hovering flock of hard-bodied boys, most of them athletes of some kind or other.

Everybody was taller than Claire.

'Watch it, freak!' Monica said, and glared at her. And then started to smile. It didn't lessen the menace in her pretty eyes. 'Oh, it's you. You ought to watch where you're going.' She half turned to her little gaggle of followers. 'Poor Claire. She's got a syndrome or something. Falls down stairs, hits her head, nearly burns down her house…' She focused back on Claire as Jennifer and Gina giggled. 'Isn't that right? Didn't your house burn?'

'Little bit,' Claire said. She was shaking, deep down, but she knew that if she backed down, she risked a lot worse. 'But I heard it's not the first time that's happened when you stop by for a visit.'

Monica's clique made a low *ooooooooooh* sound, a no-she-didn't murmur evenly split between appreciation and anticipation. Monica's eyes turned cold. – Er.

'Don't even go there, freak. Not my fault you live with a bunch of losers and jerks. Probably that Goth whore lighting candles all over the place. She's a walking fire hazard, not to mention a fashion disaster.'

Claire bit the inside of her lip and swallowed her reply, which would have had to do with who the real whore was in the conversation. She just raised her own eyebrows – well aware they weren't plucked, or perfect, or anything – and smiled like she knew something Monica didn't.

'She's not the only one. Isn't that top from Wal-Mart? The Trailer Park collection?' She turned around to go as Monica's friends *ooooh*ed again, this time with an edge of laughter.

Monica grabbed her by the backpack, yanking her off-balance. 'Tell Shane I said hi,' she said, her breath hot against Claire's ear. 'Tell him I don't care who's put out the truce flag… I'm going to get him, and you, and he's going to be sorry he *ever* screwed with me.'

Claire pulled herself free from Monica's highly polished manicured grip and said, 'He wouldn't screw you if you were the last girl on earth and it was survival of the species.'

She thought that Monica was going to scratch her eyes out with those perfectly manicured talons, and backed off fast. Monica, strangely, let her go. She was even smiling, a little, but it was a weird kind of smile, and it made Claire's stomach lurch when she looked back.

'Bye now,' Monica said. 'Freak.'

Chem class was already under way when Claire breathlessly slid into an empty seat and unpacked her notebook and text. She kept an eye out for Monica, Gina, Jennifer, or any random chemicals being flung her way – it had happened before – but she didn't run into Monica there, or on her way to her next class, or the next. By mid-afternoon she was aching from the tension, but her heart rate was pretty normal, and she'd gotten back into the groove of listening for comprehension. Not that she wasn't way ahead in the classes – she had a habit of reading the whole book at the beginning of the semester – but it was always nice when professors dropped some titbit that wasn't in the book or the published notes. Even the classes she didn't much like seemed relatively interesting. History had a quiz, which she finished in five minutes and handed in, then escaped with a silent thumbs-up from the professor.

It was late afternoon when she exited into the quadrangle outside of the science building; the crowds of students had thinned, since a lot of people tried to finish classes early and get on with the all-important party schedule. Texas Prairie University wasn't exactly Harvard on the Plains; most of the students were here to plough through two years of required courses, then transfer out to a legitimate university. So it was 'Party till you puke,' mostly.

It was funny as she looked around now, knowing what she knew about Morganville. She'd never realised what an insulated little world college was; she'd be willing to bet that ninety per cent of the kids attending had no idea what the real score was in town, or ever would. TPU was like a wildlife park, and the students were the wildlife.

And sometimes, the herd got culled.

Claire shivered, looked around for any signs of lurking Monicas, and took off for home. It wasn't a long walk, but it took her over the nicely tended (though sun-seared) grounds and out into Morganville proper's 'business district' – which really wasn't. It was a side-show for the students, all coffee shops (she wondered what poor fool Oliver had gotten to fill Eve's empty barista apron) and bookstores and trendy clothing emporiums. Buildings sported school colours – green and white – and usually had STUDENT DISCOUNT signs fading in the windows.

There was a weedy-looking guy in black standing at the corner, watching her with burning dark eyes. He looked familiar, but she couldn't think why...somebody from class, maybe? Scary, anyway. She wondered why he was staring at *her*. There were other girls on the street. Prettier ones.

Claire walked faster. When she looked back, he wasn't there anymore. Was that better, or way creepier?

Walking even faster seemed like a great idea suddenly.

As Claire passed Common Grounds, the coffee shop, she glanced inside and saw someone she thought she recognised...but what the hell would Shane's dad be doing *here*? In the middle of the day? He didn't exactly blend in with the college crowd, and every cop in town was shaking the trees for him, right?

But there he was. Granted, she'd gotten only a quick look, but how many Frank Collins look-alikes could there be in Morganville?

I should get the hell out of here, she thought, but then she wondered. If she could find out what he was doing, maybe that would help Michael and Shane with planning what to do next. Besides, it was the middle of the day, broad daylight, and it wasn't like Mr Collins didn't know where to find her if he wanted – he knew where she lived, after all.

So Claire opened the door and slipped inside, hiding behind a couple of big jocks with bulky laptop-laden backpacks who were having some earnest conversation about whether baseball stats were legitimate during the steroid years, or had to be thrown out. Yes, that *was* Shane's dad, and he was sitting in the corner of the coffee bar, sipping from a cup. Plain as day.

What the *hell*...?

She caught her breath as Oliver slipped into the seat opposite him. Oliver was a lanky guy, tall and a bit stooped, with long curling hair that was sprinkled and shot through with grey. Not very threatening, Oliver, until you saw the fangs and the real personality lurking underneath what he put on for the public. Oliver was terrifying, and she had no desire *at all* to get into any position where she'd have to deal with him again.

Claire turned to go, and ran into a broad chest clad in a soft grey T-shirt. She looked up, and saw a guy she didn't recognise – a little older than Shane, maybe, but not much. He had soft, short red hair, and he was fair-skinned and freckled. Big blue eyes, the kind of blue that made her think of clear skies or deep oceans. He was just...pretty. And kind of peaceful.

Big and solid, and wearing – of all things, in this Texas late-summer heat wave – an old, worn brown leather jacket. No backpack, but he looked like a student.

He smiled down at her. She expected him to step out of the way, but he didn't; instead, he reached down, took her hand, and said, 'Hello, Claire. I'm Sam. Let's talk.'

His fingers felt cool, like clay. And he was, under

the freckles, a little *too* pale. And there was something fey and sad in his eyes, too.

Oh, crap. Vampire.

Claire tried to pull free. He held on effortlessly. He could break bones if he wanted to – she sensed it – but he used just enough strength to keep her from getting loose. 'Don't,' Sam said. 'I need to talk to you. Please, I promise not to hurt you. Let's sit down, OK?'

'But—' Claire looked around, alarmed. The two jocks were moving away, heading for the bar to get drinks. The place was busy, and there were students everywhere – chatting, laughing, playing games, tapping away on laptops, talking on cell phones. And, of course, nobody was paying attention to her. She could make a scene and probably get away, but that would draw the attention of Oliver, not to mention Shane's dad, and she didn't want that. Low-pro was the order of the day.

Claire swallowed and let the vampire pull her to a secluded table near the window. He sat far from the hard white line of sunshine that had crept in across the wooden floor. The canopy outside screened most of it, but there was a tiny little area of risk left, she supposed.

Sam kept hold of her hand. She sat down, tried to make her voice strong and steady, and said, 'Would you mind letting go now? Since I'm sitting?'

'What? Oh. Sure.' He released her, and gave her

a smile that even her biased, suspicious (verging on paranoid) mind interpreted as...sweet. 'Sorry. You're just so warm. It feels good.'

He sounded wistful. She couldn't afford to feel sorry for him, no way in hell. *Couldn't.* 'How do you know my name?' she asked.

His blue eyes narrowed when he smiled. 'You're kidding. Everybody knows your name. You, Shane, Eve, Michael. The Founder put out a Directive. First time in, oh, I guess about thirty years, maybe forty. Pretty dramatic stuff. We're all on our best behaviour around you, don't worry.' His gaze flicked around, touched on Oliver, and came back to her. 'Well, except for people who don't really have a best behaviour.'

'People,' Claire said, and crossed her arms. She hoped it made her look tough and strong, but she really did it because she was feeling cold. 'You're not *people*'

Sam looked a bit hurt. 'Harsh, Claire. Of course we're people. We're just...different.'

'No, you *kill people*. You're...parasites!' And she had no idea why she was getting into a debate about it with a total stranger. A vampire, at that. At least he hadn't done that thing to her like Brandon had done, that mesmerising thing. Oh, and she wasn't supposed to be looking him in the eye. Crap. She'd forgotten. Sam seemed kind of, well, normal. And he did have lovely eyes.

Sam was thinking over what she'd said, as if it was a serious argument. 'Food chain,' he offered.

'What?'

'Well, humans are parasites and mass murderers, from the point of view of vegetables.'

That...almost made some kind of weird sense. Almost. 'I'm not a carrot. What do you want from me? Besides the obvious, I mean.' She mimed fangs in the neck.

He looked a little ashamed. 'I need to ask you a favour. Can you give something to Eve for me?'

She couldn't imagine anything Eve would want less than a gift from a vampire. 'No,' she said. 'Is that it? Can I go?'

'Wait! It's nothing bad, I swear. It's just that I always thought she was a lot of fun. I'm going to miss her coming in here. She always brightened up the place.' He reached in his pocket and took out a small black box, which he handed over. Claire frowned and fidgeted with it for a second, then snapped the cover open. Not that it was any of her business, but...

It was a necklace. A pretty one, silver, with a shiny coffin-shaped locket. Claire raised her eyes to Sam's, reminded herself *again* not to do that, and focused somewhere in the middle of his chest. (He had a nice chest. Kind of built, actually.) 'What's in it?'

'Open it,' he said, and shrugged. 'I'm not trying

to hide anything. I told you, it's nothing dangerous.'

She snapped the lid of the coffin open. Inside, there was a tiny silver statue of a girl with her arms crossed over her chest. Creepy, but kind of cool, too. Claire had to admit, Eve would probably be delighted.

'Look, I'm not stalking her,' Sam said. 'We're just...friends. She's not the biggest fan of the not quite breathing, thanks to that asshole Brandon – I get that. I'm not trying to be her boyfriend. I just thought she might like it.'

Sam was *not* fitting into Claire's recently built pigeon-holes, so new they still smelt of mental sawdust. VAMPIRES – BAD, one said. The one next to it said VAMPIRES – DOWNRIGHT EVIL. Those were pretty much the only two vampire slots available.

She didn't know where to put him. Sam just looked like a guy with sad eyes and a sweet smile, who could use some sun. A normal guy, one she'd probably get her heart rate up over talking to in class.

But that was probably how he got his victims, she reminded herself. She snapped the cover shut on the locket, closed the case, and slid it back across the table to him. 'Sorry,' she said. 'I'm not taking anything. If you want her to have it, give it to her yourself. Not that I think she'll ever come in here again.'

Sam looked taken aback, but he took the case

and put it in the pocket of his leather jacket. 'OK,' he said. 'Thanks for listening. Can I ask you something else? Not a favour, just information.'

She wasn't sure, but she nodded.

'It's about Amelie.' Sam had lowered his voice, and his eyes were suddenly fierce and intense. Not so normal-guy. This was what he'd really wanted, not just the gift to Eve. This was *personal*. 'You talked to her, I heard. How is she? How did she seem?'

'Why?'

He didn't break the stare. 'She doesn't talk to me anymore. None of them do. I don't care about the others, but...I worry about her.'

Claire couldn't believe what she was hearing. A vampire wanted her to talk about his vampire queen? Weirdy McWeird. 'Um...she seems...fine... She doesn't talk to you anymore? Why not?'

'I don't know,' he said, and sat back. 'She hasn't spoken to me for fifty years, give or take a few months. And no matter how many times I ask, I can't see her. They won't accept messages.' Something dark and wounded flickered in those innocent-looking eyes. 'She made me, and she abandoned me. Nobody's seen her in public in a long time. Now suddenly she's talking to you. Why?'

Fifty years. She was talking to an at-least-seventy-year-old man, with skin finer than hers.

With a gorgeous, unlined face, and eyes that had seen…well…more than she ever would, most likely. *Fifty years?* 'How old are you?' she blurted, because it was seriously freaking her out.

'Seventy-two. I'm the youngest,' he said.

'In town?'

'In the world.' He fiddled with the sugar container on the table. 'Vampires are dying out, you know. That's why we're here, in Morganville. We were being slaughtered out there, in the world. But even here, Amelie's only made two new vampires in the last hundred and fifty years.' He looked up slowly and met her eyes, and this time, she felt an echo of that thing Brandon did, that compulsion that held her in place. 'I know how it looks to you, because I've been there. I was born in Morganville; I grew up Protected. I know it sucks to be you around here. You're slaves. Just because you don't wear chains and get branded doesn't make you any less slaves.'

She flashed on an image of Shane's mother, dead in the bathtub. 'And if we run, you kill us,' she whispered. She would have expected him to flinch, or have some kind of reaction to that, but Sam's expression didn't change at all.

'Sometimes,' he said. 'But Claire, it isn't like we want to. We're trying to survive, that's all. You understand?'

Claire could almost see him standing there,

looking down at Shane's mom as she bled to death. He'd have that same gentle, sad look in his eyes. Molly Collins would have been just a pet he had to put down, that was all, and it wouldn't matter to him enough to make him lose a night's sleep. If vampires slept. Which she was starting to doubt.

She stood up so fast, her chair hit the wall with a clatter. Sam leant back, surprised, as she grabbed up her backpack. 'Oh, I understand,' Claire said through gritted teeth. 'I can't trust *any* of you. You want to know how Amelie is? Go ask. There's probably a good reason why she won't talk to you!'

'Claire!'

She stiff-armed open the door and escaped into the day. She looked back to see Sam standing there at the edge of the strip of sunlight inside Common Grounds, staring after her with an expression on his face like he'd lost his best – his only – friend.

Dammit, she was *not* any vampire's friend. She couldn't be. And she wasn't going to be, ever.

CHAPTER SIX

Claire decided on the way home that maybe it wouldn't be a good idea to blurt all of it out to Shane – not about Monica, or his dad, or the vampire Sam. Instead, she made dinner (tacos) and waited for Michael to rejoin the world. Which he did, as soon as the sun was safely under the horizon, and looked just as normal and angelic as ever.

She somehow got the message across to him that she needed to talk in private, which resulted in Michael drying dishes in the kitchen while she washed up. How that happened, she wasn't sure – it wasn't her turn – but the warm water and smooth suds were kind of soothing.

'Did you tell Shane about Monica?' Michael asked when she was done relating the day's events. He didn't seem bothered, but then, it took a lot to faze Michael. He might have been wiping the plates a little too thoroughly, though.

'No,' she said. 'He gets a little, you know, about her.'

'Yeah, he does. OK, you need to be careful, you know that, right? I'd ask Shane to go with you to class, but—'

'But that's probably what she wants,' Claire finished, and handed him another plate. 'To get us both together so she can use us against each other. Right?'

Michael nodded, eyebrows going up. 'All she has to do is grab you and she's got him. So be careful. I'm...not much use, outside of here. Or any use, actually.'

She felt bad for the flash of anger in his eyes – it wasn't directed at her but at himself. He hated this. Hated being trapped here while his friends needed him.

'I'll be fine,' she said. 'I got a new cell phone. Mom and Dad sent it.'

'Good. You've got us all on speed dial?'

'One, two, and three. And 911 on four.'

'Sweet.' Michael hip-bumped her. 'How are classes?'

'OK.' She couldn't work up any enthusiasm for them right at the moment. 'We're not talking about Shane's dad?'

'Nothing to talk about,' he said. 'You stay out of Common Grounds, and stay away from Oliver. If Shane's dad was in there, he was probably just taking a look around. Oliver might have sent him on his way. He does a good regular-guy act.' Michael ought to know, Claire reflected. Oliver had done a good enough regular-guy act to charm his way into the house, where he'd killed Michael, trying to make him a vampire. The house had saved Michael – partly. A kind of supernatural apology for having failed to protect him in the first place. The house did things like that. It was creepy, and occasionally flat-out scary, but it was at least mostly loyal to whoever was in residence.

Oliver, though...Oliver was loyal to Oliver. And that was about it.

'So we do nothing?' Claire asked.

'We do the best nothing you've ever seen.' Michael put the last plate away and tossed the towel over his shoulder like a bartender going on break. 'Meaning, *you* do nothing, Claire. That's an order.' She gave him a cockeyed mock salute. 'Yes, sir, sorry, sir.'

He sighed. 'I liked you better when you were this timid little kid. What happened?'

'I started living with you guys.'

'Oh, right.'

He fluffed her hair, smiled, and ambled off towards the living room. 'It's game night,' he said. 'I made Shane swear, no video games tonight. I think he's blowing the dust off of Monopoly. I wouldn't let him have Risk. He gets crazy with Risk.'

Didn't they all?

✷ ✷ ✷

'So, I got a new job,' Eve said brightly as they sat on the floor around the Monopoly board. Shane was kicking ass, but Michael had the railroads; Eve and Claire were just mostly watching their money stacks dwindle. *No wonder people like this game*, Claire thought. *It's just like life.*

'You got a job already?' Shane asked as Michael rattled the dice in his hand and then tossed them out on the faded, warped board. 'Jeez, Eve, throw the brakes on full employment. You're making me look bad.'

'Shane Collins, permanent slacker. If you'd book more than one interview a month, and actually, you know, *show up* to them, you might get a job, too.'

'Oh, so now you're a career counsellor?'

'Bite me. You're not even going to ask me where?'

'Sure,' Michael said as he moved his cannon across four squares. 'Where?...Oh, crap.'

'That'll be five hundred, my man. And extra for clean towels in the hotel.' Shane held out his palm.

'I got hired at the university,' Eve said, watching Michael count out cash and hand it over to Shane. 'In the student union coffee shop. I even got a raise.'

'Congratulations!' Claire said. 'And you're not working for an evil vampire. Bonus.'

'Boss-wise, a definite step up. I mean, he's a slack-jawed loser with bad breath and a drinking problem, but that pretty much describes most of the male population of Morganville...'

'Hey!' both Shane and Michael chorused, and Eve gave them both a brilliant grin.

'Excluding the hotties in the room, of course. And cheer up, guys, it includes most of the *female* population, too. Anyway. Better hours – I'm working days, so not a lot of vamp worries – and bigger pay-cheques. Plus, I get to check out campus life. I hear they party hard.'

'From the other side of the counter, all you're going to see is people dissing you and complaining about their drinks,' Shane said without looking up. 'You watch yourself, Eve. Some of those assholes on campus think that if you're wearing a name badge, you're their own personal toy.'

'Yeah, I know. I heard about Karla.'

'Karla?' Claire asked.

'She works at the university,' Eve said. 'Karla Gast. We went to school with her.' Michael and Shane both looked up and nodded. 'She was kind of a party girl in high school, you know? Real pretty, too. She went to work on campus – I don't know what she was doing – but anyway, she's missing.'

'It was in the paper,' Michael said. 'Abducted last night walking to her car.'

Claire frowned. 'Why would it be in the paper? I mean, they don't usually put stuff like that in the papers, right?' Because in Morganville, murder was sort of legitimate, wasn't it?

'They do if it wasn't vampires,' Eve said, and

nibbled on a carrot stick as she rolled the dice. 'Oooooh, pay me my two hundred, Mr Banker. If she'd been dragged off by vamps, even rogue vamps, it would have just been swept under the carpet like usual. Pay-offs to the family, end of the story. But this is different.'

'Is that, you know, unusual? Crime? Crime that isn't vampire related, I mean?'

'Kinda.' Eve shrugged. 'But people tend to get nasty around Morganville. Nasty, or drunk, or timid. One of those.'

'Which are you?' Shane asked. Eve bared her teeth at him and growled. 'Ouch. Right. Gotcha.'

'So... Eve, I heard your brother's out of jail,' Michael said. Claire was rolling dice for her move, and by the time the plastic hit the board it sounded as loud as plates shattered on a tile floor. Nobody was making a sound. Nobody was *breathing*, so far as she could tell. From the expression on his face, Michael was clearly rethinking having brought up the subject, and Eve looked...hard and fierce and (deep down) scared.

Shane was just watching, no expression at all.

Awkward.

'Um...' Claire cautiously slid her Scottie dog the six squares that she'd rolled. 'You haven't said much about your brother.' She was curious what Eve would say. Because clearly Eve was *not* happy Michael had brought it up.

'I don't talk about him,' Eve said flatly. 'Not anymore. His name is Jason, and he's a dick, and let's drop the subject, OK?'

'OK.' Claire cleared her throat. 'Shane?'

'What?' He looked down at the board where she was pointing. 'Oh. Right. Three hundred.'

She mutely handed over her last bills as Shane took the dice in hand.

'Eve, you know what he went to jail for. You don't think—,' Michael began, very slowly.

'Shut up, Michael,' Eve said tensely. 'Just shut up, OK? Is it possible he did it? Sure. I wouldn't put it past him, but he just got out yesterday morning. That's pretty fast work, even for Jason.' But she looked shaken, under the fierce expression, and even paler than normal. 'You know what? I have to get up early.

'Night.'

'Eve—'

She jumped up and headed for the stairs. Michael followed, two steps behind as she climbed towards her room, black tattered-silk skirt fluttering. Claire watched them go, eyebrows raised, and Shane continued to shake the dice.

'Guess the game's over,' he said, and rolled anyway. 'Heh. Boardwalk. I think that completes Shane's real estate empire, thank you for playing, goodnight.'

'What was Michael talking about?' Claire asked.

'Does he think Eve's brother might have taken that girl?'

'No, he thinks Eve's brother might have *killed* that girl,' Shane said. 'And the cops probably think so, too. If he did, they'll get him, and this time, he won't be getting out of jail. In fact, he probably won't even make it to jail. One of Karla's brothers is a cop.'

'Oh,' Claire said in a small voice. She could hear the murmur of conversation upstairs. 'Well...I guess I should get to bed, too. I have early classes tomorrow.'

Shane met her eyes. 'Might want to give them some privacy for a while.'

Oh. Right. She jiggled her foot under the table and started gathering up the cash and cards from the table. Her hands brushed Shane's, and he let go of the cards and took hold.

And then, somehow, she was in his lap, and he was kissing her. Hadn't meant to do that, but...well. She couldn't exactly be sorry about it, because he tasted amazing, and his lips were so soft and his hands were so strong...

He leant back, eyes half-shut, and he was smiling. Shane didn't smile all that much, and it always left her breathless and tingling. There was a secrecy about it, like he only ever smiled with her, and it just felt...perfect. 'Claire, you're being careful, right?' He smoothed hair back from her face. 'Seriously. You'd tell me if you got into trouble.'

'No trouble,' she lied, thinking about Monica's not-so-veiled threats, and that glimpse of Shane's dad seated across from Oliver in the coffee shop. 'No trouble at all.'

'Good.' He kissed her again, then moved down her jawline to her neck, and, wow, neck nibbles that took her breath away again. She closed her eyes and buried her fingers in his warm hair, trying to tell him through every touch how much she liked this, liked *him*, loved...

Her eyes came open, fast.

She did *not* just think that.

Shane's warm hands moved up her sides, thumbs grazing the sides of her breasts again, and he traced his fingers across the thin skin of her collarbone...down to where the neck of her T-shirt stopped him. Teasing. Pulling it down an inch, then two.

And then, maddeningly, he let go and leant back, lips damp. He licked them, watching her, and gave her that slow, crazy sexy smile again.

'Go to bed,' he said. 'Before I decide to come with.'

She wasn't sure she could stand up, but somehow, she got her legs to steady under her, and made it up the stairs. Michael was in Eve's room, the door was open, and they were sitting together on her bed. Michael was so bright, with his golden hair and china-blue eyes, and he didn't match the room all draped in dramatic black and red. He looked like an angel who'd taken a massive wrong turn.

He was holding Eve in his arms and rocking her, very gently, back and forth. As Claire looked in, he met her eyes and mouthed, *Close the door.*

She did, and went to her own bed.

Sadly, alone.

It occurred to Claire that she'd be smart to know what Jason Rosser looked like, in order to avoid him, but she had the strong feeling that it wouldn't be a very good idea to ask Eve for a peek at the family album. Eve was pretty touchy just now about anything to do with her brother...which, if Shane's pessimistic assessment was right, probably wasn't the wrong attitude.

So Claire went researching. Not the university library, which – while not too bad – didn't really have a lot of info about Morganville itself. She'd checked. There was some history, all carefully blanded down, and some newspaper archives.

But there was a Morganville Historical Society. She found the address in the phone book, studied the map, and calculated the time it would take to walk the distance. If she hustled, she could get there, find what she needed, and still make it to her noon class.

Claire showered, dressed in blue jeans and a black knit top with a screen-printed flower on it – one of her thrift-shop buys – and grabbed her backpack on the way to the door. She set herself a blistering pace once she hit the sidewalks, heading away from the university and into the unexplored guts of Morganville. She had the map with her, which was handy, because as soon as she was out of sight of the Glass House, things became confusing. For having been master planned, Morganville was not exactly logical in the way its streets ran. There were cul-de-sacs, dead ends, lots of unlit deserted areas.

But then again, maybe that *was* logical, from a vampire's planning perspective. Even in the hot beat of the sunlight, Claire shuddered at that idea, and moved faster past a street that ended in a deserted field littered with piled-up lumber and assorted junk. It even smelt like decay, the ugly smell of dead things left to rot in the heat. Having too much imagination was sometimes a handicap. *At least I'm not walking it at night...*

No power on earth was going to make her do that.

The residential areas of Morganville were old, mostly run-down, parched and beaten by summer. It was bound to get cooler soon, but for now, Indian summer was broiling the Texas landscape. Cicadas sang in dull dental-drill whines in the grass and trees, and there was a smell of dust and hot metal in the wind. Of all the places to find vampires, this was pretty much the last she would have expected. Just not...Goth enough. Too run-down. Too... American.

The next street was her turn, according to the map. She made it, stopped in the shade of a live oak tree, and took a couple of drinks from her water bottle as she considered how much longer a walk it would be. Not long, she thought. Which was good, because she was *not* going to miss another class. Ever.

The street dead-ended. Claire came to a stop, frowning, and checked; nope, according to the map, it went all the way through. Claire sighed in frustration and started to turn back to retrace her path, then hesitated when she saw a narrow passage between two fences. It looked like it went through to the next street.

Lose ten minutes or take a chance. She'd always been the lose-ten-minutes kind of girl, the prudent one, but maybe living in the Glass House had corrupted her. Besides, it was hot as hell out here.

She headed for the gap between the fences.

'I wouldn't do that, child,' said a voice. It was coming from the deep shadow of a porch, on a house to her right. It looked better cared for than most houses in Morganville – freshly painted in a light sea-blue, some brick trim, a neatly kept yard.

Claire squinted and shaded her eyes, and finally saw a tiny bird-like old lady seated on a porch swing. She was as brown as a twig, with drifting pale hair like dandelion fuzz, and since she was dressed in a soft green sundress that hung on her like a bag, she looked like nothing so much as a wood spirit, something out of the old, old storybooks.

The voice, though, was pure warm Southern honey.

Claire backed up hastily from the entrance to the passageway. 'I'm sorry, ma'am. I don't mean to trespass.'

The tiny little thing cackled. 'Oh, no, child, you're not trespassin'. You're bein' a fool. You ever heard of ant lions? Or trap-door spiders? Well, you walk down that path, you won't be comin' out the other side. Not this world.'

Claire felt a pure cold bolt of panic, followed by a triumphant crow from the prudent side of her brain: *I knew that!* 'But...it's daytime!'

'So it is,' the old woman said, and rocked gently back and forth on her swing. 'So it is. Day don't always protect round Morganville. You should know that, too. Now, go back the way you came like a good child, and don't come here again.'

'Yes, ma'am,' Claire said, and started to back away.

'Granma, what are you— Oh, hello!' The screen

door to the house opened, and a younger version of the Stick Lady stepped out – young enough to be a granddaughter.

She was tall and pretty, and her skin was more cocoa than wood brown. She wore her hair in braids, lots of them, and she smiled at Claire as she came to lay a hand on the old lady's shoulder. 'My granma likes to sit out here and talk to people. I'm sorry if she bothered you.'

'No, not at all,' Claire said, and nervously fiddled with one of the loose adjustment straps of her backpack. 'She, um, warned me about the alley.'

The woman's eyes moved rapidly, from Claire to the old lady and back again. 'Did she?' she said. She didn't sound warm anymore. 'Granma, you know better than that. You need to quit scaring people with your stories.'

'Don't be a damn fool, Lisa. They ain't just stories, and you know it.'

'Granma, there hasn't been any...trouble around here for twenty years!'

'Doesn't mean it wouldn't happen,' Granma said stubbornly, and pointed a stick-thin shaking finger at Claire. 'You don't go down that alley, now. I meant what I said.'

'Yes, ma'am,' she said faintly, and nodded to both women. 'Um, thanks.'

Claire turned to go, and as she did, she noticed something mounted on the wall next to the old woman's porch swing. A plaque, with a symbol.

The same symbol as was on the Glass House. The Founder's symbol.

And now that she was looking at the house, really looking, it had some of the same lines to it, and it was about the same age.

Claire turned back, smiled apologetically, and said, 'I'm sorry, but could I use your restroom? I've been chugging water out here—'

She thought for a second that Lisa was going to say no, but then the younger woman frowned and said, 'I suppose,' and came down the steps to open the white picket gate for Claire to enter. 'Go on inside. It's the second door off the hall.'

'Offer the child some lemonade, Lisa.'

'She's not staying, Granma!'

'How you know if you don't ask?'

Claire let them argue it out, and stepped inside. She didn't feel anything – no tingle of a force field or anything – but then, she didn't going in and out of the Glass House, either.

Still, she recognised it immediately...There was something about this house. It had the same quality of stillness, of *weight*, that she always felt at home. Not the same at all inside from a decorating point of view – Granma and Lisa seemed to like furniture, lots of it, all in fussy floral patterns and chintz, with rugs everywhere and a smothering amount of curtains and lace. Claire walked slowly down the hardwood hallway, trailing her fingers lightly over the panelling. The wood felt warm, but all wood did, right?

'Freaky,' she muttered, and opened the bathroom door.

It wasn't a bathroom.

It was a study, a large one, and it couldn't have been more different from the overblown frilly living room...severe polished wood floors, a massive dark desk, a few glowering portraits on the walls. Dark red velvet curtains blocking out the sun. The walls were lined with books, old books mostly, and in the cabinet there was something that looked like a wine rack, only it held...scrolls?

Amelie was seated at the desk, signing sheets of paper with a gold pen. One of her assistants, also a vampire, was standing attentively next to her, taking each sheet out of the way as she wrote her name.

Neither of them looked up at Claire.

'Close the door,' Amelie said in a gentle voice accented with an almost-French sort of pronunciation. 'I dislike the draft.'

Claire thought about running, but she wasn't stupid enough to believe she could run far enough, or fast enough, and even though the idea of shrieking and slamming the door from the *other* side was pretty tempting, she swallowed her fear and stepped all the way in before she shut it with a quiet *click*.

'Is this your house?' Claire asked. It was the only thing she could think of to ask, frankly; every other question had been shaken right out of her head because *this couldn't be happening.*

Amelie glanced up, and her eyes were just as cool and intimidating as Claire remembered. It felt a little like being frostbitten. 'My house?' she echoed. 'Yes, of course. They are all my house. Oh, I see what you ask. You ask if the particular house you entered is my home. No, little Claire, it is not where I hide myself from my enemies, although it would certainly be a useful choice. Very...' Amelie smiled slowly. 'Unexpected.'

'Then...how...?'

'You'll find that when I need you, Claire, you will be called.' Amelie signed the last paper, then handed it to her assistant – a tall, dark young man in a black suit and tie – and he bowed slightly and left the room through another door. Amelie sat back in her massive carved chair, looking more like a queen than ever, including the golden coronet of hair on top of her head. Her long fingers tapped lightly on the lion-head arms of the chair. 'You are not in the house where you were, my dear. Do you understand that?'

'Teleportation,' Claire said. 'But that's not possible.'

'Yet you are here.'

'That's *science fiction*!'

Amelie waved her graceful hand. 'I fail to understand your conventions of literature these days. One impossible thing such as vampires, this is acceptable, but two impossible things becomes science fiction? Ah well, no matter. I cannot explain the workings of it; that is a subject for philosophers and artisans, and I am neither. Not for many years.' Her frost-coloured eyes warmed just a fraction. 'Put down your pack. I've seen tinkers carrying lighter loads.'

What's a tinker? Claire wondered. She started to ask, but didn't want to sound stupid. 'Thank you,' she said, and carefully lowered her backpack to the wooden floor, then slid into one of the two chairs facing the desk. 'Ma'am.'

'So polite,' Amelie said. 'And in a time when manners are forgotten...you do understand what manners are, don't you, Claire? Behaviours that allow humans to live closely together without killing each other. Most of the time.'

'Yes, ma'am.'

Silence. Somewhere behind Claire, a big clock ticked away minutes; she felt a drop of sweat glide down her neck and splash into the fabric of her black knit shirt.

Amelie was staring at her without blinking or moving, and that was weird. *Wrong.* People just didn't *do* that.

But then, Amelie wasn't people. In fact, of all the

vampires, in many ways she was the most not-people.

'Sam asked about you,' Claire blurted, just because it popped into her head and she wanted Amelie to stop staring at her. It worked. Amelie blinked, shifted her weight, and leant forward to rest her pointed chin on her folded hands, elbows still braced on the arms of the chair.

'Sam,' she said slowly, and her gaze wandered up and to her right, fixed on nothing. Trying to remember, Claire thought; she'd noticed how people – even vampires, apparently – did that with their eyes when remembering things. 'Ah yes. Samuel.' Her gaze snapped back to Claire with unnerving speed. 'And how did you come to chat with dear young Samuel?'

Claire shrugged. 'He wanted to talk to me.'

'About?'

'He asked about you. I...think he's lonely.'

Amelie smiled. She wasn't trying to impress Claire with her vampiness – no need for that! – so her teeth looked white and even, perfectly normal. 'Of course he's lonely,' she said. 'Samuel is the youngest. No one older trusts him; no one younger exists. He has no ties to the vampire community, save me, and no ties left to the human world. He is more alone than anyone you will ever meet, Claire.'

'You say that like you...want him that way. Alone, I mean.'

'I do,' Amelie said calmly. 'My reasons are my own. However, it is an interesting experiment, to see how someone so alone will react. Samuel has been intriguing; most vampires would have simply turned brutal and uncaring, but he continues to seek comfort. Friendship. He is unusual, I think.'

'You're *experimenting* on him!' Claire said.

Amelie's platinum eyebrows slowly rose to form perfect arches over her cold, amused eyes. 'Clever of you to think such a thing, but attend: a rat who knows it is running a maze is no longer a useful subject. So you will keep your counsel, and you will keep your distance from dear sweet Samuel. Now. Why did you come to me today?'

'Why did I...?' Claire cleared her throat. 'I think maybe there's been a mistake. I was, you know, looking for a bathroom.'

Amelie stared at her for a frozen second, and then she threw back her head and laughed. It was a full, living sound, warm and full of unexpected joy, and when it passed, Claire could see the traces of it still on her face and in her eyes. Making her look almost...human. 'A bathroom,' she repeated, and shook her head. 'Child, I have been told many things, but that may yet prove the most amusing. If you wish a bathroom, please, go through that door. You will find all that you require.' Her smile faded. 'But I think you came to ask me something more.'

'I didn't come here at all! I was going to the

Morganville Historical Society—'

'I *am* the Morganville Historical Society,' Amelie said. 'What do you wish to know?'

Claire liked books. Books didn't talk back. They didn't sit there in their fancy throne chairs and look all queeny and imposing and *terrifying*, and they didn't have fangs and bodyguards. Books were *fine*. 'Um...I just wanted to look something up...?'

Amelie was already losing patience. 'Just tell me, girl. Quickly. I am not without duties.'

Claire cleared her throat nervously, coughed, and said, 'I wanted to find out about Eve's brother, Jason. Jason Rosser.'

'Done,' Amelie said, and although she didn't seem to do anything, not even lift a finger, the side door opened and her cute but deathly pale assistant leant in. 'The Rosser family file,' she told him. He nodded and was gone. 'You would have wasted your time,' Amelie said to Claire. 'There are no personnel files of any kind in the Historical Society building. It is purely for show, and the information there is inaccurate, at best. If you want to know the true history of things, little one, come to someone who has lived it.'

'But that's just perspective,' Claire said. 'Not fact.'

'All fact is perspective. Ah, thank you, Henry.' Amelie accepted a folder from her assistant, who silently left again. She flipped it open, studied what was inside, and then handed it over to Claire. 'An unexceptional family. Curious that it produced young Eve and her brother.'

It was their whole lives reduced to dry entries in long-hand on paper. Dates of births, details of school records...there were handwritten reports from the vampire Brandon, who gave them Protection. Even those were dry.

And then not so dry, because between the ages of sixteen and eighteen, Eve changed. Big-time. The school photograph at fifteen was of a pretty, fragile-looking girl dressed in conservative clothes – something even Claire would have worn.

Eve's photograph at sixteen was Goth City. She'd dyed her dark hair a flat glossy black, whited her face, raccooned her eyes, and generally adopted a 'tude. By seventeen she'd started getting piercings – one showed in the tongue she stuck out at the camera.

By eighteen, she looked pensive and defiant, and then the photographs stopped, except for some that looked like surveillance photos of Eve in Common Grounds, pulling espresso shots and chatting with customers.

Eve with Oliver.

You're supposed to be looking up Jason, Claire reminded herself, and flipped the page.

Jason was just the same, only younger; about the time that Eve had turned Goth, so had Jason, although on him it looked less like a fashion choice and more like a serious turn to the dark side. Eve always had a light of humour and mischief in her eyes; Jason had no light in his eyes at all. He looked skinny, strong, and dangerous.

And Claire realised with an icy start that she'd seen him before... He'd been on the street, staring at her just before she'd gone into Common Grounds and talked to Sam.

Jason Rosser knew who she was.

'Jason likes knives, as I recall,' Amelie said. 'He sometimes fancies himself a vampire. I should be quite careful of him, were I you. He is not likely to be as...polite as my own people.'

Claire shivered and flipped pages, speed-reading through Jason's not-very-impressive academic life, and then the police reports.

Eve had been the witness who'd turned him in. She'd seen him abduct this girl and drive away with her – a girl who was later found wandering the streets bleeding from a stab wound. The girl refused to testify, but Eve had gone on record. And Jason had gone away.

The file showed he'd been released from prison the day before yesterday at nine in the morning. Plenty of time for him to have grabbed Karla Gast on campus and...

Out with the bad thoughts, Claire. In with the good.

She flipped pages and looked at Eve's mother and dad. They looked...normal. Kind of grim, maybe, but with a son like Jason, that probably wasn't too strange.

Still, they didn't look like the kind of parents who'd just toss their daughter out on her ear and never write or call or visit.

Claire closed the file and slid it back across the desk to Amelie, who put it in a wooden out-box at the corner of her desk. 'Did you find what you wished to know?' Amelie asked.

'I don't know.'

'What a wise thing to say,' Amelie said, and nodded once, like a queen to a subject. 'You may go now. Use the door that brought you.'

'Um...thanks. Bye.' Which sounded like a dumbass thing to say to someone a billion years old, who controlled the town and everything in it, but Amelie seemed to accept it fine. Claire grabbed her backpack and hurried through the polished wood door...

...into a bathroom. With lots of floral wallpaper and really yak-worthy frilly doll-skirt toilet paper covers.

Reality whiplash.

Claire dropped her backpack and yanked open the door again.

It was the hallway. She looked right, then left. The room even smelt different – talcum powder and old-lady perfume. No trace of Amelie, her silent servants, or the room where they'd been.

'Science fiction,' Claire said, deeply unhappy, and – feeling strangely guilty – flushed the toilet before trudging back the way she'd come. The house was warm, but the heat outside was like a slap from a microwaved towel.

Oh, she was *so* going to figure that trick out. She couldn't stand the idea of it being, well, *magic*. Sure, vampires she could accept...grudgingly...and the whole mind-control thing. But not instantaneous transportation. Nope.

Lisa was sitting next to Granma on the porch swing now, sipping lemonade. There was an extra one gathering beads of sweat on the small table next to her, and she nodded Claire to it without speaking.

'Thanks,' Claire said, and took a deep, thirsty gulp. It was good – maybe too sweet, but refreshing. She drained it fast and held on to the cool glass, wondering if it was bad manners to crunch the ice cubes. 'How long have you lived here?'

'Granma's been in this house all her life,' Lisa said, and gently rubbed her grandmother's back. 'Right, Granma?'

'Born here,' the old woman said proudly. 'Gonna die here, too, when I'm good and ready.'

'That's the spirit.' Lisa poured Claire another

glass of lemonade from a half-empty pitcher. 'I find anything missing in Granma's house, college girl, and you can't hide from me in Morganville. You feel me?'

'Lisa!' Granma scolded. 'I'm so sorry, honey. My granddaughter never learnt proper manners.' She smacked Lisa on the hand and gave her the parental glare. 'This nice girl here, she never would steal from an old lady. Now, would you, honey?'

'No, ma'am,' Claire said, and drank half of the second serving of lemonade. It tasted as tart and sweet and wonderful as the first. 'I was just wondering, about the symbol next to your door...'

Lisa and Granma both looked at her sharply. Neither one of them replied. They were both wearing bracelets, she noticed, plain silver with the Founder's symbol on a metal plaque, like those MedicAlert bracelets. Finally, Lisa said, softly, 'You need to leave now.'

'But—'

'Go!' Lisa yelled it, grabbed the glass out of Claire's hand, and thumped it down on the table. 'Don't you make me throw you down the stairs in front of my granma!'

'Hush, Lisa,' Granma said, and leant forward with a creaking sound, from either the wooden porch swing or her old bones. 'Girl's got no better sense than God gave a sheep, but that's all right. It's the Founder's symbol, child, and this is the

Founder's house, and we're the Founder's people. Just like you.'

Lisa looked at her, open-mouthed. 'What?' she finally said when she got control of her voice.

'Can't you see it?' Granma waved her hand in front of Claire. 'She shines, baby. *They* see it, I guarantee you they do. They won't touch her, mark or no mark. Worth their lives if they do.'

'But—' Lisa looked as frustrated and helpless as Claire felt. 'Granma, you're seeing things again.'

'I do *not* see things, missy, and you better remember just who in this family stayed alive when everybody else fell.' Granma's faded eyes fixed on Claire, who shivered despite the oppressive, still heat. 'Don't know why she marked you, child, but she did. Now you just got to live with it. Go on, now. Go home. You got what you came for.'

'She did?' Lisa scowled fiercely. 'Swear to God, if you lifted anything from our house—'

'Hush. She didn't steal. But she got what she needed, didn't you, girl?'

Claire nodded and nervously ran a hand through her hair. She was sweating buckets; her hair felt sticky and wet. Home suddenly sounded like a real good idea.

'Thank you, ma'am,' she said, and extended her hand. Granma looked at it for a few seconds, then took it in a bird-like grip and shook. 'Can I come back and see you sometime?'

'Long as you bring me some chocolate,' Granma said, and smiled. 'I'm partial to chocolate.'

'Granma, you're diabetic.'

'I'm old, girl. Gonna die of something. Might as well be chocolate.'

They were still arguing as Claire retreated down the steps, through the neatly kept front garden, and out through the gate in the white picket fence. She looked at that alley, the one she'd almost taken, and this time she felt a shiver of warning. *Trap-door spiders.* No, she no longer had any desire to take shortcuts. And she'd learnt about as much as she could stomach about Jason Rosser. At least she knew now who to watch out for, if he started following her around again.

Claire hitched her backpack to a more comfortable position, and began walking.

CHAPTER SEVEN

There was no sign of Shane's dad or the bikers. In fact, it was very quiet in Morganville, despite Claire's fears. Travis Lowe and Joe Hess dropped by early the next morning to deliver the no-news-is-good-news party line to Eve and the house in general; they were polite and kind, and generally seemed like OK guys for cops, but they made Claire feel scared and paranoid. She supposed all cops were like that, when they were on Official Business. It didn't seem to bother Eve at all; she was up, bleary-eyed and yawning, fresh out of the shower and still wrapped in a Hello Kitty bathrobe, free of the Goth mask. Shane was, predictably, asleep, and who knew where Michael was? Watching, Claire thought. Always watching. She supposed that should have been creepy, except that in Michael's case, it was just…comforting.

'Hey, guys,' Eve said after wandering down the

stairs into the living room. She plopped on the couch, bounced, and yawned again. 'Coffee. Need coffee.'

'I made some,' Claire said, and went into the kitchen to get it. Travis Lowe followed her silently and carried the cups back out. He and his partner drank it black; Claire could barely stand it even with more milk and sugar than actual coffee. Eve was cream only, no sugar, and she sucked it down like Gatorade after a hard work-out, then collapsed against the couch cushions and sighed happily.

'Morning, Officers,' she said, and closed her eyes. 'It's too early for this.'

'Heard you got a job on campus,' Hess said. 'Congratulations, Eve.'

'Yea, me.' She made a lazy woo-hoo gesture. 'You come all this way to say that?'

'Not a long way in Morganville.' Hess shrugged. 'But no. Like I told Claire, there's no sign of your intruders. So I think you're in the clear on that. Hope that makes your day better.'

Eve shot Claire a fast, tentative look. 'Sure,' she said. 'Um...about...the other thing...?'

'You want to talk in private?' Claire asked, and stood up with her coffee cup in hand. ''Cause I can go on to school—'

'Sit,' Hess said. 'You're not going anywhere yet. And you're not going anywhere by yourself.'

'I'm…what?'

'We're giving you girls a ride to school,' Lowe said, and sipped his coffee. 'And a ride home when you're done. Consider us your Thin Blue Line Taxi Service.'

'No!' Claire blurted, appalled. 'I mean, you can't…you shouldn't…why?'

'Eve knows why,' Hess said. 'Don't you, Eve?'

Eve put her coffee cup on the side table and crossed her arms against her chest. She looked very young in pink and white, and very scared. 'Jason.'

'Yeah, Jason.' Hess cleared his throat, glanced at Claire, and continued. 'We found Karla Gast late last night. Well, actually, some of our more night-inclined colleagues found her. Dumped in a vacant lot about six blocks from here behind some piled-up lumber.'

In a flash, Claire remembered walking past the empty lot on her way to her unintended visit with Amelie. She'd even *smelt decay*. She put her coffee cup down and put both hands over her mouth, fighting an impulse to gag.

'You think—' Eve looked tense and pale. She licked her lips, swallowed, and continued. 'You think Jason was involved.'

'Yeah,' Hess said softly. 'We think. No proof, though. No witnesses, no forensic evidence, but she was definitely not killed by a vampire. Look, Jason's been spotted in the area, so I don't want you out there by yourself for now, OK? Either one of you.'

'He's my *brother*!' Eve sounded angry now, voice shaking. 'How could he do this? What kind of...of—'

'It's not your fault,' Lowe said. 'You tried to get him help. He just got sicker.'

'It *is* my fault!' she shouted. 'I'm the one who turned him in! I'm the one who didn't stop Brandon from—'

'From what?' Lowe asked, very quietly.

Eve didn't answer. She looked down at her black-painted fingernails, and picked at them restlessly.

'From moving on to an easier target,' she said. 'Once I made sure he couldn't get to me.'

'Christ,' Lowe muttered in weary disgust. 'Someday, that goddamn vamp's going to get his—'

'Trav,' Hess said. 'It ain't laundry day. Let's not air it in public.'

'Yeah, I know, but *Jesus Christ*, Joe, it ain't like this is the first time...'

It took Claire a few seconds to work out what they were all talking about, but then she remembered Eve's poetry that she'd looked through on the computer...all romantic *Aren't vampires great?* stuff until she was about fifteen, and then...no more romance. *Brandon. Brandon tried to mess with her when she was fifteen.*

And Jason was her younger brother.

'What did he do to him?' Claire asked in a very small voice. 'Brandon, I mean. Did he…bite him?'

Eve didn't look up, but her cheeks went pink to match her robe. 'Sometimes,' she said. 'And sometimes it was worse than that. We're just toys to him, you know. Dolls. We're not *real*. People aren't real at all.'

'I'm afraid the same goes for Jason now,' Hess said. 'Can't really blame the kid. He didn't have much of a chance. But I repeat, Eve, you can't blame yourself, either. You saved yourself, and that's important.'

'Yeah, I saved myself by screwing over my brother. What a hero.'

'You be careful with all that guilt,' Lowe said. 'It'll pound you down. Your parents were the ones who should have stepped in, and you know it. Anybody willing to let their kids become toys, just to get ahead…'

Claire reached out and took hold of Eve's hand. Eve, surprised, looked up – she wasn't crying, which was kind of surprising because Eve cried a *lot*. Her eyes were dry, clear, and hard. Angry.

'Why do you think I left?' she asked. 'As soon as I could. Between my parents and what Brandon made out of Jason…'

Claire couldn't think of anything to say. She just sat there, holding Eve's hand. She'd never been through any of that... She'd grown up warm and safe in a house where her parents loved her. In a town where there were no such things as vampires, where child abuse and molestation were something that happened on the evening news, and if anybody had brothers who killed people, it happened in big cities, to people she didn't know.

All this was just...too much to take in. And much too painful.

'It's going to be OK,' she finally said. Eve smiled at her sadly, but her eyes were still fierce.

'No,' she said. 'Don't think so, Claire. But thanks.'

She took a deep breath, let go of Claire's hand, and turned back to the two cops. 'Right. You guys hang out here while I get dressed.'

'Oh, sure,' Hess said, and raised an eyebrow. It made his face look crooked, but maybe that was just the way his nose was; Claire wasn't sure. 'Not like we're protecting or serving or anything.'

'You're not even on duty,' Eve said.

'Busted,' Lowe said, smiling. 'We're on our own for this. Hurry up, kid – I'd like to get to sleep sometime today before I have to fight for truth and justice again.'

Eve padded up the stairs, one hand on the railing, and Claire let out a slow, careful breath. Eve was kind of like an unexploded bomb right now.

Claire ached to make it all better, but there was no way she could do that...and no way that Eve would even let her try, she thought.

She wished Shane would wake up. She needed...well, *something*. A hug, maybe. Or one of those deliciously warm kisses. Or just to look at him, all rumpled and grumpy with his hair sticking up at odd angles, sheet creases on his face, his bare feet looking so cute and soft...

She had never thought of a guy's *feet* as sexy before. Not even movie-star feet. But Shane...there was no part of him that wasn't sizzle hot.

'More coffee?' Hess asked, and waggled his empty mug. Claire sighed and took his and Lowe's into the kitchen for refills.

She had just set the two ceramic cups down on the counter, and was reaching for the coffee pot, when a big, thick, sweaty hand closed over her mouth, and irresistibly strong arms yanked her backward. She tried to scream, and kicked, but whoever had her, really had her. She squirmed, but it didn't do any good.

'Quiet,' a rough male voice whispered in her ear. 'Shut up, or this gets ugly.'

It was already ugly, at least from Claire's terrified side of things. She went still, and the man holding her lowered her down enough to let her sneakered toes touch the floor. Didn't let her go, though.

She'd already figured out who it was – the speaker, not the one holding her – before Shane's dad stepped out into her view and leant forward, scary-close. 'Where's my son?' he asked. His breath was nasty, and stank of booze. Breakfast of Collins champions. 'Just nod. Is he in the house?' She nodded slowly. The hand muffling her mouth let her do it. 'Upstairs?' She nodded again. 'Those cops in the living room?' She nodded vigorously, and tried to think what she could do to get Detective Hess's attention. Screaming wasn't doing any good; the kitchen door was pretty solid, and it was useless to try to get sound past a hand that was about two inches thick. If they'd grabbed her when she was holding the mugs, at least she could have dropped them...

'My kid likes you,' Shane's dad said. 'That's all that keeps you alive right now, you get me? So don't push your luck. I could always change my mind, and you could get buried out back with your little friend Michael. Now, my buddy here is going to let go of your mouth, and you'd better not scream, because if you do, we're just going to have to do some killing, starting with you and ending with the cops. And that vampire-wannabe girlfriend of yours. You get me? My son is all that matters to me.'

Claire swallowed hard and nodded again. The hand pulled slowly away from her mouth.

She didn't scream. She pressed her lips together to hold in the urge.

'Good girl,' Shane's dad said. 'Now tell me what the cops are doing here. They looking for us?'

She shook her head. 'They think you're gone,' she said. 'They're here to take me and Eve to school.'

'School.' He poured contempt into the word. 'That's not a school. It's a holding pen for cattle.'

She licked her lips and tasted the sweat of the guy who was holding her. Disgusting. 'You need to go. Right now.'

'Or?'

'You can't do what you're here to do if everybody's still looking for you,' she said. She was making it up, but suddenly it made sense to her. 'If you have to kill me, and everybody here, they turn the town upside down until they find you. And they'll put Shane in jail, or worse. If you let me go and take Shane, I'll just tell them everything anyway, and they turn the town upside down—'

'Are you trying to scare me, little girl?'

'No,' Claire whispered. She could barely get the word out. 'I'm trying to tell you what will happen. They've kind of given up looking for you, but if you kill me, you lose. And if you let me go, I'm going to tell them everything.'

'Then why shouldn't I kill you?'

'Because I'll keep my mouth shut if you promise to leave Shane alone.'

He glared at her, but she could see he was thinking about it.

'Boss,' said the man holding her. He had a deep voice, rough like his throat was lined with gravel. 'Bitch got no reason to keep her word.'

'What makes you think I like the vamps any more than you do?' she shot back. 'Did Shane tell you about Brandon? I saw you in Common Grounds. Were you looking for him? Because if you weren't, you should be. He's a dick.'

Frank Collins's eyes drifted half-shut, and she was reminded sickly of Shane, somehow. 'You telling me which vamps to kill now?'

'No.' She swallowed again, acutely aware that at any second the kitchen door could swing open, and someone could come stumbling in, and everything could go to hell on the express train. 'Just a suggestion. Because as far as I can tell, he's just about the worst one. But you're going to do what you want, I know that. I just want me and my friends out of it.'

Shane's dad smiled at her. *Smiled*. And it seemed, for the first time, like a mostly genuine expression, not just a freaky twist of his lips. 'You're tougher than you look, kid. That's good. You're going to need to be, you stick around here.' He looked past her, at the biker (or so she thought – she could feel leather squeaking behind her when she struggled). 'Let her down, man. She's OK.'

The biker released her. She jerked forward, spun, and set her back to the refrigerator. She scrambled for a knife in the drawer next to her, found a wicked-looking cleaver, and held it out in front of her. 'You need to go,' she said. 'Right now. And don't come back here, or I swear, I'll tell them everything.'

He wasn't smiling anymore. Well, not as much. The biker behind him, though, was grinning.

'Girl, you don't know my son at all, do you?' he asked. 'I don't have to come back here. He's going to come to me. Eventually.'

He made a *Let's go* gesture to his six-foot bodyguard, and together they went back out the side door of the kitchen. Claire ran to pull it shut and lock it, both locks plus the newly installed sliding bolts.

Which made her wonder why it hadn't been locked before...oh. Of course. The cops had come in through the kitchen.

She took some deep breaths, rinsed the taste of that sweaty hand off her lips, and picked up the coffee cups.

Her hands were shaking so badly, there was no way she could carry anything liquid. She put them back down and went back to the door to call through, 'Making some fresh!'

She poured out the rest of the pot, loaded it again, and, by the time the machine finished, had mostly gotten herself under control.

Mostly.

Claire had a break between classes – it couldn't really be called a lunch break, because it fell at ten a.m. and she walked over to the University Centre for coffee. The UC was large and kind of seedy; the carpet was ancient, and the furniture had seen the eighties, at least, and maybe the seventies. It was one large, open atrium filled with couches, chairs, and even – tucked in one corner – a grand piano. Student-activity banners, most badly painted, draped overhead and fluttered in the weak air-conditioning.

Most of the couch groupings were already claimed by students talking or separately studying. Claire had her eye on an open study table near the corner, but she'd have to hurry; there were plenty of people looking for places to settle.

She hurried to the coffee bar at the back of the atrium, and smiled and waved as she spotted Eve behind the espresso machine. Eve waved back, pulled two shots at the same time, and dumped them into steamed milk. The line was about five deep, and Claire had plenty of time to think about what Shane's dad had said. And what he hadn't.

What was he doing there today? Really? Maybe he'd come to fetch Shane, but she wasn't sure. Shane's dad seemed to have a plan, but she had no idea what it was.

Maybe Shane would know, but she didn't want to ask.

Michael. She'd tell Michael everything, as soon as he appeared.

'Large mocha,' Claire said, and dug out the required three-fifty from her jeans pocket. It was a huge expense for her, but she figured it was only right to celebrate

Eve's first day on the job. The cashier – a bored-looking guy who was probably wishing he were anywhere else – took her cash and waved her on to the line for drinks.

She was standing there, thumbing through her English-lit book, when she heard muffled laughter, and then a wet dull thud as a drink tipped over on the counter. She looked up to see a ring of guys standing around a spilt drink, which was dripping off both sides of the counter.

'Hey, zombie chick,' one of them said to Eve, who was standing next to the counter, still pulling shots and very obviously ignoring them. 'Wanna clean that up?'

A muscle fluttered in Eve's jaw, but she silently got a handful of paper towels and began to mop up the mess. Once the counter was clean, she raised the hinged section of the bar and cleaned the floor on both sides.

The boys continued to snigger. 'You missed a spot,' said the one who'd spilt the drink. 'Over there.'

Eve had to bend over to get to the spot where he was pointing. He quickly stepped up behind her and began banging his crotch against her butt. 'Oh, baby!' he said, and they all laughed. *Laughed.* 'You're so fucking hot for a dead girl.'

Eve calmly straightened up, turned around, and stared at him. Not a word. One thing Claire could say for Goth make-up, at least it covered up blushes... She was blushing, furiously, on Eve's behalf. And shaking.

'Excuse me,' Eve finally said, and moved him aside with one hand flat against his chest. She got behind the bar again and slammed down the hatch, took the two espresso shots and dumped them into a fresh cup, stirred, put a lid on it, and put it on the bar. 'Here. On the house.'

The creep reached out, grabbed the cup, and *squeezed.* The top popped off. Coffee went everywhere, splattering Eve, the counter, the floor, the guy holding it. His buddies burst into open laughter when he said, 'Oops. Guess I don't know my own strength.'

Eve looked at the guy at the register, but he just shrugged. She took a deep breath, smiled – not,

Claire saw, her normal smile *at all* – and said, 'You ought to see a doctor about that, Bullwinkle. Plus the crotch rash. *Next!* I have a mocha for Claire!' Eve thumped down another cup and vigorously scrubbed the counter.

Claire hurried up. 'Oh my God!' she whispered. 'What do you want me to do? Get somebody?'

'Who?' Eve rolled her eyes. 'It's my first day – it's a little early to run tattling like a girlie girl. Leave it alone, Claire. Just take your coffee and go on. I'll be fine. I've got a PhD in taking shit from jocks.'

'But Shane? Should I call Shane?'

'Only if you want to be cleaning up blood instead of coffee—'

'Hey, bitch, where's *my* drink?' the guy asked loudly from behind Claire. She felt him crowding up against her a second before he body-slammed her hard against the bar. 'Oops, sorry, little girl, didn't see you there.' He didn't move back. 'Since when do we have kindergarten classes, anyway?'

Her mocha had – of course – tumbled out of her hand and was rolling across the counter, bleeding coffee. Eve caught it and set it back upright. 'Hey!' Claire squirmed to get free; he just kept her pinned.

'Hey! Asshole!' Eve echoed, louder, and pointed a finger over Claire's head, glaring. 'Back off, man, or I call the campus cops.'

'Yeah, they'll really come running.' Still, he backed up enough to let Claire twist away from him, clutching her mocha. He wasn't even looking at her. He was a big guy – Shane-big – with black gelled hair in the latest cool style and fierce blue eyes. A nice face, good lips, high cheekbones. Altogether too pretty for his own good, Claire thought. 'Get me my damn coffee. Some of us have class around here.'

Claire grabbed paper towels and began mopping up the spill on the customer side of the counter, so Eve didn't have to come around. Eve gave her a grateful look and began to pull shots. She assembled the drink in record time, slapped the top on it, and handed it to her tormentor.

Who grinned at her, tasted it, and put it back on the counter. 'Sucks,' he said. 'Keep it.'

He high-fived with his friends, and they all walked away.

'What a *jerk*!' Claire said, and Eve just raised her eyebrows, took the latte, and poured it out down the sink.

'No, he was right, it *did* suck,' she said. 'But then, he paid three bucks for it, so I win. How's the mocha?'

Claire swallowed a mouthful and gave her a thumbs-up. 'I'm sorry. I wish there was something—'

'Gotta fight our own battles, Claire Bear. Go on. I'm sure you've got some kind of studying to do.'

Claire backed away as Eve began to pull another

set of drinks; the line continued to queue up in front of the register.

The guy picking up his latte next – a tall, kind of awkward-looking boy with a round face and big brown eyes – made a point of thanking Eve, who dimpled at him and winked. He looked *much* nicer than the hard-bodied jerks who'd just left, although Claire noticed that he was wearing a fraternity shirt.

'Epsilon Epsilon Kappa?' she read out loud. 'EEK?'

He gave her an apologetic smile. 'Yeah, well, it's kind of a joke. Because of the town. You know, creepy.' He blinked and focused on her, and smiled wider. 'I'm Ian, by the way. Ian Jameson. From, ah, Reno.'

'You're a long way from home, Ian Jameson,' Claire said, and stuck out her hand. He shook it. 'Claire Danvers. From Longview.'

'I'd say you were a short way from home, but everything's far from this place,' he said. 'So, you're a freshman?'

'Yes.' She felt the dreaded blush creeping up again. 'Early admission.'

'Yeah? How early?'

She tried to shrug it off. 'Couple of semesters. No biggie.'

'What's your major?' Ian took the top off his coffee and blew on it to cool it down, then took a sip. 'Thanks again, by the way, this is really good.'

'No problem,' Eve said. She sounded much more cheerful now, and gave the sorority girls their skinny-half-caff-no-sugar lattes with a sunny, slightly manic grin.

Nobody had actually bothered to ask Claire what her major was before. Of course, it was customary for a freshman to change three or four times before settling on something, but Claire had always been pretty definite. 'Physics.'

'Really?' Ian blinked. 'Wow. That's pretty intense. You must be good at maths.'

She shrugged. 'I guess.' Modesty in action; she'd never failed to land an A, ever.

'Gonna transfer out of here, I suppose. I mean, a degree in physics from Nowhere U isn't going to do you all that much good, right?'

'I'm hoping for MIT,' Claire said. 'What about you?'

Ian shook his head. 'CE. Civil engineering. Yeah, I've got to take physics, but no way would I volunteer to take *more*. And I've got one more semester. Then I transfer out to UT Austin.'

A lot of students transferred out to the University of Texas; it was a major school for just about everything. Claire nodded. She'd considered it herself, but…MIT?

Caltech? If she had a chance, she'd take it.

'So…what's EEK? A professional fraternity?' Because there were some on campus; you paid your dues and went to some meetings and put it on your résumé later.

'It's a bunch of guys who like to party, really.' Ian looked embarrassed. 'I'm in it because I've got a couple of friends...anyway, they do throw this really cool party every year – it's a big bash. It's called the Dead Girls' Dance. All zombie-freaky scary-movie stuff.' He glanced over at Eve, who was steaming milk. 'Your friend there would fit right in as is. Most people wear costumes, though.'

Was he asking her out? No, he couldn't be. For one thing, she'd just met him. For another...well, *nobody* ever asked her out. It just didn't happen.

'It sounds neat,' Claire said, and thought, *I just used the word* neat *in a conversation with a cute boy, and I should walk away now and shoot myself.*

'It's at the EEK frat house tomorrow night. Listen, if you give me your number, I can text you the details...'

'Um...sure.' Nobody had *ever* asked before. She stumbled over the digits; he keyed it into his cell phone and smiled at her. A nice smile. A really nice smile, actually. 'Um, I don't know if I can come, though.'

'Well, if you can, you'd save my life. We geeks have to stick together while everybody else goes nuts, right? See you there tomorrow night at eight?'

'Right,' she echoed. 'Um...sure. I'll be there. Thanks. Um, Ian, right?'

'Ian.'

'Claire,' she said, and pointed at herself. 'Oh. Did I already say that?'

He laughed and walked away, sipping his latte.

It was only when he did that she realised she'd just agreed to go out on a date. An actual *date*. With a boy who *was not Shane*. How had that happened? She'd meant only to be nice, because he seemed like an OK guy, and then he'd been all charming, especially by comparison with the other guys...

She had a date.

With a boy who was not Shane.

Not good.

'Hey,' Eve said, and motioned her closer. 'So, what was that? Is he giving you a hard time or what?'

'Ummm...' Claire's mind went blank. 'No. He just... Never mind.'

Eve's eyes turned from concerned to shrewd. 'He hitting on you?'

Claire settled for a shrug. She had no idea how to tell, actually. 'I think he was just being nice.'

'Guys aren't nice,' Eve said. 'What did you tell him you'd do?'

OK, that was scary, how quickly she'd nailed it. Claire shifted her weight uncomfortably, and fiddled with her heavy backpack. 'Maybe I said I might go to this party. But it totally wasn't a date.'

'Oh, totally not,' Eve agreed. And rolled her eyes. 'Next up! Vanilla latte!...which totally describes you, by the way.'

'I'll, um, be over there,' Claire said. 'Studying.'

Eve might have wanted to stop her, but the drinks kept coming, and Claire was able to fade away and go in search of her study table. Which, miraculously, was still unoccupied. She thunked down her backpack on the battered wood and sat, sipping her mocha. The UC seemed safer than most places in Morganville... Any place packed with people reading couldn't be that bad.

Almost like a real university.

Claire was reading ahead in her history text when a shadow fell over the page. She looked up and saw a girl she slightly knew from her old dorm, Howard Hall – a freshman, like herself. Lisa? Lesley? Something like that.

'Hey,' the girl said. Claire nodded towards the empty chair opposite her, but Lisa/Lesley didn't sit. 'That Goth at the coffee bar, the one who used to work at Common Grounds – is she your friend?'

Word got around fast. Claire nodded again.

'Might want to keep her from getting herself killed, then,' Lisa/Lesley said. ''Cause she's just pulled the pin from the Monica grenade over at the counter.'

Claire winced and closed her book. She checked

her watch; well, it was probably close to time to leave for class anyway. It was bad, and shallow, but she wished that Lisa/Lesley had decided *not* to do her good deed of the day. It would have been nice to leave without another crisis.

Claire repacked her book bag and walked back towards the coffee bar. *I'm just going to tell her goodbye*, she thought. *No agenda here at all. Totally staying out of it.*

Monica, Gina, and Jennifer were leaning on the bar, blocking coffee pickup. The counter was all that separated them from Eve, who was steadily ignoring them.

'Hey, Walking Dead, I'm talking to you,' Monica was saying. 'Is it true your brother tried to kill you?'

'Yeah, was that before or after he tried to do you?' Hand gestures and everything. Wow, that was low even for Jennifer.

'Tried?' Gina snickered. 'That's not what *I* heard. I heard they were getting it on all through high school. No wonder they both turned out to be freaks.'

Eve's face was a still white mask, but her eyes...she looked crazy. In control, but just barely. Her hands were steady as she pulled espresso shots and mixed drinks; she thumped the finished products down on the counter, three across, and said, 'If you don't go away, I'm going to call my manager.'

'Ooooh,' Monica said. 'Your *manager*. Wow, I'm terrified. You think some barely-over-minimum-wage brain donor stupid enough to work *here* is going to scare me? Do you?' She leant to the side, trying to catch Eve's eyes. 'I'm talking to you, freak face.'

Gina noticed Claire standing a few feet away, and drew Monica's attention with a hand on her shoulder. 'Two freaks for one,' she said. 'They must be having some kind of special.'

'Claire.' Monica's smile widened. 'Sure, why not? You angry I'm ragging on your little lesbo girlfriend?'

'Make up your mind,' Claire said. Her voice sounded low and kind of cool, actually. Maybe it was easier doing this here in public, where she felt more comfortable. Or maybe she was actually getting used to facing down Monica. 'Are we gay, or did she sleep with her brother? 'Cause you know, kind of not making much sense.'

Monica actually *blinked*. Logic wasn't her strong suit, anyway. Claire could almost see the *Don't confuse me with facts* flicker across her brain. 'You laughing at me?'

'Yeah,' Claire said. 'A little.'

Monica smiled. A big, genuine smile. 'How about that?' she said. 'Claire's grown a pair. I guess having a badass Protector hanging over your shoulder must be a real comfort.' She threw a glance at Eve. 'But it won't last. My family means something around here. You freaks are just temporary. And...sad.'

She flipped her hair back over her shoulders, picked up her latte, and walked away. Guys' heads turned as she passed, with Gina and Jennifer in a flying-V formation behind her.

'Huh,' Eve said as she wiped down the machines with maybe a little bit more force than was necessary. 'She doesn't usually back down that easily.'

'Maybe she's got class.'

Eve snorted. 'Trust me,' she said. 'That girl's got no class at all.'

'How weird is it that we have our own personal cop limo service?' Eve asked. She and Claire were standing on the sidewalk in front of the UC, and the campus looked mostly deserted – it was seven o'clock, and the sky had darkened to a deep twilight. There were even a few premature stars out already. The sun had just gone down, and there was still a fiery orange and yellow glow on the western horizon. 'I mean, it's not like I don't have a car. I can drive.'

'I don't think they'll keep it up,' Claire offered. 'I mean, it's just a special thing. Until they catch...whoever killed that girl.'

Eve sighed and didn't answer. A blue car turned

and cruised around the circular drive, pulling to a halt in front of them. Joe Hess was driving, and Travis Lowe got out and opened the back door with a dumb-looking overdone bow. It was kind of cute, actually. Claire climbed in and slid over, and Eve got in next to her.

'Hello, girls,' Hess said, and turned to look back at them. He had dark circles under his eyes, and he seemed like he hadn't slept at all. 'Thanks for the coffee.'

Claire and Eve looked at each other. 'Sorry,' Eve said. 'I always smell like coffee; it's the perfume of the barista. I didn't actually bring any for you. But if you want, I'll go back and—'

'No way,' Lowe said as he got into the shotgun seat. 'Dark already. Let's get you gals home. Joe and me, we'll grab some later.'

'Thank you,' Claire said. 'For the ride.'

Neither of the cops answered. Detective Hess drove the other half of the circle, turned out onto the campus main drag, and within two blocks was off campus and into the dark Morganville night. Most shops were tightly closed already. As they passed Common Grounds, Claire and Eve both looked. It was full, of course, an oasis of light in the dark, empty street. No sign of Oliver. No sign of Shane's dad, either, which made Claire's conscience twinge hard. *I need to tell Shane. Soon.* She didn't see how blabbing it to Eve would help, except to make Eve even more worried. And from the pensive way Eve was staring out into the dark, there was enough of that going on already.

They were only one block from the house when a sleek black car – with tail fins, like a shark – pulled in front of them and, with shocking speed, turned sideways. Hess jammed on the brakes, and the sound of screeching tyres was like a banshee's wail. He didn't hit the other car...quite. Claire thumped back against the vinyl upholstery, panting from shock, and exchanged a wide-eyed look with Eve.

In the front seat, Hess and Lowe were doing the same things. Only with a full helping of grim, and a side of tense.

'What's happening?' Eve asked, and leant forward. 'Detectives?'

'You stay here,' Hess said, and popped his door. 'Trav. Stay with them.'

'Joe—'

'I'll be fine.' He got out, slammed the door, and walked towards the other car. A dark-tinted window rolled down, and in the glare of the headlights, Claire saw a dead-pale face she recognised.

'Hans,' she whispered. The vampire detective. She looked at Detective Lowe, and saw something strange; he had his gun out, held in his lap. And a cross in his left hand. 'Right? It's Hans.'

'You girls stay put,' Lowe said. His eyes didn't

move from the scene playing out in front of him. 'Just a routine check.'

Claire didn't know much about police procedure, but she was pretty sure it wasn't routine for one cop to block another one off in the road, right? Not even here. And it wasn't routine procedure for a detective to have his gun out, either.

Whatever conversation Hess was having, it wasn't making him happy. It was also short. He shook his head a couple of times and then finally nodded.

As he walked back to the car, Claire had a real bad feeling. His expression was too serious and too angry for it to be good news. *Shane. Oh God, maybe it's about Shane – something's happened to Shane...*

Hess opened the back door – Claire's side – and leant in. 'Girls,' he said. 'You're going to have to come with me.'

'The hell!' Lowe barked. 'I thought we were taking them home.'

'Change of plans,' Hess said. He was trying not to look angry, or worried, but Claire could still see it in his eyes. 'You're wanted downtown, girls. I'll come with you. Trav, I need you to take the car in.'

The two men exchanged a long look, and then Lowe let out a slow breath. 'Right,' he said. 'Sure. You look after them.'

'You know I will.'

Claire got out of the car, feeling more exposed and vulnerable even than usual. Hess was right there, big and comforting, but still…she saw Hans's eyes on her, and it made her feel cold.

His partner, Gretchen, got out of the passenger side and came around to open the back door. 'In,' she snapped. Claire swallowed hard and moved forward, but Eve got there first, sliding inside and all the way across.

Hess followed Claire. When Gretchen slammed the door, the three of them barely fit in the back seat.

'You all keep your mouths shut until you're asked to speak,' Hans said, and put the car in gear as Gretchen got back in. He turned the big car with a squeal of warm rubber and accelerated fast down the street.

They passed 716 Lot Street. All the lights were on, and the door was open, and someone was standing in the doorway, watching them roar by. It was too quick to tell whether it was Shane or Michael, but Claire hoped it was Shane.

She hoped that if something happened, she at least had gotten to see him before the end.

'I thought we were going to the police station,' Eve whispered as the car took some turns and wound through the confusing maze of streets.

'We're not?' Claire whispered back.

'Passed it back there. I guess we're going somewhere else.' Eve sounded flat-out scared, and when Claire reached over, she found Eve's hand was cold and shaking. They held on to each other as the car made more turns, and then slowed for some kind of barricade. 'Oh *God*. We're going to the square.'

'The square?'

'Founder's Square. It's, like, vamptown this time of night.' Eve swallowed and gripped Claire's hand more tightly. 'I'm trying to think of any way this could be a good thing.'

'Hush,' Detective Hess said quietly. 'You're OK. Trust me.'

Claire did. She just didn't trust the two vampire detectives sitting in the front seat, who were obviously more in charge.

The barricade lifted. Hans drove them through, brought the big car to a stop in an unlit parking lot, and turned to look at them. Claire first, then Eve. Hess, last of all.

Gretchen turned, too. She was smiling.

'Something we want you to see,' Hans said. Gretchen exited the car and opened the back door on Eve's side. 'Out.'

They clambered out into the cooling night air. The moon was up, casting a sickly yellow glow that didn't illuminate much. The dark seemed very deep, even though there was still some indigo lining the horizon. Not even really full night yet...

A cold, strong hand closed over Claire's upper arm. She squeaked breathlessly, and heard Eve making a sound of surprise, too. Gretchen had somehow gotten between them, holding them both by the arms.

Hans threw a look at Detective Hess. 'Stay with the car,' he said.

'I'm coming with the girls.'

'You're taking orders like a good little neutral,' Hans said. 'Unless you want to lose that status for both you and your partner. This isn't some minor incident. This has the attention of the Elders. If the girls don't cause trouble, they'll come back unharmed, but *you stay here.*'

Gretchen said, 'No, Hans. Let him come. It'll be good for him to attend.'

Hans frowned at her, then shrugged. 'Fine. But get in the way, Hess, and you're meat.'

Gretchen hustled the girls forward.

'What's going on?' Eve asked. Neither of the vampires answered. Claire turned her head and saw that Hess was behind them, but somehow, that didn't give her all that much comfort. Gretchen frog-marched them around the corner of a blank-faced brick building, and into...

A park.

Claire blinked, surprised, because this was actually very...nice. Green grass, big shady trees rustling in the darkness. There were lights, too, strung through the tree branches and shining on flowers and bushes and walking paths.

The area that bordered the park was more alive than anything she'd seen yet in Morganville. Where the stores bordering the campus were run-down and dingy, the ones facing the square were shining, polished, beautifully maintained. Beautiful in an old-world kind of way, all stone and marble and pillars. There were gargoyles, too, built onto the roofs as drain spouts.

It looked like pictures Claire had seen of old European towns, only...nicer.

Every business facing the square was open. Two outdoor restaurants were serving, and the smell of roasting meats and fresh bread made Claire's mouth water. All she'd really had for the day was coffee, and that was long gone.

And then she remembered what Eve had said. If downtown at night was vamptown, why the restaurants?

She knew when they passed close to one of them. There were groups dining, mixed vampire and human; the vampires had plates of food and were eating just as enthusiastically as the humans. 'You eat!' Claire blurted, astonished. Gretchen glanced at her with those cold, alien eyes.

'Of course,' she said. 'It provides us no nutrition, but the taste is still attractive. Why? You'll find that poisons will do you no good, if you're searching for a way to kill us.'

Claire hadn't even thought that far, actually. She was just...weirdly intrigued.

The stores they passed were incredible. Jewellers, with displays of gems and gold. Book dealers carrying ancient volumes as well as new best sellers. Clothing stores, lots of them, with tasteful and expensive styles. It was like a rich neighbourhood from a major city, like Dallas or Houston or Austin, had been transplanted directly in.

Weird.

And all the shoppers were vampires. In fact, there were lots of them around, more than Claire had ever imagined lived in Morganville; the more she saw, the more scared she felt. They were staring at her and Eve like the girls were cows on the way to the slaughterhouse, and she felt horribly alone. *I want to go home. I swear, if you let me get out of this, I'll move back with Mom and Dad. I'll never leave again...*

Gretchen steered them towards a black marble building with gold lettering at the top. ELDERS' COUNCIL, it said.

'It's OK,' Hess said quietly from behind them. 'You'll be OK, girls. Just cooperate. If they ask questions, tell the truth.'

Claire barely felt her feet on the polished black

marble steps. It was a little like moving in a dream, helpless and numb, but Gretchen's grip on her arm was all too real. And painful. Ouch. Bruises later.

Hans opened the big polished door, and they went inside.

Of all the things Claire expected to see, she somehow hadn't expected a television set, but there one was, tuned to a twenty-four-hour news channel showing flickering pictures of a war – bombs exploding, soldiers shooting. And standing in front of it, arms folded, was Oliver. He wasn't wearing his hippie-dippie Coffee Shop Guy clothes; he was wearing a suit, black, tailored, and sharp as a knife. His greying hair had been pulled back into a ponytail, and he was wearing a tie. No, not a tie, exactly. Kind of like a scarf, with a diamond pin through it to hold it in place. Maybe it had been fashionable when Oliver was younger.

'Some things never change,' he said, staring at the television. 'People continue to kill over the stupidest possible excuses. And they call *us* monsters.'

On the last word, his gaze snapped to Claire, and she shivered. Oliver had nice eyes, but somehow, they scared her even more than Gretchen's ice-cold ones. Maybe it was because she still wanted to like him, no matter what he'd done. *He killed Michael!* she reminded herself. Well, he'd mostly killed him, anyway.

'Hello,' Oliver said to her, and nodded. He moved his stare to Eve. 'Eve. We've missed you at the shop.'

'B—' Eve swallowed what she'd been about to say, which Claire was ninety-nine per cent sure was *Bite me.* 'Thanks.' Which for Eve was amazingly cautious. If anybody had been shocked and angry about Oliver turning out vampire, it had been Eve.

Oliver nodded and walked across the large, empty room – empty except for the silently playing television and thick plush maroon carpet – and opened a set of double doors. He wasn't the doorman; he walked on through and into the next room. Gretchen pushed Claire and Eve forward. The carpet was squishy soft under Claire's feet, and she caught the scent of fading flowers. Roses. Lots of roses.

It hit her full force when they entered the next room, which was a big circular place with burgundy velvet curtains all around, with pillars in between. A low-key chandelier cast a medium-bright glow. Same carpet, but this room had furniture – chairs laid out in neat rows, in three sections with aisles between.

It took Claire a second to realise that she was walking into a *funeral parlour*. When she did, she stopped, and stumbled as Gretchen continued to drag her relentlessly onward, past the rows of empty folding chairs, all the way to the front, where

Oliver was standing near another velvet curtain.

'Sir,' Joe Hess said, coming out from behind Claire and Eve. 'I'm Detective Hess.'

Oliver nodded. 'I know you.'

'Shouldn't there be others present here for this?' The tension in Hess's voice, and his body, warned Claire that Oliver's interrogating them on his own was a very bad thing.

'There are others present, Detective Hess,' said a light, cool voice from the far corner of the room, which Claire could have *sworn* was empty one second before.

She gasped and looked, and there was Amelie, standing there as if she'd been carved in stone before the building came up around her. And her bodyguards – or servants – were standing in a group near her. She'd brought four of them. Claire wondered if that was a signal of how much trouble she and Eve were in.

'There is a third coming,' Amelie said, and settled herself in a chair as if it were a golden throne. She was wearing black, like Oliver, but her attire was a long elegant suede skirt suit, with a severe white shirt under the tailored jacket. She crossed her legs, which were pale and perfect, and folded her hands in her lap.

Oliver wasn't looking happy. 'Who are we waiting for?' he asked.

'You know the laws, Oliver, even if you choose

to find ways to cheat them,' Amelie said. 'We are waiting for Mr Morrell.'

They didn't have to wait long; in a matter of less than a minute, Claire heard voices coming from the anteroom outside, and a jingle of keys. She'd never seen the man who walked in, flanked by two uniformed cops, but she knew one of the cops: Richard Morrell, Monica's brother. So the portly, balding man with the smug expression was probably her dad.

The mayor of Morganville.

He was dressed in a suit, too – blue, pin-striped, with wide lapels. Kind of pimpish, really, and the pants were a little too long. He had too many rings on his fingers, all in gold, and he was smiling.

'Oliver,' he said cheerfully. The smile vanished fast when he spotted Amelie sitting so quietly off to the side, with her entourage. His face composed itself into something a whole lot more...respectful. 'Founder.'

'Mayor.' She nodded to him. 'Good. We can begin.'

Gretchen let go of Claire's arm. She winced at the returning flow of blood to her tingling hand, and rubbed at the place where Gretchen had been gripping her. Yeah, that was going to be a bruise. Definitely. She risked a look at Eve, who was doing the same thing. Eve looked dead scared.

Oliver reached over and pulled a hidden cord,

and the burgundy velvet curtain behind him opened.

There was a body lying on the marble slab, surrounded by rich red roses, bunches of them in floor vases. The corpse looked blue-white, rubbery, and utterly, horribly *dead*. Claire felt a cloud creep over her, heard a buzzing in her ears, and nearly collapsed, but somehow she managed not to faint.

'Oh my God,' Eve whispered, and brought both hands to her mouth.

'It's Brandon,' Claire said, and looked at Oliver. 'It's Brandon, right?' Because that cold, white face didn't look human anymore, and she couldn't match it up to the living person – vampire – she'd feared. The one who'd threatened her, chased her home, nearly killed her and Eve...

Oliver nodded. He pulled back the velvet covering Brandon from the neck down, revealing black open wounds. Some of them still smoked. Claire caught the smell of cooking meat, and this time, her knees buckled. Detective Hess caught her arm and steadied her.

'He was tortured,' Oliver said. He sounded neutral – disinterested, even. 'It took a long time. Someone very much enjoyed this. Almost as if there was a...personal agenda at work.'

Mayor Morrell motioned his son forward. Richard wasn't nearly the psycho his sister was. In fact, Claire kind of liked him, as much as she could like anybody from his family who worked for vampires. He seemed almost fair.

Richard examined the wounds in Brandon's body. He actually *touched* them, which made Claire throw up in her head, if not actually through her mouth. 'Looks like some kind of weapon straight to the heart. Probably a stake,' Richard said, and looked up at his father. 'Whoever did this was serious. This wasn't just random; this was done slowly. I don't know what they wanted out of him, but whatever it was, they probably got it. I can see shadows of wounds that closed over before he died. That's hours, at least.'

Silence. Deep, dark silence. Richard straightened up and glanced at Claire and Eve. If he recognised them, he gave no sign. 'These two girls have something to do with it?'

'Perhaps,' Oliver said. Claire didn't see him move, but all of a sudden he was right in front of her, looking down. 'Perhaps they know something. You didn't like Brandon very much, did you, Claire?'

'I—' She didn't know what to say. *Don't lie*, Hess had said. Did the vamps have some kind of lie detector power? Maybe even mind-reading? 'No, I didn't like him. But I wouldn't want to see this happen to anybody.' *Not even you*. She said that to herself, though.

He had such kind eyes. That was the horrible

thing about him, this warm feeling that she could trust him, *should* trust him, that somehow she was letting him down by not—

'Don't,' Eve said sharply, and pinched her arm. Claire yelped and looked at her. 'Don't look him in the eye.'

'Eve,' Oliver sighed. 'I'm very disappointed in you. Don't you understand that it's my responsibility, as Brandon's Patron, to get to the bottom of this? To find the ones responsible? You're not the innocent Claire may be; you know the penalties for killing one of us. And you know the lengths to which we'll go to find out the truth. If I can get it from her without pain, don't you want me to do that?'

Eve didn't answer. She kept her eyes focused somewhere around the middle of his chest. 'I think you'll do whatever you want,' she said grimly. 'Just like vamps always do. You didn't ask me, but I'm glad Brandon's dead. And I'm glad he suffered, too. However much it was, it wasn't enough.'

That was when Nice Oliver vanished. Just...gone. Claire saw a flicker of movement, nothing more, and then he had hold of Eve's black-dyed hair and he was yanking her head back at a painful angle.

And there was nothing human in his eyes. Unless pure, flaming rage was human.

'Oh,' he breathed into Eve's ear. 'Thank you for

saying that. Now I don't have to be so careful anymore.'

Detective Hess stepped forward, fists clenched; Richard Morrell got in his way. 'Easy, Joe,' he said. 'It's under control.'

Didn't look that way to Claire. She was breathing too fast, feeling faint again, and she could see Eve's knees buckling. The menace in the room – the body on the table – it was all just...terrifying.

Shane's dad did that. Claire felt sick and even more terrified once she had the thought, because now somehow she had to keep it to herself.

And she knew they were going to ask.

Oliver sniffed at Eve's exposed neck. 'You've been working at a coffee shop,' he said. 'On campus, I suppose. Funny. I wasn't asked for any references.'

'Let go,' Eve said faintly.

'Oh, I can't do that. It makes it harder to hurt you.' Oliver smiled, then opened his mouth, and his fangs – snake fangs, deadly sharp – snapped down into place. They weren't like teeth, really; they were more like polished bone, and they looked *strong*.

He licked Eve's neck, right over the pulse.

'Oh God,' she whispered. 'Please don't do that. Please don't let him do that.'

'Ask the girl a question, Oliver. We don't have time for your hobbies.' Mayor Morrell said it in a bored tone, like all of this was keeping him from something more important. He inspected his manicure and buffed his fingernails against his suit jacket. 'Let's move this train down the track.'

Amelie wasn't saying or doing *anything*.

'I'm Protected,' Eve said. 'You can't hurt me.' She didn't sound very confident, though, and Claire looked at Amelie, sitting in the front row of chairs, studying the scene closely, as if it was all some show put on for her benefit. Her expression was polite, but cool.

Please help, Claire thought. Amelie's pale gold eyebrow raised just slightly. *Can you hear me?*

If she could, Amelie gave no other sign. She simply sat, calm as Buddha.

'Let's just say that Amelie and I have an understanding in matters such as this,' Oliver said. 'And Eve, love, that understanding is that I can use any methods to pursue humans who break the peace. Regardless of Protection. Regardless of *who* that Protection is from. Now, I think we should have a little talk about your home invaders.'

'Our...what?' Eve was struggling not to meet his eyes, but he was so close, it was almost impossible to avoid him. 'I don't know who they were.'

'You don't. You've very sure about that,' he said. His voice had dropped to a low, lethal whisper, and Claire tried to think of something to say, something to do, that would help Eve. Because clearly, Eve wasn't going to help herself, and she couldn't just stand by and see her…hurt. She *couldn't*.

'I know,' she said, and she felt everyone shift their collective attention onto her. Scary. Claire cleared her throat. 'They were bikers.'

'Bikers.' Oliver let go of Eve's hair and turned towards Claire. 'I see. You're attempting to distract me with the obvious, and, Claire, that is not a good idea. Not a good idea at all. We know all that, you see. We know when they came to town. We even know who called them.'

Claire felt all the blood drain from her head. Her stomach flipped over, and kept flipping, and Oliver walked away from Eve and yanked another cord.

Another curtain slid aside, next to Brandon's body.

Two men, on their knees, bound and gagged and held in place by really scary-looking vampires. One of the prisoners was a biker.

Shane was the other.

Claire screamed.

CHAPTER EIGHT

In the end, they sat her down in a chair and had Gretchen hold her down with those strong, iron-hard hands pressing on her shoulders. Claire continued to struggle, but fear and shock were winning out over anger. And Shane wasn't moving. He was watching her, but he couldn't say anything around the gag, and if Shane wasn't struggling, maybe there wasn't anything to be gained from it.

Eve spun around and slapped Oliver. An open-hand, hard smack that echoed like a gunshot off of all the marble in the room. There was a collective intake of breath. 'You son of a bitch!' she spit. 'Let Shane go! He has nothing to do with this!'

'Really.' A flat word, not even really a question. Unlike a human's, Oliver's face didn't show any sign of a handprint from the slap, and it had definitely been hard enough. He barely looked as if he'd felt it at all. 'Sit down, Eve, while I tell you the facts of your rather pathetic life.'

She didn't. Oliver put his hand flat on her chest, right at the notch of her collarbone, and shoved. Eve sprawled in a chair, glaring at him.

'Detective Hess,' Oliver said. 'I suggest you explain to my dear ex-employee exactly what she risks the next time she touches me in anger. Or, come to think of it, touches me at all.'

Hess was already moving, sitting in the chair beside Eve and leaning towards her. He whispered to her, urgent words that Claire couldn't catch. Eve shook her head violently. A trickle of sweat ran from her messy hair down the side of her face, making a flesh-coloured track through the white make-up.

'Now,' Oliver continued once Hess stopped, and Eve was sitting still. 'We're not technological idiots, Eve. And we do own the telephone providers in this area, particularly the cell phone providers. Shane placed a call from your home to a number that, much to our surprise, we found to be assigned to a device we located on his friend Mr Wallace.' Oliver pointed to the biker. 'GPS is a marvellous invention, by the way. We're quite grateful for all the hard work humanity has put into keeping track of itself. It makes finding people so much easier than it used to be in the old days.'

'Shane didn't do anything,' Claire said. 'Please. You have to let him go.'

'Shane was found at the crime scene,' Oliver said. 'With Brandon's body. And I hardly think we can say he wasn't involved, if he was friendly enough with Mr Wallace to be exchanging telephone calls.'

'No, he didn't—!'

Oliver slapped her. She never saw it coming, just felt the impact and saw red for a second. Her whole body shook with the force of how much she wanted to hit him back, and she felt the stinging imprint of his hand on her cheek like a brand.

'You see, Eve?' Oliver asked. 'An eye for an eye. Of course, my interpretation is a bit free of the Scriptures.'

Shane was screaming around his gag, and now he was fighting, but the vampires were holding him down on his knees without breaking a sweat. Eve's eyes were huge and dark, and Hess was holding her down in the chair as she struggled to come after Oliver.

Don't, Claire thought wildly. Because her friends had just told Oliver exactly what he wanted to know: that hurting her would get something out of them.

'Oliver,' Amelie said. Her voice was soft and very gentle. 'Is there a question you are posing to the children? Or are you merely indulging yourself? You say you already know the boy called this man. What more information do you need?'

'I want to know where his father has gone,' Oliver said. 'One of them knows.'

'The girls?' Amelie shook her head. 'It seems unlikely that someone like Mr Collins would trust in either of them.'

'The boy knows, then.'

'Possibly.' She tapped her lips with one pale finger.

'Yet somehow, I doubt he will tell you. And there is no need for any cruelty to discover the truth, I believe.'

'Meaning?' Oliver turned fully towards her, crossing his arms.

'Meaning that he will come to us, Oliver, as you very well know. In order to save the boy from the consequences of his actions.'

'So you withdraw your Protection from the boy?'

Amelie looked at the body lying on the slab. After a moment of silence, she rose gracefully and walked to what was left of Brandon, trailed ghost-white fingers over his distorted face, and said, 'He was born before King John, did you know that? Born a prince. All those years, ending. I grieve for the loss of all that he saw that we will never know. All the memories that can never enrich us.'

'Amelie.' Oliver sounded impatient. 'We can't allow his killers to run free. You know that.'

'He was yours, Oliver. You might spare a

moment for his loss before you run baying after blood.'

Amelie's back was to him, so she couldn't have seen it, but Claire did: there was hate in Oliver's eyes, hate twisting his face. He got it under control before Amelie turned towards him.

'Brandon had his flaws,' Oliver said. 'Of all of us, he was the one who enjoyed the hunt the most. I don't think he ever came to terms with the rules of Morganville. But it's those rules we have to observe now. By sentencing these criminals.'

Sentencing? What about a trial? Claire started to ask, but a cold hand clapped over her mouth from behind, and she looked up to see Gretchen bending over her, fangs out, holding a hushing finger to her own mouth. Eve was likewise gagged by Hans. Next to them, Detective Hess folded his arms and looked deeply troubled, but he didn't speak.

Amelie looked at Oliver, then past him, at Shane.

'I warned you,' she said quietly. 'My Protection can only extend to you so far. You betrayed my trust, Shane. For the sake of kindness, I will not break faith with your friends; they remain under my Protection.' She shifted her pale gaze to Oliver, and gave him a slow, regal incline of her head. 'He is yours. I withdraw Protection.'

Claire screamed out a protest, but it was lost against the gag of Gretchen's hand. Amelie bent over and placed a kiss on Brandon's waxy forehead.

'Goodbye, child,' she said. 'Flawed as you were, you were still one of the eternal. We won't forget.'

Claire heard someone yell outside the room, and Amelie whipped around so quickly that she was a blur, then *moved*...and something hit the marble pillar next to where she'd been and exploded with a sharp popping sound.

A bottle. Claire smelt gas, and then heard a thick, whooshing sound.

And then the curtains exploded into flame.

Amelie snarled, bone-white and utterly not *people*, all of a sudden, and then she was dragged out of the way and down, with a moving bunker of bodyguards crowding around her. Gunfire exploded in the room, and somebody – Detective Hess? – shoved Claire forward to the carpet and covered her, too. Eve was down, too, curled into a protective ball, her black-fingernailed hands covering her head.

And then, there was fighting – grunts and smacks and wood being thrown against walls and smashed during struggles. Claire couldn't get any sense of what was going on, except that it was brutal and it was over fast, and when the choking fog of smoke began to clear, Hess finally backed off and let her sit up.

There were two men dead in the entrance of the

room. Big guys, in leather. There was one still moving.

Amelie pushed aside her bodyguards and stalked past Claire as if she didn't exist. She glided down the aisle and to the one biker still feebly trying to crawl away. He was trailing a dark streak on the maroon carpet. Claire got slowly to her feet, grateful for Detective Hess's arm around her, and exchanged a look of sheer horror with Eve, on his other side.

Amelie never got to the biker. Oliver was there ahead of her, dragging the wounded man up and, before Claire could blink, snapping his neck with a dry sound.

The body dropped to the carpet with a limp thump. Claire turned and hid her face against Hess's jacket, trying to control a surge of nausea.

When she looked back, Amelie was staring at Oliver. He was staring right back. 'No point in taking chances,' he said, and gave her a slow, full smile. 'He might have killed you, Amelie.'

'Yes,' she said softly. 'And that wouldn't have been in anyone's best interests, would it, Oliver? How fortunate I am that you were here to...save me.'

She didn't move or gesture, but her bodyguards swarmed and surrounded her, and the whole mass of them moved out, walking around (or over) the dead men.

Oliver watched her go, then turned back to

sweep a glare around the entire room, stopping on Shane.

'Your father thinks he can act without consequences, I see,' he said. 'How sad for you. Put these two where they belong. In cages.'

The biker and Shane were pulled to their knees and dragged off, behind the curtains. Claire lunged forward, but Gretchen grabbed her and put her hand over Claire's mouth. Claire winced as her arm was twisted up behind her back, and she realised she was crying, unable to breathe for the pressure of the hand on her mouth and the stuffiness building up in her nose.

Eve wasn't crying. Eve was staring at Oliver, and even when Detective Hess let go of her, she didn't move.

'What are you going to do to them?' she asked. She sounded unnaturally calm.

'You know the laws,' Oliver said. 'Don't you, Eve?'

'You can't. Shane had nothing to do with this.'

Oliver shook his head. 'I won't debate my judgement with you. Mayor? You'll sign the papers? If you're done cowering, that is.'

The mayor had been down in a defensive crouch behind an urn; he got up now, looking flushed and angry. 'Of course I'll sign,' he said. 'The nerve of these bastards! Striking *here*? Threatening—'

'Yes, very traumatic,' Oliver said. 'The papers.'

'I brought a notary. It'll be all nice and legal.'

Gretchen let go of Claire, sensing her will to fight was trickling away. 'Legal?' Claire gasped. 'But...there hasn't even been a *trial*! What about a jury?'

'He had a jury,' Detective Hess told her. His tone was gentle, but what he was saying was harsh. 'A jury of the victim's peers. That's the way the law works here. Same for humans. If a vampire ever got brought up on murder charges, it would be humans deciding whether he lived or died.'

'Except no vampire has ever been brought up on charges,' Eve said. She looked nearly cold and pale enough to be a vampire herself. 'Or ever will. Don't kid yourself, Joe. It's only the humans who get the sharp end of justice around here.' She looked at the dead guys lying on the carpet at the entrance to the room. 'Scared the shit out of you, though, didn't they?'

'Don't flatter them. They had no hope of succeeding,' Oliver said. He looked at Hans. 'I have no further use for these two.'

'Wait! I want to talk to Shane!' Claire yelled. Gretchen propelled her towards the exit with a shove. It was move, or fall over the dead, bloody bodies.

Claire moved. Behind her, she heard Eve doing the same.

She blinked away tears, wiped angrily at her face

and nose, and tried to think what to do next. *Shane's dad*, she thought. *Shane's dad will save him.* Although, of course, the dead guys she was stepping over indicated that rescue had already been attempted, and that hadn't gone so well. Besides, Shane's dad wasn't here. He hadn't stuck around when Shane got caught. Maybe he didn't care. Maybe nobody cared but her.

'Easy,' Detective Hess said, and stepped in beside her to take her by the elbow. He managed to make it feel like escorting, instead of arresting. 'There's still time. The law says that the convicts have to be displayed on the square for two nights so that everyone can see them. They'll be in cages, so they'll be safe enough. It's not the Ritz, but it keeps Brandon's friends from ripping them apart without due process.'

'How—' Claire's throat closed up on her. She cleared it and tried again. 'How are they going to—?'

Hess patted her hand. He looked tired and worried and grim. 'You won't be here when it happens,' he said. 'So don't think about it. If you want to talk to him, you can. They're putting them in cages now, at the centre of the park.'

'Oliver said take them back,' Gretchen said from behind them. Hess shrugged.

'Well, he didn't say when, did he?'

⋈ ⋈ ⋈

The Founder's Park was a large circle, with walkways like spokes in a wheel, all leading to the centre.

And at the centre were two cages. Cells just big enough for a man to stand up, not wide enough to stretch out. Shane would have to sleep sitting up, if he slept, or curled in a foetal position.

He was sitting, knees up, head resting on his arms, when Eve and Claire arrived. The biker was yelling and rattling his bars. Not Shane. He was...quiet.

'Shane!' Claire almost flew across the open space, grabbed the cold iron bars in both hands, and pressed her face between them. 'Shane!'

He looked up. His eyes were red, but he wasn't crying. At least, not now. He managed to move around in the small, cramped cage until he was sitting closer to her, and reached through the bars to lay his hand against her cheek, stroking it with his thumb. It was the cheek that Oliver had slapped, she realised. She wondered if it was still red.

'I'm sorry,' Shane said. 'My dad... I had to go. I couldn't let him do this. I had to try to stop it, Claire, I had to—'

She was crying again, silently. With his thumb, he wiped away the tear that fell. She could feel his hand shaking. 'You didn't do anything, did you? To Brandon?'

'I didn't like the son of a bitch, but I didn't hurt

him, and I didn't kill him. That was already done when I got there.' Shane laughed, but it sounded forced. 'Just my luck, huh? Charging off to be the hero, I get to be the villain instead.'

'Your dad—'

He nodded. 'Dad'll get us out. Don't worry, Claire. It'll be OK.'

But the way he said it, she knew he didn't believe it, either. She bit her lip to hold back a fresh wave of sobbing, and turned her head to kiss his palm.

'Hey,' he said softly. He moved closer to the bars, pressing his face between them. 'I always said you were jailbait, but this is ridiculous.'

She tried to laugh. She really did.

His smile looked broken. 'I'm going to consider this protective custody. At least this way, I can't do anything that'd get me in real trouble, right?'

She leant forward to kiss him. His lips felt just the same, soft and warm and damp, and she didn't want to move away. Not ever.

He sat back first, leaving her stranded there tingling and once again on the verge of tears. *Dammit!* Shane could *not* be blamed for this. It wasn't *fair*!

'I'll talk to Michael,' she said.

'Yeah.' Shane nodded. 'Tell him…well, hell. Tell him I'm sorry, OK? And he can have the PlayStation.'

'Stop it! Stop it… You're not going to die, Shane!'

He looked at her, and she saw the bright spark of fear in his eyes. 'Yeah,' he said softly. 'Right.'

Claire clenched her fists until they ached, and looked at Eve, who'd been standing quietly in the background. As Eve came towards the cage, Claire turned away and went to Detective Hess. 'How?' she asked again. 'How are they going to kill him?'

He looked deeply uncomfortable, but he looked down and said, 'Fire. It's always fire.'

That nearly made her cry again. Nearly. Shane already knew, she thought, and so did Eve. They'd known all along. 'You have to help him,' she said. 'You have to! He didn't do *anything*!'

'I can't,' he said. 'I'm sorry.'

'But—'

'Claire.' He put both hands on her shoulders and pulled her into a hug. She realised she was trembling, and then the tears came, a huge flood of them, and she held to the lapels on his coat and cried like her heart was breaking. Hess stroked her hair. 'You bring me proof that he had nothing to do with Brandon's death, and I swear to you, I'll do everything I can. But until then, my hands are tied.'

The idea of Shane burning in that cage was the most horrible thing she had ever imagined. *Get hold of yourself*, she thought furiously. *You're all he has!* So she pulled in deep, shaking breaths and stepped back from Hess's embrace, scrubbing the tears from her face with the sleeve of her T-shirt.

Hess offered her a tissue. She took it and blew her nose, feeling stupid, and felt Eve's hand on her shoulder before she even knew Eve was there behind her.

'Let's go,' Eve said. 'We've got things to do.'

It had been Michael in the doorway when they'd driven by on their way to Founder's Square, and it was Michael in the doorway when the car pulled to a halt at 716 Lot Street. Gretchen opened the back door to allow Eve and Claire to scramble out. Claire looked back; Hess was still in the back seat, watching them go. He wasn't making a move to get out with them. 'Detective?' she asked. Eve was already halfway up the walk, moving fast. Claire knew that the first rule of Morganville was 'Never hang around out in the dark,' but she did it anyway.

'I'm going back to the station,' he said. 'Hans and Gretchen will drop me off. It's OK.'

She didn't like the idea of leaving anybody alone with Hans and Gretchen, but he was the adult, and he had to know what he was doing, right? She nodded, backed up, and then turned and ran the rest of the way up the steps and into the house.

Michael had pulled Eve inside, but not far in; she nearly ran into the two of them when she charged over the threshold. She slammed the door and locked it – Shane or Michael had replaced the locks again, and added more – and spun around to see that Michael had Eve in a bear hug, pressing her against him so tight that she nearly disappeared. He looked at Claire in total misery over Eve's shoulder. 'What the hell is going on? Where's Shane?'

Oh God, he didn't know. Why didn't he know? 'What happened?' she blurted. 'Why did you let him leave?'

'Shane? I didn't *let him* do anything. Any more than I let you go running off unprotected in the middle of the day. His dad called. He just…left. It was still daylight. There wasn't anything I could do.' Michael pushed Eve back a little and looked at her. 'What happened?'

'Brandon's dead,' Eve said. She didn't try to soften it, and her voice was as hard as an iron bar. 'They've got Shane in a cage on Founder's Square for his murder.'

Michael sagged back against the wall as if she'd punched him in the stomach. 'Oh,' he whispered. 'Oh my God.'

'They're going to kill him,' Claire said. 'They're going to burn him alive.'

Michael closed his eyes. 'I know. I remember.' Oh, *crap*, he'd seen it done before. So had Eve. She remembered them saying so before, though they'd spared her the details. Michael just breathed for a few seconds, and then said, 'We have to get him out.'

'Yeah,' Eve agreed. 'I know. But by *we*, you

mean me and Claire, right? Because you're of no damn use at all.'

She might as well have punched him *again*, Claire thought; Michael's mouth dropped open, and she saw the agony in his eyes. Eve must not have seen it. She turned and clomped away, brisk and efficient.

'Claire!' she called back. 'Come on! Move it!'

Claire looked miserably at Michael. 'I'm sorry,' she said. 'She didn't mean that.'

'No, she did,' he said faintly. 'And she's right. I'm no use to you. Or to Shane. What good am I? I might as well be dead.'

He turned and slammed his hand into the wall, hard enough to break bones. Claire yelped, scrambled backward, and ran after Eve. When Michael went all avenging-angel, well, it was definitely scary. And he didn't look like he wanted witnesses to whatever was happening inside.

Eve was already going up the stairs. 'Wait!' Claire said. 'Michael...shouldn't we—?'

'Forget about Michael. Are you in or out?'

In. She guessed. Claire cast another look back at the hallway, where the sound of flesh hitting wood continued, and winced. Michael couldn't hurt himself, not permanently, but it sounded painful.

Probably not as painful as what he was feeling.

When Claire reached the doorway, Eve was yanking open drawers, pulling out frilly stuff, and throwing it aside. Black lace. Netting. Fishnet hose. 'Ah!' she said, and brought out a big, black box. It must have been heavy. It made a hollow *thunk* as she slammed it down on top of the dresser, rattling her collection of Evil Bobbleheads, which all started nodding uneasily. 'Come here.'

Claire went, worried; this was a brand-new Eve, one she wasn't sure she liked. She liked the vulnerable Eve, the one who cried at the drop of a hat. This one was harsh and hard and liked to order people around.

'Hold out your hand,' Eve said. Claire did, tentatively. Eve slapped something round and wooden into it.

Pointed on one end.

A home-made stake.

'Vampire killer's best friend,' Eve said. 'I made a bunch when Brandon was bothering me. I let him know, the next time he came sniffing around me he was going to get a woody. A *real* one.'

'Aren't these…illegal?'

'They'll get you thrown *under* the jail. Or killed and dumped in some empty lot somewhere. So don't get caught holding.'

She pulled out more stakes, and set them on the top of the dresser. Then some crude home-made crosses, extra large. She passed one to Claire, who gripped it in numbed fingers. 'But...Eve, what are we *doing*?'

'Saving Shane. What, you don't want to?'

'Of course I do! But—'

'Look.' Eve pulled out some more stuff and dumped it on the pile of stakes – lighter fluid, a Zippo lighter. 'The time for playing nice is over. If we want to get Shane out of there, vampires have to die. That means we start a war nobody wants, but tough. I'm not watching Shane burn. I won't do that. *They* want this. Oliver wants it. Fine, he can have it. He can choke on it.'

'Eve!' Claire dropped the cross and stake, grabbed her shoulders, and shook her. 'You *can't*! You know it's suicide – you've told me that before! You can't just...kill vampires! You'll end up in a cage right next to—'

Oh, God. She hadn't seen it before, but now she knew what was different about Eve. What was missing in her eyes.

'You want to die,' Claire said slowly. 'Don't you?'

'I'm not afraid of it,' Eve said. 'No big deal, right? Tra-la, off to paradise just like my parents always told me, pearly gates and all that. Besides, nobody's going to help us, Claire. We have to stick together. We have to help ourselves.'

'What if I find some evidence?' Claire asked. 'Detective Hess said—'

'Detective Hess stood there and did *nothing*. That's what they're all going to do. *Nothing*. Just like Michael.'

'God, Eve, stop it! That's not fair. Michael can't leave the house! You know that!'

'Yeah. Not much help, is it?' Eve began stuffing her arsenal of vampire-killing equipment into a black gym bag. 'It's time for a little payback around here. There are other people who're tired of sucking up to the vamps. Maybe I can find them if you're going to punk out on me. I need people I can rely on.'

'Eve!'

'With me or out of the way.'

Claire retreated to the doorway, and bumped into a warm body. She yelped and lunged forward, turning to face...

Michael.

His face was like a chalky mask, and his eyes were big and wounded and angry. He took Claire's hand and pulled her through the doorway, out into the hall.

Then he took hold of the doorknob, and looked at Eve. 'You're not going anywhere,' he said. 'Not while I can stop you.'

He slammed the door and locked it with an old-fashioned key. Seconds later, Eve hit the other side with a bang and began rattling the knob. 'Hey!' she screamed. 'Open it! Right now!'

'No,' Michael said. 'I'm sorry, Eve. I love you. I'm not letting you do this.'

She screamed and battered harder. 'You *love me*? You *asshole*! *Let me go!*'

'Can you really keep her in there?' Claire asked anxiously.

'I can for tonight,' Michael said, his eyes fixed on the door as it vibrated under the force of her kicks and blows. 'The windows won't open, or the doors. She's stuck. But when the sun comes up...' He turned to look at Claire. 'You said if you could find evidence, Detective Hess would step in for Shane?'

'That's what he said.'

'It's not enough. We need Amelie on his side. And Oliver.'

'Oliver's the one who put him in the cage! And Amelie – she walked away. I don't think we can get anything from her, Michael.'

'Try,' he said. 'Go. You have to.'

Claire blinked. 'You mean...go out there? At night?'

Michael looked exhausted suddenly. And very young. 'I can't do it. I can't trust Eve enough to let her out of her room, much less go out and talk to some of the most powerful vampires in town. Call Detective Hess, or Lowe. Don't go alone...but Claire, I need you to do this. I need you to make it right. I can't—'

It was written all over his face, the things he couldn't do. The limits he'd crashed into with so much force it had left him broken and bleeding in the wreckage.

'I know,' Claire said. 'I'll try.'

It was dark, it was Morganville, and she was sixteen years old. Not the best idea ever, going out of the house again, but Claire put on her darkest pair of jeans, a black shirt, and a big, gaudy cross that Eve had given her. She felt queasy at the idea of stakes. Doubly queasy at the idea of actually stabbing somebody with one.

I still have Protection, Amelie said so.

She hoped that would actually mean something.

Claire called Detective Hess's number from the card Eve had left pinned to the board in the kitchen. He answered on the second ring, sounded tired and depressed.

'I need a ride,' Claire said. 'If you're willing. I need to talk to Amelie.'

'Even I don't know how to get to Amelie,' Hess said. 'Best-kept secret in Morganville. I'm sorry, kid, but—'

'I know how to get to her,' she said. 'I just don't want to walk. Given...the time.'

There was a second of silence, and then the sound of a pen scratching against paper. 'You shouldn't be out at all,' Hess said. 'Besides, I don't think you're going to get anywhere. You need to find somebody who can back up Shane's story. That means one of his dad's biker buddies. There may be one or two running around loose, but I don't think talking sweet to them's going to get you much.'

'What about his dad?'

'Trust me, you're not going to find Frank Collins. Not before the powers that be do, anyway. Every vampire in town is out tonight, combing the streets, looking for him. They'll find him eventually. Not a lot of places he can hide when it's an all-out effort.'

'But...if they catch him, that's kind of a good thing. He could tell them Shane didn't do it!'

'He could,' Hess agreed. 'But he's just crazy enough to think burning in a cage alongside his kid is going out in a blaze of glory. Some kind of victory. He might say Shane was part of it just to punish him. We can't know.'

She couldn't deny that. Claire swallowed hard. 'So...are you going to give me a ride or not?'

'You're determined to go out,' Hess said. 'In the dark.'

'Yes. And I'll walk if I have to. I just hope I don't – have to.'

His sigh rattled the phone speaker. 'All right. Ten minutes. Stay inside until I honk the horn.'

Claire hung up the phone and turned, and nearly bumped into Michael. She yelped, and he reached out and steadied her. He kept hold of her arms even after she didn't need the steadying support anymore. He felt warm and real, and she thought – not for the first time – how weird it was that he could seem so *alive* when he really wasn't. Not exactly. Not all the time.

He looked like he had something he wanted to say, but he didn't know how to say it. And finally, he looked away. 'Hess is coming?'

'Yeah. Ten minutes, he said.'

Michael nodded. 'You're going to see Amelie?'

'Maybe. I've got exactly one shot. If that doesn't work, then...' She spread her hands. 'Then I guess I talk to Oliver instead.'

'If...you do see Amelie, tell her I need to talk to her,' he said. 'Will you do that for me?'

Claire blinked. 'Sure. But...why?'

'Something she said to me before. Look, obviously I can't go to her. She has to come here.' Michael shrugged and gave her a tiny curve of a smile. 'Not important why.'

That raised a little red flag in the back of her mind. 'Michael, you're not going to do anything, well, crazy, right?'

'Says the sixteen-year-old about to walk out the door in the dark to go see a vampire? No, Claire. I'm not going to do anything crazy.' Michael's eyes glittered suddenly with some fierce emotion. It looked like rage, or pain, or some toxic mix of both. 'I hate this. I hate letting you go. I hate Shane for getting himself caught. I hate *this*—'

What Michael was really saying, Claire understood, was *I hate me.* She totally got that. She hated herself on a regular basis.

'Don't punch anything, OK?' Because he had that look again. 'Take care of Eve. Don't let her go crazy, OK? Promise? If you love her, you need to take care of her. She needs you now.'

Some of the fierceness faded out of his eyes, and the way he looked at her made her go all soft and warm inside. 'I promise,' he said, and rubbed his hands gently up and down her arms, then let go. 'You tell Hess that if anything happens to you – anything – I'm killing him hard.'

She smiled faintly. 'Ooooh, tough guy.'

'Sometimes. Look, I didn't ask before – is Shane OK?'

'OK? You mean, did they hurt him?' She shook her head. 'No, he looked pretty much in one piece. But he's in a cage, Michael. And they're going to kill him. So no, he's not *OK.*'

The look in his eyes turned a little wild. 'That's the only reason I'm letting you go. If I had any choice—'

'You do,' she said. 'We can all sit here and let him die. Or you can let Eve go on her wild-ass rescue mission and get herself killed. Or you can let sweet, calm, reasonable Claire go do some talking.'

He shook his head. His long, elegant hands, which looked so at home wrapped around a guitar, closed into fists. 'Guess that means there's no choice.'

'Not really,' Claire agreed. 'I was kind of lying about that choice thing.'

Detective Hess was surprised when she gave him the address. 'That's old-lady Day's house,' he said. 'She lives there with her daughter. What do you want with them? Far as I know, they're not involved in any of this.'

'It's where I need to go,' Claire said stubbornly. She had no idea where Amelie's house was, but she knew of one door into it. She'd been thinking about ways to explain how you could open a bathroom door and be in a house that might be halfway across town, but all she could think of was folded space, and even the most wild-haired physicists said that was nearly impossible.

But she liked folded space better as an explanation than crazy booga-booga vampire magic.

'You going prepared for trouble?' he asked. When she didn't answer, he reached into the glove compartment of the car and pulled out a small jewellery-type box.

'Here. I always carry spares.'

She opened it and found a delicate silver cross on a long chain. She silently put it around her neck and dropped it down the neck of her shirt. She already had a backup, one of Eve's handmade wooden ones, but this one felt…real, somehow. 'I'll give it back to you,' she said.

'No need. Like I said, I've got more.'

'I don't take jewellery from older men.'

Hess laughed. 'You know, I thought you were a mousy little thing when I first saw you, Claire, but you're not, are you? Not underneath.'

'Oh, I am mousy,' she said. 'All this scares the hell out of me. But I don't know what else to do, sir, except try. Even a mouse bites.'

Hess nodded, the laughter fading out of his face. 'Then I'll try to give you the chance to show some teeth.'

He drove the half mile or so, navigating dark streets with ease. She saw glimpses of people moving in the dark, pale and quick. The vampires were out in force, he'd said, and he was right. She caught a burning reflection of eyes as the car turned a corner. Vampire eyes reflected light like a cat's. Disturbing.

Hess pulled to a halt in front of the old Victorian-style house. 'You want me to come up with you?' he asked.

'You'd just scare them,' Claire said. 'They know me. Besides, I'm not exactly threatening.'

'Not until they get to know you,' Hess said. 'Stay out of the alley.'

She paused, her hand on the door. 'Why?'

'Vampire lives at the end of it. Crazy old bastard. He doesn't come out of there, and neither does anybody who wanders in. So just stay out.'

She nodded and ducked out into the dark. Outside, the Morganville shadows had a character all their own. A neighbourhood that had been a little shabby in the daytime was transformed into a freak-show park at night, gilded by cold silver moonlight. The shadows looked like holes in the world; they were so black. Claire looked at the house, and felt its *presence*. It was like the Glass House, all right. It had some kind of living soul, only where the Glass House seemed mildly interested in the creatures scuttling around inside of it, this place...she wasn't sure it even liked what was going on.

She shuddered, opened the picket gate, and hurried up to knock on the door. She kept knocking, frantic, until a voice shouted through the wood, 'Who the hell's that?'

'Claire! Claire Danvers, I was here, you remember? You gave me some lemonade?' No answer. 'Please, ma'am, please let me in. I need to use your bathroom!'

'You *what*? Girl, you better step off my granma's porch!'

'Please!' Claire knew she sounded desperate, but then…she was desperate. Not to mention just one step shy of crazy. '*Please, ma'am, don't leave me out here in the dark!*'

That was only a little bit of acting, frankly, because the dark kept getting heavier and closer around her, and she couldn't stop thinking about the alley, the crazy vampire hiding at the end like some giant tarantula waiting to jump—

She nearly screamed as the door was suddenly opened, and a hand closed around her arm.

'Oh, for God's sake, get in!' snapped Lisa. She looked irritated, tired, and rumpled; Claire had clearly rattled her right out of bed. She was wearing pink satin pyjamas and fluffy bunny slippers, which didn't make her look any less pissed off. She yanked, Claire stumbled forward across the threshold, and Lisa slammed and multiply locked the door behind her.

Then she turned, crossed her arms, and frowned at Claire. It was a formidable frown, but the pink pj's and bunny slippers undermined it.

'What the *hell* are you doing here? Do you know what time it is?' Lisa demanded. Claire took a deep breath, opened her mouth…and didn't have to say anything.

Because Granma was standing in the hallway entrance, and with her was Amelie.

The contrast couldn't have been more striking.

Amelie looked every inch the glorious, perfect ice queen, from her carefully braided and coiled hair to her unlined face to the sleek white dress she wore – she'd changed from the black suit she'd worn to the Elders' Council building. She looked like one of those Greek statues made out of marble. Next to her, Granma seemed ancient, exhausted, and breakable.

'The visitor is here for me,' Amelie said calmly. 'I've been expecting her. I do thank you, Katherine, for your kindness.'

Who's Katherine? Claire looked around, and realised after a few seconds that it had to be Granma. Funny, she couldn't imagine Granma ever having had a first name, or being young; Lisa looked kind of thrown by it, too.

'And I appreciate your vigilance, Lisa, but your caution is unnecessary,' Amelie continued. 'Please return to your—' For a second, Amelie hesitated, and Claire couldn't imagine why until she saw that the vampire's gaze was fixed on the sight of Lisa's bunny shoes. It was only a second, a little crack in the marble, but Amelie's eyes widened just a bit, and her mouth curved. *She has a sense of humour.* That, more than anything else, made Claire feel lost. How could vampires have a sense of humour? How exactly was that fair?

Amelie recovered her poise. 'You may return to your sleep,' she said, and bowed her head gracefully to Lisa and her granma. 'Claire. If you would attend me.'

She didn't wait to see if Claire would, or explain what 'attend me' meant; she just turned and glided down the hallway. Claire exchanged a look with Lisa – this time, Lisa looked worried, not angry – and hurried after Amelie's retreating figure.

Amelie opened the bathroom door and stepped through into the same study Claire had visited before, only now it was night, and a fire was roaring in the enormous hearth to warm the chilly room. The walls were thick stone, and looked very old. The tapestries looked old, too – faded, tattered, but still keeping a sense of magnificence, somehow. The place looked way spookier by firelight. If there were electric lights, they weren't on. Not even the books crowding the shelves made the place warm.

Amelie crossed to a chair near the hearth and gracefully motioned Claire to one across from her. 'You may sit,' she said. 'But be warned, Claire, what I expect you want from me is not in my power to grant.'

Claire settled carefully, not daring to relax. 'You know why I'm here.'

'I'd be a fool if I thought it was any reason other than young Shane,' Amelie said, and smiled very sadly. 'I can recognise loyalty when I see it. It shines strongly from you both, which is one reason I have

trusted you so much on insignificant acquaintance.'
She lost her smile, and her pale eyes turned to frost
again. 'And that is why I cannot forgive what Shane
has done. He broke faith with me, Claire, and that
is intolerable. Morganville is founded on trust.
Without it, we have nothing but despair and death.'

'But *he didn't do anything*!' Claire knew she
sounded like a whiny little girl, but she didn't know
what else to do. It was that or cry, and she didn't
want to cry. She had the feeling she'd be doing
plenty of that, no matter what. 'He didn't kill
Brandon. He tried to save him. You can't punish
him for being in the wrong place!'

'We have no one's word of that save Shane's.
And make no mistake, child, I know why Shane
returned to Morganville in the first place. It is
regrettable that his sister was so brutally and
unnecessarily killed; we tried to make amends with
his family, as is custom. We even allowed them to
leave Morganville, which you understand is *not*
common, in hopes that Shane and his parents might
heal their grief in less…difficult surroundings. But it
was not possible. And his mother broke through the
block surrounding her memories.'

Claire shifted uncomfortably in her chair. It was
too big, and too high up; her toes barely touched
the ground. She gripped the arms firmly, tried to
remind herself that she was strong and courageous,
that she *had* to be, for Shane. 'Did you kill her?

Shane's mother?' she asked, as bluntly as she could. It still sounded timid, but at least she'd gotten the question out.

For a second she thought Amelie wasn't going to answer her, but then the vampire looked away, towards the fire. Her eyes looked orange in its glow, with dots of reflective yellow in the centre. She shrugged, a gesture so small, Claire barely even saw it. 'I have not lifted a hand against a human in hundreds of years, little Claire. But that is not what you ask, is it? Am I responsible for his mother's death? In a larger sense, I am responsible for anything that is done in Morganville, or even beyond its borders if it relates to vampires. But I think you ask if I gave an explicit order.'

Claire nodded. Her neck felt stiff, and her hands would have been shaking if they hadn't been grabbing the arms of the chair so hard her knuckles cracked.

'Yes,' Amelie said, and turned her head back to meet Claire's eyes. She looked cool, merciless, and absolutely without conscience. 'Of course I did. Shane's mother was one of the rare cases who, by focusing on a single event in their past, are able to overcome the psychic block that is placed on them when they depart this place. She remembered her daughter's death, and from that, she remembered other things. Dangerous things. As soon as we became aware this was happening, it was brought to my attention, and I gave the order to kill her. It was to be done quickly and without pain, and it was a mercy, Claire. Shane's mother had been in so much pain for so long, do you understand? She was damaged, and some damages cannot be healed.'

'Nothing heals if you're dead,' Claire whispered. She remembered Shane on the couch, blurting out all the horror of his life, and she wanted to throw up on Amelie's perfect lap. 'You can't do things like that. You aren't God!'

'For the safety of all who live here? Yes, Claire, I can. I must. I am sorry my decisions do not meet with your approval, but nevertheless, they are mine, and the consequences are also mine. Shane is a consequence. My agents warned me at the time that they believed the boy might have been tainted by his mother, that his block was slipping, but I chose not to expand the tragedy by killing a boy who might not have been a threat.' Amelie shrugged again. 'Not all of my decisions are cruel, you see. But the ones which are not are usually wrong. Had I killed Shane then, and his father, as well, we would not now be facing this...bloody and painful farce.'

'Because he'd be *dead*!' Claire felt tears sting hard in her eyes and at the back of her throat. 'Please. Please don't let this happen. You can find out the truth, can't you? You have powers. You can tell that Shane didn't kill Brandon...'

Amelie said nothing. She turned back towards the fire.

Claire watched her miserably for a few seconds, and felt tears break free to run down her cheeks. They felt ice-cold in the overly warm room. 'You can tell,' she repeated. 'Why won't you even *try*? Is it just because you're angry at him?'

'Don't be infantile,' Amelie said distantly. 'I do nothing out of anger. I am too old to fall into the trap of emotion. What I do, I do for expedience, and for the sake of the future.'

'Shane *is* the future! He's *my* future! And he's innocent!'

'I know all that,' Amelie said. 'And it does not matter.'

Claire stopped, stunned. Her mouth was open, and she tasted woodsmoke on her tongue until she closed it and swallowed. 'What?'

'I know Shane is innocent of the crime of which he is accused,' Amelie said. 'And yes, I could countermand Oliver. But I will not.'

'*Why?*' It burst out of Claire like a scream, but it was really just a whimper, all the fight kicked out of it.

'I have no reason to explain myself. Suffice to say that I have chosen to place Shane in that cage for a purpose. He may live, or he may die. That is no longer in my hands, and you may save both your breath and your hopes; I shall not stand up dramatically at the last moment as they light the pyres, and save your lover. Should it come to that, Claire, you must be prepared for the harsh reality that the world is not a fair or just place, and all your wishing cannot make it so.' Amelie sighed, very lightly. 'A lesson I learnt long, long ago, when the oceans were young, and sand was still rock. I am old, child. Older than you can possibly understand. Old enough that I play with lives like counters in a game. I wish this was not so, but damn me if I can change what I am. What the world is.'

Claire said nothing. There didn't seem to be anything left to say, so she just cried, silently and hopelessly, until Amelie pulled a white silken handkerchief from her sleeve and gracefully held it out to her. Claire dabbed at her face with it, honked her nose, and hesitated with the silken square clutched in her hand. She'd grown up with disposable tissues; she'd never actually held a handkerchief before. Not one like this, all beautiful embroidery and monogramming. You didn't throw these away, right?

Amelie's lips curved into that distant smile. 'Wash it and return it to me someday,' she said. 'But go now. I grow tired, and you will not change my mind. Go.'

Claire slid off the chair and stood up, turned, and gasped. There were two of Amelie's bodyguards standing *right there*, and she hadn't even known they were behind her the whole time. If she'd tried anything...

'Go to sleep, Claire,' Amelie said. 'Let things be. We shall see how the cards fall in our game.'

'It's not a game: It's Shane's life,' Claire shot back. 'And I'm not sleeping.'

Amelie shrugged and folded her hands neatly in her lap. 'Then go about your quest,' she said. 'But do not come back to me, little Claire. I will not be so well-disposed to you again.'

Claire didn't look back, but she knew the bodyguards followed her all the way to the door.

'Was there not something else you wanted to tell me?' Amelie asked, just before she went out. Claire glanced back; the vampire was still staring into the fire. 'Did you not have another request?'

'I don't know what you're talking about.'

Amelie sighed. 'Someone asked you for a favour.'

Michael. Claire swallowed hard. 'Michael wants to talk to you.'

Amelie nodded. Her expression didn't change.

'What do I tell him?' Claire asked.

'That is entirely your affair. Tell him the truth – that you did not care enough to deliver his message.' Amelie waved a hand without even looking towards her. 'Go.'

❧ ❧ ❧

Lisa was sitting in the living room, frowning, arms folded, when Claire came back down the hall. She still looked fierce, never mind the bunny slippers, as she stood up to open the locks on the front door. *Warrior princess on vacation*, Claire thought. She guessed you grew up tough in Morganville, especially if you lived in a house Amelie could visit any time she felt like it.

'Bad news,' Lisa said. 'Right?'

Did it show that much? 'Right,' Claire said, and wiped at her eyes again with the handkerchief. She shoved it in her pocket and sniffled miserably. 'But I'm not giving up.'

'Good,' Lisa said. 'Now, when I open this door, you're gonna want to hurry. Go straight to the car out there. Don't look left or right.'

'Why? Is there something…?'

'Morganville rules, Claire. Learn them, live them, survive them. Now *go!*' Lisa yanked open the door, put a hand flat on Claire's back, and propelled her out onto the porch. A second later, Lisa slammed the door, and Claire heard the rattle of the locks being turned. She got her balance, jumped down the steps, and hustled down the dark path and through the picket gate, and yanked open the passenger door of the car. She scrambled in and hit the lock, and then relaxed.

'I'm OK,' she said, and turned to Detective Hess. He wasn't there.

The driver's seat was empty. The keys were still in the ignition, the engine was idling, and the radio was playing softly. But the car was completely empty, except for her.

'Oh God,' Claire whispered. 'Oh God, oh God, oh God.' Because she *could* drive the car, but that would mean stranding Detective Hess, if he'd gone off doing police things. Stranding him without his partner to help him. She'd seen enough cop shows to know that wasn't a good idea. Maybe he'd just gone off to talk to somebody and was coming right back...or maybe he'd been snatched out of the car by some hungry vamp. But didn't Hess have some kind of special Protection?

She had no idea what to do.

While she was thinking about it, she heard voices. Not loud, but a steady stream of conversation. It sounded like Detective Hess, and he wasn't far away. Claire cautiously rolled down the window and listened hard; she couldn't make out any words, but there were definitely voices.

Claire unlocked her door and eased it open, straining to catch the words, but they were just sound, no meaning. She hesitated, then slipped out of the car, eased the door shut, and hurried towards the sound of the voices. Yes, that was Detective Hess; she recognised his voice. No question about it.

She didn't even realise where she was going – she

was so intent on listening – until she realised how *dark* it was, and the words weren't getting any clearer, and she wasn't at all sure now that *was* Detective Hess's voice after all.

And she was halfway down an alley with tall, rough board fence on both sides, trapping her.

She'd gone into the alley. Why the hell had she done that? Hess had warned her. Granma had warned her. And she hadn't listened!

Claire tried to turn around, she really tried, but then the whispers came again, and yes, for sure that was Detective Hess, there was no safety back there in the car, the car was a trap waiting to spring, and if she could just get to the end of the alley she'd be safe, Detective Hess would keep her safe, and she'd be—

'Claire.'

It was a cold, clear voice, falling on her like ice down her back, and it shocked her right out of the trance she'd fallen into. Claire looked up. On the second story of Granma's house, bordering the alley, a slender white figure stood in the window, staring down.

Amelie.

'Go back,' she said, and then the window was empty, curtains blowing in the wind.

Claire gasped, turned, and ran as fast as she could out of the alley. She could feel it at her back, pulling at her – *it*, whatever *it* was, it wasn't a vampire as she understood vamps in Morganville; it was something else, something worse. *Trap-door spider*, that was how Granma and Lisa had described it. Panic whited out its song in her head, and she made it – somehow – to the end of the alley and burst out into the street.

Detective Hess was standing at the car, looking straight at the alleyway. Gun drawn and held at his side. He visibly relaxed at the sight of her, came around, and hustled her to the passenger side of the car. 'That was dumb,' he said. 'And you're lucky.'

'I thought I heard you,' she said faintly. Hess raised his eyebrows.

'Like I said. Dumb.' He shut the door on her, came around, and put the car in gear.

'Where'd you go?'

He didn't answer. Claire looked back. There was something in the shadows in the alley, but she couldn't tell what it was.

Just that its eyes reflected the light.

It was coming up on deep night, when most sensible people were fast asleep in their beds with their doors bolted and windows securely locked, and Claire was knocking on the door of Common Grounds. It had a CLOSED sign in the window, but the lights were on in the back.

'You're sure you want to do this,' Hess said.

'You sound just like my subconscious,' Claire

said, and kept knocking. The blinds twitched and tented; locks rattled.

Oliver opened the door of the coffee shop, and the smell of espresso and cocoa and steamed milk washed over her. It was warm, welcoming, and so very wrong, considering what she knew about him.

He looked very humanly harassed at her arrival. 'It's late,' he said. 'What is it?'

'I need to talk to you about—'

'No,' he said very simply, and looked at Hess over her head. 'Detective Hess, you need to take this child home. She's lucky to still be alive today. If she wants to continue that winning streak, then she ought to be a little more cautious than to run around Morganville in the dead of night, knocking on my door.'

'Five minutes,' Claire promised. 'Then I'll go. Please. I never did anything to hurt you, did I?'

He stared at her for a few cool seconds, and then stepped back and held the door open. 'You, too, Detective. I hate to leave anyone with a pulse outside of shelter this evening.'

I'll bet, she thought. Oliver's peace-and-love hippie act no longer worked on her. Amelie had a kind of noble dignity that let her get away with pretending concern; Oliver was different. He was trying to be like Amelie, but not quite making it.

And I'll bet that pisses him off, too.

Hess urged her across the threshold and

followed her in. Oliver locked up, walked to the coffee bar, and, without being asked, began to put together three drinks – cocoa for Claire, strong black coffee for Detective Hess, and a pale tea for himself. His hands were steady and sure, the activity so normal that it lulled Claire into relaxing just a little as she sat down at a table. She ached all over with exhaustion and the tension she'd run through her body at Amelie's.

'Miles to go before you sleep,' Oliver said, as he stirred the cocoa. 'Here. Steamed milk and spiced cocoa. Hot peppers. It does have an amazing effect.'

He brought it to the table and handed it off to her, put Hess's coffee down, and retrieved his own brewing teacup before sitting. All very normal-life casual.

'You're here about the boy, I would suppose,' Oliver said. He dunked his tea bag and watched the results critically. 'I really must get a new supplier. This tea is pathetic. America just doesn't understand tea at all.'

'He's not *the boy*. His name is Shane,' Claire said. 'And he's not guilty. Even Amelie knows that.'

'Does she?' Oliver raised his gaze to fix it on hers. 'How interesting, because I, in fact, don't. Brandon was hideously and cruelly tortured, then murdered. He might have had his flaws—'

'What, like molesting children?'

'—but he was born into a different time, and some of his habits were difficult to change. He had his bright side, Claire, as do we all. And now that's gone, along with any harm he might have done.' Oliver wouldn't let her look away. 'Hundreds of years of memory and experience, poured out like water. Wasted. Do you think it's so simple to forget such a thing for me? For any of us? When we look at Brandon's body, we see ourselves at the mercy of humans. At *your* mercy, Claire.' He glanced at Detective Hess. 'Or yours, Joe. And you must admit, that's a terrifying prospect.'

'So you'll just kill anyone who frightens you. Who *could* hurt you.'

'Well...yes.' Oliver took the tea bag out of his cup and set it aside on the saucer, then sipped. 'A habit we learnt from you, really. Humans are all too ready to slaughter the innocent with the guilty, and if you were older, Claire, you would know this. Joe, I'm sure, is not so naive.'

Hess smiled thinly and sipped coffee. 'Don't talk to me. I'm just the driver.'

'Ah,' Oliver said. 'How generous of you.' They exchanged some kind of a look that Claire didn't know how to interpret. Was that anger? Amusement? A willingness to get up and beat the crap out of each other at a moment's notice? She couldn't even figure out what Shane and Michael were thinking, and she knew them. 'Is she then aware of the price of your services?'

'He's trying to get you rattled, Claire. There's no price.'

'How interesting. And what a departure.' Oliver dismissed Hess and got back to Claire, who hastily took a sip of her cocoa. *Ohhhhhh*...it just kind of exploded in her mouth, rich cocoa, warm milk, and a spicy edge that she didn't expect. Wow. She blinked and took another sip, carefully. 'I see you like the cocoa.'

'Um...yeah. Yes, sir.' Because somehow, when Oliver was being civilised, she felt compelled to still call him *sir*. Mom and Dad had a lot to answer for, she decided. She couldn't even be rude to evil vampires who'd caged her boyfriend and were preparing to roast him alive. 'What about Shane?'

Oliver leant back, and his eyelids drifted down to half-mast. 'We've covered this subject, Claire. Quite thoroughly. I believe you might even have the bruises to remind you of my opinion.'

'He didn't do it.'

'Let us deal in facts. *Fact*, the boy came back to Morganville with the clear intention of disrupting the peace, at the very least, and more likely killing vampires, which is an automatic death sentence. *Fact*, he concealed himself from us, along with his intentions. *Fact*, he communicated with his father and his father's friends both before they came to Morganville and after. *Fact*, he was at the scene of the crime. *Fact*, he has offered little in his own defence. Need I go on?'

'But—'

'Claire.' Oliver sounded sad and wounded. He leant forward, braced his elbows on the table, and placed his chin on top of his folded hands. 'You're young. I understand that you have feelings for him, but don't be a fool. He'll drag you down with him. If you force me to it, I'm sure I could uncover evidence that you knew about the presence of Shane's father in Morganville, and you had knowledge of their agenda. And that, my dear girl, would mean the end of your precious Protection, and put you in a cage alongside your boyfriend. Is that what you want?'

Hess put a warning hand on her arm. 'Enough, Oliver.'

'Not nearly enough. If you came to bargain, I think you have nothing to offer me that I can't get elsewhere,' Oliver said. 'So please take yourselves—'

'I'll sign whatever you want,' Claire blurted. 'You know, swear myself to you. Instead of Amelie. If you want. Just let Shane go.'

She hadn't been planning to do it, but when he'd mentioned *bargain* it had just taken on a life of its own inside her, and leapt right out of her mouth. Hess groaned and ran a hand over his hair, then covered his mouth, evidently to keep himself from telling her what an idiot she was.

Oliver continued to gaze at her with those steady, kind eyes.

'I see,' he said. 'It would be love, then. For love of this boy, you would tie yourself to me for the rest of your life. Give me the right to use you as I see fit. Do you have any idea what you're offering? Because I would not offer you the conditional contracts that most in Morganville sign, Claire. No, for you, there would be the old ways. The hard ways. I would own you, body and soul. I would tell you when to marry and whom to marry, and own your children and all their issue. I was born in a time when this was custom, you see, and I am not in a charitable mood just now. Is this what you want?'

'Don't,' Hess said sharply. He gripped Claire's forearm and pulled her up to her feet. 'We're going, Oliver. Right now.'

'She has the right to make her own choices, Detective.'

'She's a *child*! Oliver, she's sixteen years old!'

'She was old enough to conspire against me,' he said. 'Old enough to find the book that I spent half a hundred years pursuing. Old enough to cut off my one and only chance to save my people from Amelie's intolerable iron grip. *Do you think I care about her age?*' Oliver's friendly courtesy was all gone, and what was left was like a man-sized snake, with a cruel light flickering behind his eyes, and fangs flicking down in warning. Claire let Hess pull her out from behind the table, towards the door. He'd drawn his gun.

'I may not let you leave,' Oliver said. 'You realise that?'

Hess spun and raised the gun, pointed it straight at Oliver's chest. 'Silver bullets washed in holy water, with a cross cast right in.' He clicked back the hammer. 'You want to test the line, Oliver? Because it's right here. You're standing on it. I'll take a lot of shit from you, but not this. Not that kind of contract, and not with a kid.'

Oliver hadn't even bothered to stand up.

'I take it you don't want your coffee poured to go? A pity. Do watch your back, Detective. You and I will have a talk, one of these days. And Claire...come back anytime. If the hours run thin, and you want to make that deal, I will listen.'

'Don't even think about it,' Hess said. 'Claire, open the door.' He held his gun trained on the vampire, unblinking, while Claire unlocked the three dead bolts and swung it open. 'Get in the car. Move.' He backed out behind her as she ran to the car and dived inside. Hess banged the door to Common Grounds closed, hard enough to crack glass, and slid over the hood of the car in a move she'd only ever seen in action movies, and was in the car and starting it before she could take a breath.

They raced off into the night. Claire checked the back seat, suddenly terrified she'd turn around to see Oliver grinning at her, but it was empty.

Hess was sweating. He wiped at the drops with the back of his hand. 'You don't fool around when you get yourself in trouble, I'll give you that,' he said. 'I've lived here all my life, and I've never seen anybody get that out of Oliver. Ever.'

'Um...thanks?'

'It wasn't a compliment. Listen, under no circumstances do you *ever* go back to Common Grounds, get me? Avoid Oliver at all costs. And no matter what happens, don't make that deal. Shane wouldn't want it, and you'd live to regret it. You'd live a long time, and you'd hate every horrible second of it.' Hess shook his head and took a deep breath. 'Right. That's the end of the line for you tonight. You're going home, I'm seeing you safe inside, and I'm going home to hide in a closet until this blows over. I suggest you do the same.'

'But Shane—'

'Shane's dead,' Hess said, so quietly and matter-of-factly that she thought he meant it, that somehow someone had slipped in and killed him and *she hadn't even known*...but then he went on. 'You can't save him. Nobody can save him now. Just let go and watch yourself, Claire. That's all you can do. You've pissed off both Amelie and Oliver in one night. Enough already. A little common sense would be welcome from you right about now.'

She sat in dull, grim silence the rest of the way home.

Hess was as good as his word. He walked her from the car up the steps, watched her open the front door, and nodded wearily as she stepped inside. 'Lock it,' he said. 'And for God's sake, go get some rest.'

Michael was right there, warm and comforting, when she closed the door. He was holding his guitar by the neck, so he'd clearly been playing; his eyes were red-rimmed, his face tense. 'Well?' he asked.

'Hello, Claire, how are you?' Claire asked the air. 'No death threats, right? Thanks for going out in the dark to bargain with two of the scariest people on earth.'

He at least had the good manners to look embarrassed about it. 'Sorry. You OK?'

'Duh. No fang marks, anyway.' She shuddered. 'I do *not* like those people.'

'Vampires?'

'Vampires.'

'Technically, not people, but then, neither am I, now that I think about it. So never mind.' Michael put an arm around her and steered her towards the living room, where he sat her down, put a blanket around her shoulders. 'I'm guessing it didn't go well.'

'It didn't go at all,' she said. She'd been depressed on the ride home, but having to actually report on her failure was a whole new level of suck. 'They're not letting him go.'

Michael didn't say anything, but the light died in his eyes. He went down on one knee next to her and fussed with the blanket, tucking it tighter around her. 'Claire. *Are* you OK? You're shaking.'

'They're cold, you know,' she said. 'They make me cold, too.'

He nodded slowly. 'You did what you could. Rest.'

'What about Eve? Is she still here?'

He glanced up at the ceiling, as if he could see through it. Maybe he could. Claire really didn't know what Michael could and couldn't do; after all, he'd been dead a couple of times already. Wouldn't do to underestimate somebody like that. 'She's asleep,' he said. 'I...talked to her. She understands. She won't do anything stupid.' He didn't look at Claire when he said that, and she wondered what kind of talking that might have been.

Her mother had always said, when in doubt, ask. 'Was it the kind of talk where you gave her something to live for? Like maybe, um, you?'

'Did I... What the hell are you talking about?'

'I just thought maybe you and her—'

'Claire, *Jesus*!' Michael said. She'd actually

made him flinch. Wow. That was new. 'You think banging me is going to make her forget about charging out to commit cold-blooded vampire slaying? I don't know what kind of standards you have on sex, but those are pretty high. Besides, whatever's between me and Eve...well, it's between me and Eve.' *Until she tells me about it later*, Claire thought. 'Anyway, that's not what I meant. I...persuaded her. That's all.'

Persuaded. Right. The mood Eve had been in when Claire left? Not too likely...

And then Claire remembered the voices whispering to her in the alley, and her blind, stupid assumption of safety leading her into danger. Could Michael do that?

Would he?

'You didn't—' She touched her temple with one finger.

'What?'

'Screw with her head? Like *they* can?'

He didn't answer. He fussed with the blanket around her shoulders some more, fetched her a pillow, and said, 'Lie down. Rest. It's only a couple of hours until dawn, and I'm going to need you.'

'Oh, God, Michael, you didn't. You *didn't*! She'll never forgive you!'

'As long as she lives to hate me later,' he said. 'Rest. I mean it.'

She didn't intend to sleep; her brain was whirling

like a tyre rim scraping pavement, shooting off sparks in every direction. Lots of energy being expended, but she wasn't going anywhere fast. *Have to think of something. Have to…*

Michael started playing, something soft that sounded melancholy, all in minor keys, and she felt herself begin to drift…

…and then, without any sense of going, she was gone.

The blanket around her smelt like Shane.

Claire burrowed deeper into its warmth, murmuring something that might have been his name as she woke; she felt good, relaxed, safe in his embrace. The way she'd been the other night when they'd spent it here on the couch, kissing…

All that faded fast when the events of the past day flooded back, stripping away the comfort and leaving her cold and scared. Claire sat up, clutching the blanket, and looked around. Michael's guitar was back in its case, and the sun was over the horizon. So, he was gone again, and she and Eve…she and Eve were on their own.

'Right,' she whispered. 'Time to get to work.' She still needed to find some kind of viable strategy to break Shane out of that cage on Founder's Square. Which meant research…maybe Detective Hess could tell her something about how many guards there were, and where. Clearly, there was some kind of security process for keeping out the human losers like her, but any security could be broken, right? At least, that's what she'd always heard. Maybe Eve knew something that could help.

If Eve wasn't back on suicide watch this morning, anyway. Claire thought wistfully about a hot shower, decided maybe it could wait, and wandered into the kitchen to put on coffee. Eve wasn't going to be happy, but she'd be even less happy without caffeine. Claire waited while the pot filled, then carried a black mug full of the stuff upstairs. The key to Eve's door was hanging on a hook, with a note taped to it. Michael's handwriting. It read, *Don't let her leave the house.* By implication, of course, it meant Claire was supposed to stay here, too.

As if she could even think about doing that, with Shane's last hours running out. And who knew what was happening to him out there? She thought about the cold fury in Oliver, the indifference in Amelie, her stomach twisting. She grabbed the key, turned it in the lock, and opened Eve's bedroom door.

Eve was sitting, fully dressed and made-up in zombified glory, on the edge of her bed. She'd put her hair into two pigtails, one on each side, and she'd done her make-up with great care. She looked like a scary porcelain doll.

An *angry* scary porcelain doll. The kind that

they made horror movies about, with stabby knives.

'Coffee?' Claire asked weakly. Eve looked at her for a second, took the coffee, got up, and walked out of the bedroom towards the stairs. 'Oh boy.'

By the time Claire made it downstairs, Eve was standing in the middle of the living room, looking up at nothing. She'd put the coffee down, and her hands were on her hips. Claire paused, one hand still clutching the banister, and watched Eve turn a slow circle as if she was looking for something.

'I know you're there, you coward,' she said. 'Now hear this, crazy supernatural boy. *If you ever fuck with me again, I swear, I will walk out this door and never come back*. You get me? One for yes, two for no.'

He must have said yes, because some of the stiffness went out of Eve's shoulders. She was still mad, though. 'I don't know what's lower, you playing vamp tricks on me, or locking me in my room, but either way, you are so busted, man. Being dead can't save you. When you get back tonight, I am completely kicking your ass.'

'He was sorry,' Claire said. She sat down on the first step as Eve turned a glare of righteous anger in her direction. 'He knew you were going to be mad, but he couldn't... He cares about you, Eve. He couldn't just let you go out and get yourself killed.'

'Last time I checked, I was over eighteen and nobody's *property*!' Eve yelled, and stomped her foot. 'I don't care if you're sorry, Michael... You're going to have to work really hard to make this up to me! Really hard!'

Claire saw the breeze ruffle Eve's hair. Eve closed her eyes for a second, swaying, mouth open in a round, red O.

'OK,' she said weakly. 'That was different.'

'What?' Claire asked, and jumped to her feet.

'Nothing. Um, nothing at all. Right.' Eve cleared her throat. 'What happened last night? Did you get them to let Shane go?'

Claire's throat just locked up on her in misery. She shook her head and looked down. 'But it's no use going out there with stakes and crosses,' she said. 'They'd be ready. We need another plan.'

'What about Joe? Detective Hess?'

Claire shook her head again. 'He can't.'

'Then let's go talk to some people who can,' Eve said reasonably. She picked up her coffee and drained it in long, chugging gulps, set the mug aside, and nodded. 'Ready.'

'Who are we going to see?'

'It may shock you, but living in Morganville my entire pathetic life isn't a complete waste. I know people, OK? And some of them actually have backbones.'

Claire blinked. 'Um...OK. Two minutes.'

She dashed upstairs for the fastest shower and change of clothes in her life.

CHAPTER NINE

It stood to reason that Eve would know places to go that Claire didn't, but for some reason it surprised Claire where those places were. A Laundromat, for instance. And a photo-processing place. In each case, Eve made her wait in the car while she talked to somebody – a human somebody, Claire was almost sure. But nothing came out of it, either time.

Eve got back in her big, dusty Cadillac looking grim and already wilting in the morning's heat. 'Father Jonathan's on a trip,' she said, 'I was hoping we could get him to talk to the mayor. They go back.'

'Father Jonathan? There's a priest in town?'

Eve nodded. 'The vampires don't care about whether or not he celebrates Mass, as long as he doesn't display any crosses. Communion's kind of interesting; the vamps keep the wafers and wine under guard. Oh, and forget about the holy water.

If they ever caught him making the sign of the cross over anything liquid, they'd make sure his next congregation has an address behind the pearly gates.'

Claire blinked, trying to get her head around it. 'But...he's on a trip? Out of town? What?'

'Gone to the Vatican. Special dispensation.'

'The *Vatican* knows about Morganville?'

'No, idiot. When he leaves town, he's like anybody else: no memory of the vamps. So I don't think we can count on the Vatican Strike Team storming in to save Shane, if that's what you were thinking.'

It wasn't, but it was kind of comforting to imagine paramilitary priests in bullet-proof armour, with crosses on the vests. 'So what now, then? If you can't get to Father Jonathan?'

Eve started the car. They were parked in the tiny photo-store parking lot, next to a big industrial-sized Dumpster. They were the only car in the parking lot, although a white van was just turning into the lot and squealing to a stop, in the space next to them. It was still pretty early – before nine a.m. – and what passed for traffic in Morganville was slowly filtering around the streets. The photo-processing place claimed to be open twenty-four hours; now, that was a job Claire figured she didn't want. Did vampires take pictures? What kind? Maybe the trick was not to look at what came spitting out of the machine, just shuffle the prints into an envelope and hand them over...but then, that was probably the trick outside of Morganville, too.

She checked the clock again. 'Eve! What about your job?'

'I can get another one.'

'But—'

'Claire, it wasn't that good of a job. Look at what I had to put up with. Jocks. Jerks. Monica.'

Eve started to back out of the parking lot, then slammed on the brakes when another car pulled in behind her, blocking her in. 'Dammit,' she breathed, and fumbled for her cell phone. She pitched it to Claire. 'Call the cops.'

'Why?' Claire twisted to look out the back, but she couldn't see who was driving the other car.

She was looking in the wrong place. The threat wasn't the car behind them; it was the white van next to the passenger side of the Cadillac, and as she started punching 911, a sliding panel came open, and someone reached out and pulled on the handle of Claire's door.

It was locked. She wasn't a total idiot. But two seconds later, it didn't matter, because a crowbar hit the window behind her, smashing it into a million little sparkly pieces, and Claire reflexively jerked forward, hands over her head. She fumbled the phone into the floorboards, and tried frantically to find it. Eve was cursing breathlessly.

'Get us out of here!' Claire yelled.

'I can't! We're blocked in!'

Claire grabbed the phone triumphantly, finished pushing buttons for 911, and pressed SEND just as a hand reached in from the back seat and slammed her face-first into the dash.

After that, things got a little distant and fluffy around the edges. She remembered being taken out of the car. Remembered Eve yelling and fighting, then going quiet.

Remembered being bundled into the van and the door sliding shut.

And as her head began to clear up again, except for a monster-sized headache centred right over her eyes, she remembered the van, too. She'd seen it before. She'd *been* in it before.

And just like before, Jennifer was driving, and Monica and Gina were in the back. Gina was holding her down. The girls looked flushed. Crazy. Not good.

'Eve,' Claire whispered.

Monica leant closer. 'Who, the freak? Not here.'

'What did you do to her?'

'Just a little cut, nothing too serious,' Monica said.

'You ought to be worried about yourself, Claire. My daddy wanted to get a message to you.'

'Your...what?'

'Daddy. What, you don't have one of those? Or do you just not know which John was the sperm donor?' Monica sneered. She was wearing a tight pair of blue jeans and an orange top, and she looked as glossy as a magazine page. 'Oh, don't bother, mouse. Just stay down... You won't get hurt.'

Gina pinched Claire, hard. Claire yelled, and Monica grinned in response. 'Well,' she amended, 'maybe hurt a *little*. But a tough chick like you can take it, right, genius?'

Gina pinched Claire again, and Claire gritted her teeth and managed to keep it to just a whimper this time. Easier, since she was already prepared for the pain. Gina looked disappointed. Maybe she should scream her lungs out no matter what, save herself the trouble of Gina having to work harder for it...

'You were following us,' Claire said. She felt nauseated, probably from smacking her head into the dashboard, and she was deeply worried about Eve. *A little cut*. Monica wasn't the type to do anything halfway.

'See? I told you she was a genius, didn't I?' Monica sat down in one of the padded leather seats that lined the van, and crossed her legs. She had on cute platform shoes that matched her orange tank top, and she inspected her nails – also done in orange – for signs of chipping. 'You know what, genius? You're right. I was following you. See, I wanted to bring you in quietly, but no, you and Zombie Girlfriend had to make it all difficult. Why aren't you in class, anyway? Isn't that, like, against your religion or something, cutting class?'

Claire struggled to sit up. Gina glanced at Monica, who nodded; Claire edged away from Gina and put her back up against the sliding door of the van. She rubbed her stinging arm where Gina had given her pinches. 'Shane,' she said. 'That's what your dad wants to see me about, isn't it?'

Monica shrugged. 'I guess. Look, I don't like Shane; that's no secret. But I never intended for his sister to get killed in that fire. It was a stupid school thing, OK? No big deal.'

'No big deal?' Of everything Monica had ever said to her – and there'd been some jaw-droppers – that was maybe the worst. '*No big deal?* A kid died, and you destroyed their whole family! Don't you get it? Shane's mom—'

'Not my fault!' Monica was suddenly flushed. Not used to being blamed, Claire guessed; maybe nobody ever had blamed her except Shane. 'Even if she remembered, if she'd kept her mouth shut, she'd have been fine! And Alyssa was an accident!'

'Yeah,' Claire said. 'I'm sure that makes it all better.' She felt gritty and tired, never mind the sleep she'd had, or the shower. The floor of the van was filthy. 'What the hell does your father want with me, anyway?'

Monica stared at her in silence for a few seconds, then said, 'He doesn't think Shane killed Brandon.'

'You're kidding.'

'No. He thinks it was Shane's dad.' Monica's perfectly lipsticked mouth curved into a slow smile. 'He'd like for you to tell Shane's dad that and see what happens. 'Cause if he was any kind of a father, he wouldn't stand by and let his baby boy take the heat for him. Literally.'

'So he wants me to tell Shane's dad the mayor is willing to make a deal?'

'Shane's life for his father's,' Monica said. 'No real dad could resist something like that. Shane's not important, but Dad wants this over. Now.'

Claire had a very bad feeling squirming in the pit of her stomach, like she'd swallowed earthworms. 'I don't believe it. They'd never let Shane go!' Not if Oliver had any say in it, anyway.

Monica shrugged. 'I'm just delivering a message. You can tell Frank whatever you damn well want, but if you're smart, you'll tell him something to get him out in the open. Get me? Amelie's Protection only goes so far. You can still be hurt. In fact, Gina would probably enjoy that a lot, even if she gets a slap on the wrist for punishment.'

'And think about your friend, back there all by herself,' Gina said. She was smiling, a wet, crazy sort of smile. 'All kinds of things can happen to girls out on their own in this town. All kinds of *bad* things.'

'Yeah, well, Eve should know,' Monica said. 'Look who her brother is.'

Claire's head knocked back against metal as the van bumped over what felt like railroad tracks, setting off a nuclear vibration in her head with the already-fierce headache in the front. 'So,' Monica said. 'You know what you have to do, right? Go to Shane's dad. Convince him to trade himself for Shane. Or...you may find out just how unfriendly Morganville can really be.'

Claire didn't say anything. The things she wanted to say would, she figured, get her killed; whether or not Monica and Gina would be punished for it later wasn't much of a comfort.

She finally gave them one sharp, unwilling nod.

'Home, James!' Monica called up to Jennifer, who gave the OK sign and turned a corner. Claire tried to peer out, but she didn't recognise the street. Somewhere close to campus, though. She saw the bell tower next to the UC rising up on the right-hand side.

She grabbed for a handhold as Jennifer slammed on the brakes. Monica wasn't so lucky; she spilt out of her seat and onto the floor, screaming and cursing. 'Dammit! What the hell was that, Jen, Driving for Dummies?'

Jen didn't say anything. Her hands slowly

came up in a position of surrender.

The door behind Claire slid open, and a big hand grabbed her by the back of the neck and hauled her backward into the hot sunlight. *Not a vampire*, she thought, but that wasn't much of a comfort, because a burly, muscular arm stretched out past her, and it was holding a sawn-off shotgun. She recognised the blue flame tattoos licking down his arm and onto the back of his hand.

One of the bikers.

She looked around and saw three more, all armed, pointing weapons at the van – and then, she saw Shane's father walking up, as easy as if the whole town and every vampire in it hadn't been hunting him through the night. He even looked rested.

'Monica Morrell,' he said. 'Come on down! See what you've won.'

Monica froze where she was, holding on to one of the hanging leather straps. She looked at the guns, at Gina, who was kneeling with her hands in the air, and then helplessly at Claire.

She was afraid. Monica – crazy, weird, pretty Monica – was actually scared. 'My father—'

'Let's talk about him later,' Frank said. 'You get your sweet ass down here, Monica. Don't make me come and get you.'

She retreated farther into the van. Shane's dad grinned and motioned two of his bikers inside. One grabbed Gina by the hair and dragged her out to sprawl in the street.

The other one grabbed Monica, struggling and spitting, and handcuffed her to the leather strap in the back. She stopped fighting, amazed. 'But—'

'I knew you were going to do the opposite of what I told you,' Frank said. 'Easiest way to keep you in the van was to tell you to get out.' He opened the driver's-side door and stuck a gun in Jennifer's face. 'You, I don't need. Out.'

She slid down, fast, and kept her hands high as Frank pushed her towards the bikers. She sat down next to Gina on the curb and put her arms around her. Funny, Claire had never thought of those two as being friends in their own right, just as hangers-on for Monica. But now they seemed...real. And really scared.

'You.' Shane's dad turned to look directly at Claire. 'In the back.'

'But—'

One of the bikers put his gun close to her head. She swallowed and scrambled into the van, claiming the leather seat that Monica had so recently tumbled out of. Shane's father got in after her, then a sweaty load of bikers. One of them got in the driver's seat, and the van lurched into gear.

It hadn't taken but a minute, Claire figured. In Morganville, at this hour, nobody probably even noticed. The streets looked deserted.

She looked at Monica, who stared back, and for the first time, she thought she really understood what Monica was feeling, because she felt it, too.

This was a very bad thing.

The van lurched through a long series of turns, and Claire tried to think of an easy way to get to her cell phone, which was in the pocket of her jeans. She'd dropped Eve's back at the car, when Monica had slammed her face-first into the dashboard... She managed to get her fingers hooked in her pocket, casual-like, and touched the metal case. *All I have to do is dial 911*, she thought. Eve had probably already reported the abduction, if Eve was OK enough to talk. They could trace cell phones, right? GPS tracking or something?

As if he'd read her mind, Shane's dad came to her, stood her up, and patted her down. He did it fast, not lingering like some dirty old man, and found the phone in her pocket. He took it. Monica was yelling again, and trying to kick; one of the bikers was doing the same thing as Frank, although Claire thought it was more feeling up than patting down. Still, he found her cell, too – a Treo – and slid open the van door to pitch them out into the street. 'Kill 'em!' he yelled to the driver, who pulled the van into a U-turn and went back the other way. Claire didn't hear the crunch, but she figured the phones were nothing but electronic bits.

The turning and lurching continued. Claire just hung on, head down, thinking hard. She couldn't get word out, but Eve would have. Detective Hess, Detective Lowe? Maybe they'd come running.

Maybe Amelie would send her own people to enforce her Protection. That would be pretty fabulous right about now.

'Hey,' Monica said to Shane's dad. 'Stupid move, asshole. My dad's going to have every cop in Morganville on you in seconds. You're never going to get away, and once they have you, they'll throw you in a hole so deep, even the sewer will seem like heaven. *Don't touch me, you pig!*' Monica writhed to get away from the stroking hands of the biker next to her, who just smiled and showed gold-capped teeth.

'Don't touch her,' Shane's dad said. 'We're not animals.' Claire wondered where all this sudden White Knight syndrome came from, because he'd been willing to let his boys do whatever to her and Eve back at the Glass House. 'Take her bracelet.'

'What? No. *No!* It doesn't come off, you know that!'

The biker reached down and took a small pair of bolt cutters from a pouch on his belt. Claire gasped in horror as the biker grabbed Monica's arm. *Oh God*, she thought, *he's going to cut off her hand...*

But he just sliced through the metal bracelet, instead, yanked it off her wrist, and tossed it to

Shane's father. Monica glared at him, trembling, and slapped him. Hard.

He drew back a hand to slap her back. 'Leave it,' Shane's father said. He was staring at the bracelet. The outside was the symbol, of course; Claire couldn't read it, but she figured it was Brandon's symbol, and now that Brandon was dead, she wondered who picked up his Protection duties. Maybe Oliver...

On the inside was inscribed Monica's full name: MONICA ELLEN MORRELL. Shane's dad grunted in satisfaction.

'You want a finger, too?' the biker asked, snipping the shears. 'No trouble.'

'I think this makes the point for us,' Shane's dad said. 'Get us underground, Kenny. Move.'

The guy driving – Kenny, at least now Claire knew one of their names – nodded. He was a tall man, kind of thin, with long black hair and a blue bandanna. His leather vest had a naked girl on a Harley on the back, and it matched the tattoos down the arm that Claire could see. Kenny expertly navigated the confusing streets and turns of Morganville, moving fast but not dangerously fast, and then all of a sudden...darkness.

Kenny flicked on the lights. They were in a storm drain, a huge concrete tunnel big enough to fit the van – though barely – and it was heading down at a steep angle into the dark. Claire fought to get her breath. She didn't really like closed-in places, or the dark... She remembered how freaked-out she'd been sealed in the hidden pantry room at the Glass House, not so many days ago. No, she didn't like this. She didn't like it at all.

'Where are you taking us?' she asked. She meant it to sound tough, but instead it sounded like what she was: a scared sixteen-year-old, trying to be brave. Great.

Frank Collins, hanging on to one of the leather straps, looked at her with something strange in his eyes – almost, she thought, respect. 'Not taking *you* anywhere,' he said. 'You get to deliver the message.' And he pitched her Monica's severed bracelet. 'Tell the mayor that if I don't hear that my son's been set free before tomorrow at dawn, pretty little miss here gets to find out what fire is really like. We've got us a nice blowtorch.'

She didn't like Monica. In fact, she kind of hated her, and she thought Morganville would be a much better place if Monica just...disappeared.

But nobody deserved what he was talking about.

'You can't do that,' she said. 'You can't.' But she knew, looking around at the grinning, sweaty crew he'd brought with him, that he could do that, and a lot worse. Shane was right. His dad was seriously sick.

'Kenny up there's going to pull up to a ladder soon,' Frank continued. 'And I'm going to want you to get out of the van, Claire. Go up the ladder and push open the grate. You'll be right in front of the Morganville City Hall. You walk up to the first cop you see and you tell him you need to see the mayor about Frank Collins. And you tell him that Frank Collins has his daughter, and she's going to pay for the life she already took, not to mention the one they're about to. Got it?'

Claire nodded stiffly. Monica's bracelet felt cold and heavy in her fingers.

'One more thing,' Frank said. 'I'm going to need you to tell them just how serious I am. And you'd better be persuasive, because if I don't hear something from the mayor before dawn, we'll be using those bolt cutters to send him some more reminders. And she's fresh out of bracelets.'

The van lurched to a stop, and Frank threw open the sliding door. 'Out,' he said. 'Better make it good, Claire. You want to save my son, don't you?'

He didn't say anything about saving Monica, she noticed. Nothing at all.

Monica looked at her, no longer sleek and magazine glossy. She seemed small and vulnerable, alone in the van with all those men. Claire hesitated, then got up from her seat and grabbed a leather strap to steady herself. Her knees felt like water. 'This is crazy,' she said. 'Hang in there. I'll get help.'

Tears glittered in Monica's eyes. 'Thanks,' she

said softly. 'Tell my dad—' She didn't finish, and she sucked in a deep breath. The tears cleared away, and she gave Claire a half-crazy smile. 'Tell my dad that if anything happens to me, he can hold you personally responsible.'

The door slammed shut between them, and the van sped off into the dark. Claire was glad she had her hand on the ladder, because the lights went away fast, and she was left in a dark so close and hot and filthy that she wanted to curl up into a ball.

Instead, she climbed, feeling for the slimy rungs in the dark and waiting for something – something with teeth – to lunge onto her back at any second. Vampires lived down here, they had to. Or at least, they used these tunnels as highways; she'd always wondered how they got around during the day. These weren't sewer tunnels, just storm drains built extra large. And since Morganville wasn't exactly built on a floodplain, chances were, the water had never been more than ankle-high in these things since they'd been constructed.

Claire climbed, and when she squinted just right, she saw flickers of what looked like daylight. There was a grate overhead, covered with some kind of protective material to keep the sun from filtering down into the tunnel. She braced herself on the rungs, hooked her left arm through one of the iron bars, and heaved with her right to push the grate up.

Hot Texas sun washed over her in a warm, sticky flood, and Claire gasped and raised her face to it in gratitude. After taking a few fast breaths, she pushed herself up another rung and thumped the grate back on its hinges to climb out.

Just as Shane's dad had said, she was standing in front of the Morganville City Hall – which was, unfortunately, *not* on Founder's Square. It was a big Gothic castle of a building, all red sandstone in rough-cut blocks, and people were coming and going on their way to or from work, or filing paperwork – just carrying out their daily lives, whatever that meant in Morganville.

She rolled out onto the grass and flopped there, breathing hard. A couple of faces appeared overhead, blocking out the sun. One of them was wearing a policeman's uniform cap.

'Hello,' Claire said, and shaded her eyes. 'I need to talk to the mayor. Tell him I have information about his daughter, and Frank Collins.'

The mayor had changed out of the suit he'd worn to put Shane in a cage the night before; he was wearing a green golf shirt with black slacks and loafers. Very preppy. He was in the hallway, talking into his cell phone, looking tense and angry. Claire was escorted past him, into his office, and deposited in a big red leather chair by two members of Morganville's finest; she didn't recognise either of them. When she asked after Detectives Hess and Lowe, she got nothing. Nobody even admitted to knowing their names.

Claire was feeling more than a little light-headed. She had no idea how long it had been since she'd eaten, but the world was starting to take on a surreal melty edge that really wasn't a very good sign. Between the stress, the poor sleep, and the lack of food, she was going to be loopy soon.

Keep it together, Claire. Pretend you're cramming for a test. She'd gone without sleep for three days once, prepping for her SAT, and she hadn't eaten much beyond Jolt cola and Cheetos. She could do this.

'Here,' said a voice from beside her, and a red can of Coca-Cola appeared, held in a big male hand. 'You look like you could use something to drink.'

Claire looked up. It was Richard, Monica's cop brother. The cute one. He looked tired and worried. He pulled up another chair close to hers and leant forward, elbows on his knees. Claire busied herself with the Coke, popping the top and taking a fast chug of the icy sweet contents.

'My sister got carjacked,' he said. 'You know that, right?'

Claire nodded and swallowed. 'I was there. I was in the van.'

'That's exactly why I wanted to talk to you

before I let you see my dad,' Richard said. 'You were in the van with Jennifer and Gina and Monica.'

Claire nodded again.

'Let me ask you this, then. How did you signal them?'

She blinked. 'How did I what?'

'How did you plan the set-up? What was your system? Did you text message them? You know, we can pull those records, Claire. Or was it some kind of trap you led my sister into?'

'I don't know what you're—'

Richard looked up at her, and she fell silent, because he didn't look so friendly this time. Not friendly at all. 'My sister's a crazy psycho – I know that. But she's still *my sister*. And nobody lays their hands on a Morrell in this town, or somebody – maybe a whole bunch of somebodies – pays for it. Get the point? So whatever you know, whatever your relationship is with these invaders, you'd better come to it quick, or we're going to start digging. And Claire, that's going to be a fast, bloody kind of process.'

She wrapped both hands around the Coke can and raised it to her mouth for another trembling gulp, then said, 'I didn't lead them to your sister. Your sister abducted *me*. Right out of the Photo Finish parking lot. Ask Eve. Oh God...Eve...Gina cut her. Is she OK?'

Richard frowned at her. 'Eve's all right.'

That eased a terrible knot in her stomach. 'What about Gina and Jennifer?'

'Also fine. They called in the carjacking. Gina said—' He turned something over in his mind, and then said, more slowly, 'Gina said a lot of things. But I should have remembered who I was talking to. If there's anybody in Morganville crazier than my sister, it's Gina.'

She couldn't disagree with that. 'The guys who took over the van—'

'Shane's father,' Richard interrupted. 'We already know all that. Where is he now?'

'I don't know,' she said. 'I swear! He let me out in the storm drain and told me to climb the ladder and talk to your father. That's why I'm here.'

'Leave the kid alone, Richard.' Mayor Morrell stalked in, slamming the office door behind him, and paused to glare at the two extra police officers standing guard. 'You. Out. If my son can't handle some sixteen-year-old stick of a girl, he deserves what he gets.'

They left, fast. Claire put the Coke can aside on a table as the mayor sank into his big, plush leather chair. He no longer looked quite as smug as he had back at Founder's Square, and he definitely looked angry.

'You,' he snapped. 'Talk. Now.'

She did, spilling it out in a tumbling stream of words. Shane's father hijacking the van and pitching Gina and Jennifer out. Destroying the cell phones. Threatening Monica and sending Claire as his messenger of doom. 'He's serious,' she finished. 'I mean, I've seen him do things. He's seriously not afraid to hurt people, and he definitely doesn't like Monica.'

'Oh, and suddenly you're her bestest little friend? Please. You hate her guts, and you've probably got reason,' Richard said. He got up to pace the room. 'Dad, look, let me do this. I can find these guys. If we put every available man and vampire on the streets—'

'We did that last night, son. Wherever these guys go, they're going someplace we can't follow.' The mayor's red-rimmed eyes fastened back on hers. He cracked his knuckles. He had big hands, like his son. Hard hands. 'Oliver wants this over. He wants to move up the timetable, burn the kid tonight and get them out in the open. It's not a bad plan. Call their bluff.'

'You think Frank Collins is bluffing?' Richard asked.

'No,' the mayor said. 'I think he'll do exactly what he said he'd do, only a whole lot worse than we can imagine. But what Oliver wants...'

'You're just going to let him do it? What about Monica?'

'Oliver doesn't know they've got her. Once I tell him—'

'Dad,' Richard said. 'It's *Oliver*. He's not going to give a crap and you know it. Acceptable losses. But it's not acceptable to me, and it shouldn't be to you, either.'

Father and son exchanged looks, and Richard shook his head and continued to pace. 'We need to find a way to get her back. Somehow.'

'You.' The mayor pointed a thick finger at Claire. 'Tell me the whole thing again. Everything. Every detail, I don't care how minor. Start from the first time you saw these men.'

Claire opened her mouth to answer, and caught herself just in time. *No, you idiot! You can't tell them the truth! The truth gets Shane fried for sure...* She wasn't a good liar, she knew that, and there was too much time slipping by while she was scrambling around in her head, trying to pick up the threads of where to start the story...

'I guess... I saw some of them when they broke into the house,' she said tentatively. 'You know, when we called the cops about the home invasion? And then I saw...'

She froze and closed her eyes. She'd seen something important. *Very* important. What was it? Something to do with Shane's dad...

'Start with the van,' Richard said, and short-circuited her attempt at catching the memory. She dutifully recounted it all again, and then again, answering specific questions as fast as she could. Her head ached, and despite the cold Coke, her throat did, too. She needed sleep, and she wanted to roll up in blankets and cry herself into a coma. *Oliver wants to move up the timetable, burn the kid tonight.* No. No, they couldn't let it happen, they couldn't...

But they could. Without question.

'Let's start over,' Richard said. 'From the beginning.'

She burst into despairing tears.

It took hours before they were done with her. Nobody offered to drive her home.

Claire walked, feeling like she was drifting half out of her body, and made it all the way home without a single incident. It was still daylight, which helped, but the streets seemed unnaturally quiet and deserted. Word was out, she guessed. Humans were keeping their heads down, hoping the storm would pass.

As Claire slammed the door, Eve came bolting down the stairs, raced to her, and wrapped her in a breathless full-body hug. 'Bitch!' she said. 'I can't believe you scared the crap out of me like that. Oh my *God*, Claire. Can you believe those jerks at the police station wouldn't even take my statement? I even had a wound! A real wound with blood and everything! How'd you get away? Did Monica hurt you?'

Eve didn't know. Nobody, had told her at the police station.

'Shane's dad stopped the van,' Claire said. 'He took Monica as a hostage.'

For a second, neither one of them moved, and then Eve whooped and held up her hand for a high five. Claire just stared at her, and Eve compensated by clapping both hands over her head. 'Yesssss!' she said, and did a totally geeky victory dance. 'Couldn't happen to a nicer psycho!'

'Hey!' Claire yelled, and Eve froze in mid-celebration. It was stupid, but Claire was angry; she knew Eve was right, knew she had no reason at all to think Monica was ever going to be anything but a gigantic pain in the ass, but... 'Shane's dad's going to burn her if they go through with the execution. He has a *blowtorch*.'

The glee dropped out of Eve's expression. 'Oh,' she said. 'Well...still. Not like she didn't ask for it. Karma's a bitch, and so am I.'

'Oliver's trying to get them to kill Shane *tonight*. We're out of time, Eve. I don't know what to do anymore.'

That knocked the last of Eve's smugness right out from under her. She didn't seem to know, either. She licked her lips and said, 'There's still time. Let me make some phone calls. And you need to get some food. And some sleep.'

'I can't sleep.'

'Well, you can eat, right?'

She could, as it turned out – and she needed to.

The world had taken on a grey colour, and her head was aching. A hot dog – plain except for mustard – chips, and a bottle of water solved some of that, though not the ache in her heart, or the sick feeling that had nothing to do with hunger.

What are we going to do?

Eve was on the phone, calling people. Claire slumped on the couch, tipped over, and curled up under the blanket. It still smelt like Shane's cologne.

She must have slept for a while, and when she woke it was almost as though someone had flipped a switch or whispered in her ear, *Wake up!* Because she was upright in seconds, heart racing, and her brain was running to catch up. The house was quiet, except for the usual ticks and pops and moans that old houses got. A breeze rattled dry leaves outside.

And it took Claire a second to realise that she couldn't see the tree that shaded the window because *it was dark*.

'No!' She catapulted off the couch and raced to find a clock. It was exactly what she'd feared. No eclipses or sudden unexplained collapses of the normal day-night continuum; no, it was just dark because it was night.

She'd slept for hours. *Hours*. And Eve hadn't woken her up. In fact, she wasn't even sure Eve was still in the house.

'Michael!' Claire went from room to room, but

he was nowhere to be seen. 'Michael! Eve! Where are you?'

They were in Michael's room. He opened the door, and he was half-dressed – shirt open, jeans hanging low-slung around his hips, revealing a chest and abs that even now Claire *had* to notice – and Eve was curled up in the bed, under the covers.

Michael quickly stepped out, buttoning his shirt. 'You're awake.'

'Yeah.' Claire suppressed a burst of pure fury. 'If you're done screwing around, maybe we can talk about Shane *dying tonight.*'

Michael dipped his chin a little, staring her straight in the eyes. 'You do *not* want to go there, Claire,' he said flatly. 'You really don't. You think I don't know? I don't care? *Fuck.* What do you think Eve's been doing all day while you—'

'Slept? Yeah, I fell asleep! You could have woken me up!'

He came forward a step. She backed up a step, then another, because his eyes…not Michael's usual expression. Not at all.

'So you could sit and rip your guts out, too?' he asked softly. 'Enough of that going around, Claire. You needed to sleep. I let you sleep. Get over it.'

'So what's the brilliant plan you guys came up with while I was napping, then? What is it, Michael? What the hell do we do now?'

'I don't know,' he said, and whatever tight

control he'd been hanging on to ripped loose at the roots. 'I don't know!' It was a yell, and it came right out of his guts. Claire backed up another step, feeling an icy flush race over her skin. 'What the hell do you want me to do, Claire? What?'

Her eyes filled up with tears. 'Anything,' she whispered. 'God, please. Anything.'

He grabbed her and hugged her. She sagged against him, trembling, not quite crying but...not quite not, either. It was a hopeless sort of feeling, as if they were loose and drifting and there was no land in sight.

Like they were lost. All lost.

Claire sniffled and stepped back, and when she did, she saw Eve standing in the doorway, watching them. Whatever Eve was thinking, it wasn't good, and it wasn't anything that Claire ever wanted to see again.

'Eve—'

'Whatever,' Eve said flatly. 'There's still one vampire who might help us. If we can find him and get him to agree. He could get into Founder's Square without any problem. He might even be willing to open up Shane's cage if we create some kind of diversion.'

Michael turned towards her. 'Eve.' He didn't sound guilty, at least. He sounded worried, though. 'No. We talked about this.'

'Michael, it's the last thing we can do. I know

that. But we need to go for it now, if we're going to do it at all.'

'What vampire?' Claire asked.

'His name is Sam,' Michael said, 'and this is going to sound weird, but he's my grandfather.'

'*Sam?* He's your...your—'

'Grandfather. Yeah. I know. Freaks me the hell out, too. It has all my life.'

Claire had to sit down. Fast.

When she recovered her breath, she told Eve and Michael about running into Sam at Common Grounds. About the present Sam had tried to give her for Eve.

'I didn't take it,' she said. 'I didn't know...well, it just didn't seem...right.'

'Damn straight,' Michael said.

Eve wasn't looking at him. 'Sam's OK,' she said.

'I thought you hated vampires.'

'I do! But... I guess if there's a most-hated-vampire list, he's at the bottom. He always seems so lonely,' Eve said. 'He came into Common Grounds pretty much every night and just talked for hours. Just talked. Oliver always watched him like a hawk, but he never did anything, never threatened anybody. Not like Brandon. In fact, I sometimes wondered—'

'Wondered what?'

'If Sam was there keeping an eye on Brandon.

Maybe on Oliver, although I didn't know that at the time. Looking out for...'

'For the rest of us?' Michael nodded slowly. 'I don't know how true it is, because I always avoided him, but family talk always said Sam was a good guy, before he was changed. And he is the youngest of all of them. The most like...well, like us.'

Eve had gone over to the dark window, and was looking out, hands behind her back. 'You know anything else about him? Family secrets, I mean?'

'Just that supposedly he took on the vampires and won.'

'Won? He's one of them! How exactly is that winning?'

Michael shook his head, moved up behind her, and put his hands on her shoulders. He kissed the nape of her neck gently. 'I don't know, Eve. I'm just telling you what I heard. He got some kind of agreement out of the vampires. And it was because Amelie loved him.'

'Yeah, loved him enough to kill him and turn him into a bloodsucking fiend,' Eve said grimly. 'How sweet. Romance isn't dead. Oh, wait. It is.'

She pulled free of Michael and walked into the kitchen. Michael looked at Claire mutely. She shrugged.

When they got downstairs, they found that Eve was making bologna and cheese sandwiches. Claire wolfed down one in about six bites, then took a second sandwich. The other two looked at her. 'What?' she asked. 'I'm starved. Honest.'

'Be my guest,' Michael said. 'I hate bologna. Besides, not like I can starve.'

Eve snorted. 'I made you roast beef, genius.' She handed him one. 'So go on. This is the first I've heard from you about the History of Sam. What made him so special to be the last vampire ever?'

'I don't really know,' Michael said. 'The only thing Mom ever told me was what I just told you. The point is, Sam's never really fit in with the vampires. Amelie doesn't like to be reminded of weakness, and he was a constant neon sign. She really cared about him. So she cut him off... Last I heard, she wouldn't see him or talk to him. He hangs around humans a lot more than other vampires.'

'And that's why I said he could help us,' Eve said. 'Or at least, he'd be willing to listen. Bonus if he's family.'

'So where do we find him?' Claire looked from Michael to Eve, then back again. 'At Common Grounds?'

'Off-limits to you,' Eve said. 'Hess told me what happened with you and Oliver.'

'Something happened?' Michael mumbled around his roast beef. 'Why don't I know this? God, I needed this. Tastes great.'

Eve rolled her eyes. 'Yeah, sandwiches take great

skill. I'm thinking of teaching a class. Meanwhile, back on the subject, Claire is not going anywhere near Common Grounds. I said so. If anybody's going, it's me.'

'No,' Michael said. Eve glared at him.

'We had this talk,' she said. 'You may be dead sexy, and I mean, like, really dead and really sexy, but you don't get to tell me what to do. Right? And no head-shrinker stuff, either, or I swear to God, I'll pack my shit and move!'

Claire scraped her chair back, walked over to the cordless phone lying on the counter, and dialled from the business card still stuck to the refrigerator with a magnet. Four rings, and a cheerful voice answered on the other end and announced she'd reached Common Grounds. 'Hi,' Claire said. 'Can I talk to Sam, please?'

'Sam? Hold on.' The phone clattered, and Claire could hear the buzz of activity in the background – milk being steamed, people chatting, the usual excitement of a busy coffee shop. She waited, jittering one leg impatiently, until the voice came back on the line. 'Sorry,' it said. 'He's not here tonight. I think he went to the party.'

'The party?'

'You know, the zombie frat party? Epsilon Epsilon Kappa? The Dead Girls' Dance?'

'Thanks,' Claire said. She hung up and turned to face Michael and Eve, who were staring at her in outright surprise. She held up the phone. 'The power of technology. Embrace it.'

'You found him.'

'Without going into Common Grounds,' Claire pointed out. 'He's at a party on campus. The big frat thing. The one—' She paused, felt a chill, then a rush of heat. 'The one I was invited to. It was kind of a date. I was supposed to meet this boy there. Ian Jameson.'

'Guess what?' Eve said. 'We're both going. Time to put on the dead look, Claire.'

'The...what?'

Eve was looking at her critically while she munched her sandwich. 'Size one, maybe two, right? I've got some things that would fit you.'

'I'm not getting dressed up!'

'I don't make the rules, but everybody knows you don't get into the Dead Girls' Dance without making an effort. Besides, you'll look way cute as a teeny little Goth girl.'

Michael was frowning at them both now. 'No,' he said. 'It's too dangerous for you to be out at night without an escort.'

'Well, we're fresh out of escorts. I think Claire broke Detective Hess last night. And I'm *not* going to just sit and wait, Michael. You know that.' Eve locked eyes with him, and softened as he reached across the table and took her hand. 'No head stuff. You promised.'

'I promised,' he agreed. 'Never happen again.'

'Cute as you are when you worry, it's a party – there are hundreds of people there. It's safe enough.' Eve held his gaze steadily. 'Safer than Shane is, in that cage, waiting to die. Unless you're giving up on him.'

Michael let go of her hand and walked away. He stiff-armed his way out of the kitchen door.

'Guess not,' Eve said softly. 'Good. Claire. We need to find out what the timeline is. Whether they've moved it.'

'I'll do it,' Claire said, and punched in the number from another card. It was Detective Hess's private number, the one pencilled in on the back, and it rang four times before he picked up. He sounded bleary and exhausted. 'Sir? It's Claire. Claire Danvers. I'm sorry to wake you—'

'Not asleep,' he said, and yawned. 'Claire, whatever you're thinking, don't. Stay home, lock the doors, and keep your head down. I mean it.'

'Yes, sir,' she lied. 'I just want to know – there was talk about moving up the...the execution?'

'The mayor said no,' Hess said. 'Said he wanted due process, and called for Shane's dad to give himself up. Looks like a Mexican stand-off to me: he's got Shane;

Shane's dad has Monica. Nobody wants to blink.'

'How long...?'

'Before sunrise. Five in the morning,' Hess said.

'It'll all be over before dawn. For Monica, too, if Shane's dad isn't just bluffing.'

'He's not bluffing,' Claire said numbly. 'Oh God. That's not much time.'

'Better than what Oliver wanted. He wanted to do it at sunset tonight. The mayor backed him off, but only to the legal deadline. There won't be any last-minute stays of execution.' Hess shifted; his chair creaked. 'Claire, you need to prepare yourself. There's no miracle coming; nobody's going to have a change of heart. He's going to die. I'm sorry, but that's the way it is.'

She didn't have the heart to argue with him, because she knew, deep down, that he was right. 'Thank you,' she whispered. 'I have to go now.'

'Claire. Don't try. They'll kill you.'

'Goodbye, Detective.'

She hung up, put the phone down on the counter, and braced herself with stiffened arms. When she looked up, Eve was watching her with bright, strange eyes.

'All right,' Claire said. 'If I have to be a zombie, I'll be a zombie.'

Eve smiled. 'Cutest zombie ever.'

Claire had never worn this much make-up in her life, not even at Halloween. 'You wear this every day?' she asked as Eve stepped back to look at her critically, make-up sponge still in hand. 'It feels weird.'

'You get used to it. Close your eyes. Powder time.' Claire obeyed, and felt the feathery touch of the powder brush as it glided over her face. She fought back an urge to sneeze.

'OK. Now, eyes,' Eve said. 'Hold still.'

It went on like that for a while, with Claire passively sitting and Eve working whatever dark magic she was working. Claire didn't know. There was no mirror, and she was weirdly reluctant to see what was happening to her, anyway. It felt a little like she was losing herself, although that was stupid, right? How you looked wasn't *you*. She'd always believed that, anyway.

Eve finally stepped back, studied her, and nodded. 'Clothes,' she said. Eve herself had put on a black corset thing, a tattered black skirt, and a necklace of skulls with matching earrings. Black lipstick. 'Here you go.'

Claire took off her blue jeans and T-shirt with great reluctance, then sat down to put on the black hose. They had white death's-head symbols in a line, and she couldn't figure out if they were supposed to go front or back. 'Where do you find this stuff?' she asked.

'Internet. Skulls go in the back.'

After the adventure of the hose, the black leather skirt – knee-length, jingling with zippers and chains – seemed almost easy. Claire's legs felt cold and exposed. She hadn't been in a skirt in…when? Not since she was twelve, probably. She'd never liked them.

The top was a black net thing, stretchy and tight, see-through with a black skull and crossbones printed on it. 'No way,' she said. 'It's transparent!'

'You wear it over a camisole, genius,' Eve said, and tossed a black silky thing to her. Claire slipped it over her head, then fought her way into the clingy embrace of the skull shirt. 'Watch the make-up!' Eve warned. 'OK, you're good. Excellent. Ready to take a look?'

She wasn't, but Eve didn't seem to notice. She steered her into the bathroom, turned on the light, and put her arm around Claire. 'Ta da!' Eve said.

Oh my God, Claire thought. *I can't believe I'm doing this.*

She looked like Eve's skinny little sister. A dead-on junior freak in training.

Well, at least she'd blend in, and if anybody was looking for her, they'd never, ever recognise her. She wouldn't recognise herself. And somehow she just *knew* there'd be pictures on the Internet later.

Claire sighed. 'Let's go.'

Eve drove the black Cadillac onto campus and parked in the faculty lot – a blatant violation, but then, Eve didn't give a crap about campus tickets, either. It was the closest parking to the frat house. So close, in fact, that Claire could see the lights blazing from every window, and hear the low thudding thump of the bass rattling through the car.

'Wow,' Eve said. 'They've gone all out this year. Good old EEK.'

There was a graveyard around the house – tilting tombstones, big creepy-looking mausoleums, some decaying statues. There were also zombies – or, Claire guessed, party guests – lurching around and doing their best *Night of the Living Dead* parody for their friends' cameras.

The dull roar of the party was audible even through the car's closed windows.

'Stay close,' Eve said. 'Let's find Sam, yeah? In and out.'

'In and out.' Claire nodded.

They got out and ran the short distance to the graveyard.

At close range, the tombstones were either foam rubber or Styrofoam, and the mausoleum was a dressed-up storage building, but it looked great. Zombie hands were reaching up out of the dirt. Nice touch, Claire thought. She came close to one, and it turned and groped her ankle. Claire screamed and jumped back into Eve, who caught her. 'Jesus, guys, grow up,' Eve said, and crouched down to look at the ground. 'Where are you?'

'Right here!' A trapdoor covered with sod lifted up, and a geeky-looking frat boy wearing a pledge board stuck his head out. 'Uh, sorry. Just kidding. I have to—'

'Grope girls and look up their skirts. Yeah. Tough work, pledge.' Eve stood up and brushed dirt from her knees. 'Carry on.'

He grinned at her and thumped the trapdoor back down. His hand came up again through a hole in the ground.

'Wow,' Claire said. 'How many of them are there? In the ground?'

'Just the pledges,' Eve said. 'Come on. If Sam's here, he'll be talking to people. He loves to talk.'

If Sam could talk, and anyone could hear him, it was more than Claire could imagine. The music was pounding so loud that she felt it like physical waves through her body, and she had to fight back an urge to cover her ears. Eve had put Claire's hair up in little pigtails, and she missed having it over her ears to block out the roar. 'I need earplugs!' she yelled in Eve's ear. Eve mimed a *What did you say?* 'Never mind!'

The Epsilon Epsilon Kappa fraternity house was trashed. Claire suspected it was usually trashed, but this was extra special – plastic cups everywhere, drinks soaking into carpet, a chair broken in the corner, and drunks sleeping on the sofa. And this was just the foyer. Two guys stepped into their path and held out their hands in the universal gesture for *Don't even think about it*; they were big, muscular guys dressed in white face paint with black T-shirts that said UNDEAD SECURITY on them. 'Invitations?' one of them yelled. Claire exchanged a look with Eve.

'Ian Jameson invited me!' she screamed back. 'Ian Jameson!'

The security guys had a list. They checked it, and nodded. 'Upstairs!' one yelled. 'Last door on the left!'

She didn't intend to find Ian, but she nodded anyway. She and Eve pressed between the two security guys – who were maybe a *little* too close and stepped over the threshold into the wildest party Claire had ever seen in her entire life.

Not that her experience was wide, but still...she was pretty sure Paris Hilton would have classified this as wild. Despite the fact that alcohol was banned on campus, she was also pretty sure the punch that was being ladled out of gigantic coolers was alcoholic (it also had severed hands, eyeballs, and assorted plastic gross-outs floating in it, and was blood red). A lot of the people at the party already showed the telltale signs of being wasted – stumbling, laughing too loud, making wild gestures. Spilling drinks all over themselves and others, which really didn't seem to bother people because, hey, zombies! Not neat freaks. Everybody wore white make-up, or had some kind of rubbery disgusting mask (though that was mostly the guys).

The main room was kind of a dance floor, people pressed up against each other and swaying. Claire stood in the doorway, frozen with sudden dread. It looked like a room full of dead people. Worse – dead, drunk, *horny* people.

'Come on,' Eve yelled impatiently, and grabbed her by the hand. She plunged into the crowd without hesitation, craning her head to look around. 'At least he's a redhead!' Because most of those at the party were wearing black wigs, or had dyed their hair like Eve's. Claire's had suffered a temporary blacking from some kind of spray-on stuff Eve had assured her would wash right out. Claire tried to shield herself from unnecessary body-to-body contact, but it was pretty much useless; she was closer to a whole bunch of guys than she'd ever been in her life.

A hand tried to go up her skirt as she pressed through the crowd. She yelped and jumped, moving faster. Somebody else swatted her on the ass.

'Faster!' she yelled at Eve, who had slowed down to get her bearings. 'God, I can't breathe in here!'

'This way!'

Claire felt filthy – not just from getting groped, which continued to happen, but because she was sopping with other people's sweat by the time Eve squirmed them through to a small clear space on the other side of the room, next to the stairs. It must have been the Wallflower Corner; there were some shy-looking girls, all dressed in mock-Goth finery, grouped together for comfort and (Claire suspected) protection. She felt an instant sympathy for them. 'Great party!' Eve screamed over the pounding beat of the music. 'Wish I could enjoy it!'

'Any sign of Sam?'

'No! Not in here! Let's try the other rooms!'

After the chaos of the main dance room, the kitchen felt like a study hall, even though it was still filled with people talking too loud and gesturing too much. More punch-filled coolers in here, which was driving Claire crazy; she was thirsty, but no way was she adding being drunk to her problems just now. Too much was at stake.

Her ears were still ringing. At least, in here, there was room to breathe. Claire reflexively searched for her cell phone, remembered it getting crunched under the wheels of the white van, and cursed under her breath. 'What time is it?' she asked Eve, who consulted her own black Razr (decorated, of course, with skulls).

'Ten,' she said. 'I know. We have to hurry.'

Somebody grabbed Claire by the arm, and she recoiled in fright, but then she recognised him under the make-up – Ian, the guy who'd told her about the party. The one whose name they'd used to get inside. 'Claire?' he asked. 'Wow. You look great!'

He looked less geeky now, more edgy, with spiked black hair and vampire-style make-up. Claire wondered uneasily how many actual vampires were infiltrating this party tonight. Not a pleasant thought. 'Oh...hi, Ian!' Eve was scanning the room, and as Claire glanced at her, Eve shook her head and mimed going to the next room. Claire begged her not to go, at least with her eyes, but the thick make-up probably disguised her desperation.

'I'm so glad you came!' Ian said. He hardly had to raise his voice at all to be heard over the roar; he just had that kind of voice, and plus, it was a blessedly dull roar in here. 'Can I get you some punch?'

'Um...do you have anything that's not, you know...?'

'Right, yeah. How about some water?'

'Water would be wonderful.' Where the hell was Eve? She'd ducked behind two tall guys and now Claire couldn't see her, and she felt alone and very vulnerable just standing here in her fake Goth get-up, and God, this make-up itched; how did Eve stand it? Claire wanted a shower, wanted to scrub her face clean, and wanted to put on plain jeans and a plain T-shirt and never be adventurous again.

Shane. Think about Shane. She felt an uncomfortable twist of guilt that she'd ever let him slip out of her thoughts, even for a minute.

Ian came back with a bottle of water, the top

already off. 'Here you go,' he said, and handed it over. He was drinking water, too, not the punch stuff. 'Crazy, huh?'

'Crazy,' she agreed. In a town full of vampires, this was just about the craziest idea she could imagine, putting a bunch of drunk, horny college kids in a place where vampires could blend right in. 'Did you see where my friend went?'

'Girls,' Ian sighed. 'Always travel in packs. Yeah, she went into the library. Come on.'

Claire gulped water as she followed him, stepping carefully over the legs of several people who'd decided the kitchen floor looked like a good place to sit down for a chat. And oh God, what was that couple in the corner doing? She blushed under the make-up and looked quickly away, focusing on the back of Ian's neck. He'd missed a spot on the make-up. It looked pink.

The next room had people, too, but not quite as many as the kitchen and it was practically deserted compared to the dance room. *Library* was a generous word. It had books, but not as many as Claire would have thought, and most of them were old textbooks. Some were being defaced by people wielding black markers and pens, giggling with one another over the results.

No sign of Eve.

'Huh,' Ian said. 'Hang on.' He went to ask a question of another guy, taller, dressed in a silky-looking black shirt open halfway down to reveal a strong, muscular chest. It took a while. Claire swigged more water, grateful for the moisture because even the library was steaming hot, and almost wiped at her face before she remembered the careful make-up job.

There was no sign of Sam in this room, either. While Ian was talking, Claire went over to one of the girls defacing books. She looked vaguely familiar – maybe somebody from chemistry? Anna something?

'Hi...Anna?' It must have been right; the girl looked up. 'Have you seen Sam? Red hair...maybe wearing a brown leather jacket...?' Although he had to have taken it off, in this heat. 'Blue eyes?'

'Oh, sure. Sam. He's upstairs somewhere.' Anna went back to her book sabotage, which seemed to involve drawing devils and pitchforks. *Upstairs*. Claire needed to get upstairs, but most importantly, she needed to find Eve. Fast.

Ian came back. 'She went upstairs,' he said. 'She's looking for a guy named Sam, right?'

'Yeah,' Claire said. 'Would you mind if—?'

'No, sure, I'll go with you.' He looked at the drained bottle in Claire's hand. 'Want some more?'

She nodded. He grabbed a bottle from an ice-filled cooler and handed it over. She cracked the seal and took another life-giving mouthful as Ian led the way to the stairs.

The heat was making her feel slow and disconnected. She wanted to pour the cold water over her face, but realised just in time – again – about the make-up. Stupid make-up.

The stairs seemed to go on forever, and it was like dancing around land mines; people were sitting on just about every step, some talking, some mumbling to themselves, some passing joints back and forth. *Oh man.* She really needed to get out of here, fast.

The upstairs landing seemed like a paradise of open space, and Claire clung to the handrail and breathed for a few seconds. Ian came back to get her. 'You OK?' he asked. She nodded. 'I don't know which room he's in. We'll just have to look.'

She followed him. He swung open the first door on the hall, and behind him she saw about ten people talking very intensely. They all looked at Ian with a definite *Get out* vibe, and as he shut the door, Claire realised that all ten of them were vampires.

Not Sam, though, but given what Sam had told her, and what she'd heard from Michael and Eve, that made sense. He'd be hanging around the humans, right? The vampires didn't want any part of him.

'Wrong room,' Ian said unnecessarily, and moved to the next one. She couldn't see over his shoulder, but he closed it in a hurry. '*Really* wrong room. Sorry.'

There were about ten doors on the hallway, but they didn't get that far. Claire was feeling kind of light-headed – in fact, she was dizzy. Maybe it was the heat. She took another gulp from the bottle, but that just seemed to make her feel nauseous. As Ian opened the fourth door, she said, 'I don't feel so good.'

Ian smiled and said, 'Well, that was fast,' and shoved her into the room. 'I thought I was going to have to work a little harder, but you're pretty easy.'

There were three other guys in the room. She didn't know any of them... No, wait, one looked familiar.

The jerk from the UC coffee bar, the one who'd been so mean to Eve. He was one of them. She turned towards Ian, confused, but he was locking the door.

Her knees felt wobbly, and so did her head. Something was wrong. Something was very, very wrong...but she hadn't had anything to drink. She'd been careful...

Not careful enough. The first water bottle he'd brought her, he'd opened it first.

Stupid, Claire. Stupid, stupid, stupid. But he'd seemed so...nice.

'You don't want to do this,' she said, and backed up as one of the guys reached for her. There wasn't a lot of space. It was somebody's bedroom, most of it taken up by a bed, a dresser with the drawers hanging half-open. Dirty laundry piled in a corner. *Oh God.* It hit her hard that Eve had no idea where she was, she had no cell phone, and even if she screamed, no one would hear her over the music. Or care.

She remembered what Eve had done that terrible evening after the biker shoved his way in. *You need a weapon.* Yeah, but Eve was older and bigger, and wasn't drugged at the time...

She nearly tripped over a baseball bat sticking out from under the bed. She grabbed it and took up a bleary, weaving batting stance. 'Don't touch me!' she said, and screamed at the top of her lungs. 'Eve! *Eve!* I need help!'

She took a wild swing at Ian, who was strolling forward, and he ducked it easily. She reversed and slammed the butt end of the bat towards him, and that one, he didn't duck. It hit him squarely in the mouth, and he staggered back, bleeding.

'You *bitch*!' he said, and spit blood. 'Oh, you are gonna pay for that.'

'Hold up,' said the coffee bar jerk, who was leaning against the door with his arms folded. 'You put the full dose in her bottle, right? And she drank it?'

Ian nodded. He fished around in the laundry pile and found a sock to press against his mouth and nose. Good. She hoped it was filthy. And had athlete's foot on it.

'Then all we have to do is wait a couple of minutes,' the jerk said. 'She's not going anywhere except to la-la land.' He high-fived his buddies. Ian continued to glare at her. They were all between her and the door. There was a window, but it was the second floor and she wasn't even steady enough to stand, much less free-climb. Claire gripped the bat in sweaty, numbed hands, and saw sparkles at the edges of her vision. Everything looked bleary. She felt waves of heat sweep over her, and then an icy chill. Michael? Was Michael here? No, Michael couldn't leave the house...

Somehow, she was sliding down to a sitting position on the floor. The bat was still clutched in her hands, but she was tired, very tired, and she felt so sick and hot...

Somebody rattled the doorknob. Claire summoned up whatever was left of her strength and screamed, 'Help! Get help! Eve!'

Ian said, and grinned at Claire with bloody teeth, 'Just somebody looking for a place to screw. Don't worry, baby. We won't hurt you. Not that you'll remember, anyway.'

She pretended to be worse off than she really was (although truthfully, she was pretty bad) and, mumbling, let her eyes drift half-closed.

'That's it,' the coffee bar jerk said. 'She's out. Get her on the bed.'

She'd never really done this before, but she was

imagining hard how Eve would have handled it. She let the bat kind of wobble and fall to rest in her lap, aligned with her leg, as if it had gotten too heavy to hold up. (Not quite. Just nearly.)

And when Ian walked up to grab her, she brought the bat straight up with as much force as she could manage. It smacked him right where it would hurt the most, and Ian crumpled with a high-pitched, breathless scream, huddled in on himself.

Claire forced her legs to hold her, and slid back up to a standing position. She was leaning for support, and lucky to be in a corner, where the two angled walls let her look like she wasn't about to topple over. Her arms were shaking, and the guys would have seen that if she'd tried to raise the bat, so she tapped it casually against her leg. 'Who wants some?' she asked. 'I won't hurt you. Much.'

It was all show, and they only had to wait. Coffee Bar Jerk knew that, all too well, and she could feel the drug – what the hell was it? – stealing away her concentration, her strength, making her slow and stupid and all-too-easy prey.

Shane, she thought, and forced herself to stand upright just a little longer. *Shane needs me. I'm not letting this happen.*

'You're bluffing,' Coffee Bar Jerk said, and came around the bed. Claire took a swing at him, missed, and smacked the bat into the wood so hard it rattled her teeth.

He grabbed the bat on the backswing and easily twisted it out of her grip. He tossed it to one of the other two guys, who caught it one-handed. 'That,' he said, 'was really stupid. This could have been real nice and easy, you know that, right?'

'I have Amelie's Protection,' Claire said.

He grabbed her by the throat of her sheer black skull-printed shirt, and dragged her forward. Her legs folded when she tried to pull away.

'I don't care,' he said. 'I'm not from this stupid town. None of us are. Monica said that was the way to go, to get around the dumbass rules, whatever they are. Whoever Amelie is, she can kiss my ass. After you're done doing it.'

The door to the hall gave a dry, metallic pop, and swung slowly open. Claire blinked and tried to focus her eyes, because there was someone standing there. No, two someones. One had red hair. Wasn't there something about red hair...? Oh yeah. Sam had red hair. Sam the vampire. Sam I Am. Michael's grandpa, wasn't that just too weird?

The door no longer had a knob on the outside. The one on the inside fell out with a dull thud to the carpet and rolled under the bed.

'Claire!' Oh, that was *Eve*. 'Oh my God...'

'Excuse me,' Sam said, 'but what did you say about Amelie?'

Coffee Bar Jerk let go of Claire's top, and she slid back down the wall. She fumbled around for something to use for a weapon, but all she came up with was another set of filthy socks that had missed the laundry. For some reason, that seemed funny. She giggled and rested her head against the wall to let her neck relax. Her neck was working too hard.

'I said that Amelie can kiss my ass, Red. And what are you going to do about it? Stare me to death?'

Sam just stood there. Claire couldn't see anything about him change, but it was like the room just went...cold. 'You really don't want to do this,' Sam said. 'Eve, go get your friend.'

'Yeah, Eve, come on in, we've got a nice big bed!' Ian giggled. 'I hear you know how to have a real good time.' He tossed the bloody sock he'd been pressing to his nose down on the floor and got ready to grab Eve if she came inside. Sam looked at the discarded sock for a second, then picked it up and squeezed it, drizzling blood into the palm of his hand.

And then he licked it up. Slowly. Meeting the eyes of every guy facing him.

'I said,' he whispered, 'you really don't want to do this.'

Claire heard a great big buzzing in her head, like a hive full of bees. *Oh, I'm going to pass out, because that was gross.*

'Shit,' Ian whispered, and backed up. Fast. 'You're sick, man!'

'Sometimes,' Sam agreed. 'Eve, go get her. Nobody's going to touch you.'

Eve cautiously edged past him, hurried to Claire, and gave her a fast embrace before she hauled her upright again. 'Can you walk?'

'Not very well,' Claire said, and gulped down nausea. The world kept coming in hot and cold flashes, and she felt like she was going to throw up, but somehow it was all smeared and funny, even the terror in Eve's eyes.

Not so funny when Coffee Bar Jerk decided to grab Eve, though.

He lunged over the bed, reaching for Eve's wrist – Claire was too fuzzy to know why he was doing it. Maybe he was hoping to use her as some kind of shield against Sam. But whatever he meant, it was a bad decision.

Sam moved in a flicker, and when Claire blinked, Coffee Bar Jerk was up against the wall, eyes wide, staring at Sam's face from a distance of about three inches.

'I said,' Sam whispered, 'nobody was going to touch her. Are you *deaf*?'

Claire didn't see it, but she imagined he probably flashed some fang right about then, because Coffee Bar Jerk whimpered like a sick dog.

The other boys moved out of Eve's way

without even trying to stop her.

'Monica,' Claire said. 'I think it was Monica. She got Ian to ask me.'

'What?'

'Monica got him to ask me. Told them to do this.'

'*Bitch!* OK, I take it all back. She needs a good blowtorching.'

'No,' Claire said faintly. 'Nobody deserves that. Nobody.'

'Great. Saint Claire, the patron saint of the kick-me sign. Look, keep it together, OK? We need to get out of here. Sam! Come on! Leave them!'

Sam didn't seem inclined to listen. 'Manners, boys,' he said. 'Looks to me like nobody ever taught you any. It's time you had a lesson before somebody else gets hurt.'

'Hey, man—' Ian was holding out his hands in surrender. 'Seriously. Just having fun. We weren't going to hurt her. No need to go all Charles Bronson. We didn't even really touch her. Look. Clothes still on.'

'Don't even try.' Sam continued to stare at Coffee Bar Jerk, who was looking less like a predator, and more and more like a scared kid faced with the big, bad wolf. 'I like these girls. I don't like you. Do the maths. Consider yourself subtracted.'

'Sam!' Eve's voice was loud and flat. 'Enough

with the macho hero stuff. We came to find you. Let's get out of here and talk.'

'I'm not leaving,' Sam said, his eyes fixed on the boy he was holding. 'Not until Disney Princess here apologises, or his head comes off, one of the two.'

'Sam! What we need to talk about is *important*, and Disney Princess is *not*!'

For a second Claire thought nothing Eve could say would get through, but then she saw Sam smile – it wasn't a nice smile – and he let Coffee Bar Jerk slide back to the floor. 'Fine,' he said. 'Consider yourself horribly tortured. Make sure you think about all the ways I could have hurt you, because if I hear about anything like this happening again, I want you to know what's coming.'

Coffee Bar Jerk nodded shakily, and kept his back to the wall as he slid over to join his posse.

Sam turned towards the girls, and came forward to touch Claire lightly on the shoulder. 'Are you all right?'

Claire nodded, a loose flop of her head. That was a mistake; she nearly pitched over, and it took all of Eve's strength to keep her on her feet.

When she was able to open her eyes and focus again, Sam had moved away, to the door.

'What?' Eve asked. 'And by the way, you're blocking the escape hatch.'

'Hush,' Sam said softly, barely loud enough to be heard over the pounding, relentless beat of the music.

And then Claire heard the screaming.

In a blink, Sam was gone from the doorway. Eve moved out into the hallway, craning her head to look over the rail, and Claire looked, too.

It was chaos down there, and not the happy chaos of a dance. Knots of screaming, pushing people, desperately jamming up the exits from the big open room, all in black clothes, white faces, some splashes of red here and there...

Blood. There was *blood*.

Sam grabbed both her and Eve by the shoulders, swung them around, and pushed them back inside the room. He looked at Ian, who was still cowering against the wall. 'You. O Positive. How many exits?'

'What?... Oh *shit*, did you just call me by my blood type?'

'*How many exits?*'

'The stairs! You have to take the stairs!'

Sam cursed under his breath, went to the closet, and yanked it open. It was a walk-in, pretty large, filled with junk. He shoved Claire and Eve inside and held the door open. 'You,' he said to the four boys. 'If you want to live, get in. Touch these girls and I'll kill you myself. You know I'm serious, yeah?'

'Yeah,' Ian said faintly. 'Not a finger on 'em. What's happening? Is it, like, one of those shooting things?'

'Yes,' Sam said. 'It's like that. Get in.'

The boys piled into the closet. Eve dragged Claire to the farthest corner, shoving piles of rank-smelling athletic shoes out of the way, and sat her down. Eve crouched next to her, ready for action, and glared at the guys. They kept their distance.

Sam slammed the door.

Darkness.

'What the hell is going on?' Coffee Bar Jerk demanded. His voice was shaking.

'People are getting hurt,' Eve said tightly. 'Could be you if you don't shut up.'

'But—'

'Just *shut the hell up*!'

Silence. The music was still pounding downstairs, but over it Claire could hear the screaming. She started to go into that funny grey place, but jerked herself back with an effort and squeezed Eve's tense hand. 'It's OK,' Eve whispered to her. 'You're OK. I'm so sorry.'

'I was doing OK,' Claire said. Surprised, actually, that it was true. 'Thanks for saving me.'

'I didn't do anything but find Sam. He found you.' Eve stopped. 'All right, who's touching me?'

A high-pitched male voice out of the darkness. 'Oh shit! Sorry!'

'Better be.'

There was a tense silence in the dark.

And then Claire heard heavy footsteps coming down the hallway.

'Quiet,' Eve whispered. She didn't need to say it. Claire felt it, and she knew everybody else did, too. There was something bad out there, something worse than four horny, stupid, cruel boys.

She felt something brush against her. A hand. One of the boys, she didn't know which one – was it Ian who'd slumped against the wall nearest to her?

She took it and squeezed. He squeezed back, silently.

And Claire waited to see if they were going to die.

CHAPTER TEN

The screaming stopped, and the music cut off in mid-rave. That was worse, somehow. The silence felt...cold. Claire held on grimly to consciousness. The effects seemed to be coming and going. Maybe she was going to be OK.

A floorboard creaked *right outside the closet door.*

Claire felt a tremor go through the boy whose hand she held, and she pressed herself harder against the wall and stared at the closet door. It was a big black rectangle outlined in warm yellow.

There was a flicker of shadow, and a snarl, and a man's full-throated yell, and the sound of a body hitting the floor.

Then the boom of a gun going off. Claire jumped, and felt Eve and the boy jump, too. 'Oh God,' he whispered. He was shaking all over. Claire supposed that was one thing that being roofied was good for – it kept your heart rate down in an emergency. She felt pretty calm, all things considered. Or maybe she was just getting used to being scared out of her mind.

Running footsteps. The banister in the hall creaked. More shouts from downstairs, feet pounding on the stairs, heading down...

And then the distant, shrill sound of sirens.

'Cops,' somebody whispered, maybe Coffee Bar Jerk. He sounded a whole lot less arrogant. 'We'll be OK. We're going to be OK.'

'Yeah, until these two turn us in,' muttered another boy. 'For, you know. The thing.'

'You mean for *attempted rape*?' Eve whispered fiercely. 'Jesus, listen to you. *The thing*. Call it what it is, you asshole.'

'Look, it was just... I'm sorry, OK? We didn't want to hurt her. We just—'

'She's *sixteen*, man.'

'What?'

'Sixteen. So you can thank me now for saving you serious jail time, because attempted rape is a hell of a lot better than *actual* rape. The statutory kind. Did Monica put you up to it?'

'I...uh...yeah. She said...she said Claire was good to go, that she just needed it rough. She wanted to be sure we got her here.'

'Shhhhhh,' Claire whispered frantically. She heard another floorboard creak. Everybody fell silent.

The door swung open, blinding them with a wash of light, and Claire squinted at the man standing there.

Red hair.

'Out,' Sam said. 'Move.'

The boys got up and filed out, looking a whole lot less arrogant than before and clustered together in the corner. It had been Ian whose hand she'd held, after all,

Claire saw. He was looking at her in a weird, new way, as if he actually saw her for the first time.

'I'm sorry about your nose,' she said. He blinked.

'It's not so bad,' he offered. 'Look, Claire—'

'Don't.'

'You still going to tell the cops?' That was Coffee Bar Jerk.

'No,' Claire said.

'Bullshit! Yes,' Eve said. 'A world of yes. So you'd better not try this again. Ever. And besides, if you do, the last thing you have to worry about is the cops. Right, Sam?'

Sam nodded without speaking.

'Let's get out of here. Claire? Can you walk?'

'I can try.'

But the world just slipped out from under her when she got up, and she fell into Eve's arms. Eve juggled her awkwardly, trying to find the right way to hold her up, and suddenly Claire was floating about four feet off the ground.

Oh. Sam had her, and he was holding her as if she were as heavy as a bag of feathers.

'Hey,' Coffee Bar Jerk said. Sam stopped on his way to the door. 'Sorry, seriously. It was just...Monica said—'

'Stop, man,' Ian said. 'Monica just gave us the idea. We were the ones who did it. No excuses.'

'Yeah,' Coffee Bar Jerk said. 'Whatever, man. Won't happen again.'

'If it does,' Sam said, 'never mind the police. I'll find you.'

Things were melting into one another. Claire felt sick and disoriented, and only having her arms around Sam's cool, strong neck kept her from floating away on a tide of chemicals. When she opened her eyes she caught flashes... The EEK frat house was trashed. Furniture broken, walls bashed, people lying on the floor...

And some of them were bloody.

Eve stopped and pressed her fingers to the throat of a boy wearing full vamp gear, including the teeth; his blue eyes were open, staring at the ceiling. He didn't move.

'He's dead,' she whispered.

There was a wooden stake in his chest.

'But...he wasn't a vampire,' Claire said. 'Right?'

'They didn't care. He looked like one, and he must have gotten in the way,' Sam said. 'There are two vampires dead in the other room. This one was a mistake.'

'In the other room?' Claire asked. 'How do you know?'

'I know.' Sam stepped over the body and moved around a busted-up couch. Glass crunched under his feet. The sirens were getting closer now, late to the party as usual.

'Was it Frank's guys?' Eve asked. 'The bikers?'

Sam didn't answer, but he didn't really have to. How many rampaging anti-vamp gangs could there be in Morganville?

Claire closed her eyes and let her head drop against Sam's chest, meaning just to rest for a second.

And...she just left the world for a while.

Claire woke up to the sound of voices and a headache the size of Cleveland inside of her skull; her mouth was dry as a bone, and her tongue a thick roll of felt covered in sandpaper. Also, hello, nausea.

She was lying in her own bed, at home.

Claire rolled out, ran to the bathroom, and took care of the sickness first, then looked in the mirror. It was horrible. Her face was smeared with make-up, her black eyeliner smudged every which way, her black-sprayed hair sticking up in thick clumps.

Claire started the shower, stripped off the Goth disguise, and sat in the tub with the water pounding down. There wasn't enough soap in the world, really, but she tried, scrubbing hard. Scrubbing until her skin was stinging.

She froze at the sound of a knock on the bathroom door. 'Claire? It's Eve. You OK?'

'Yeah,' she said. 'I'm OK.' Her voice sounded thick and weak.

Eve must have taken her at her word, because she went away. Claire wished she hadn't, somehow; she needed somebody to ask; she needed somebody to be there for her. *I was almost...*

The worst part of it was that they weren't monsters, those guys. In fact, they were probably OK most of the time. How was that even possible? How could people be good and bad at the same time? Good was good; bad was bad – you had to draw a line, right? *Like with the vampires?* some part of her mind whispered. *Where's Amelie, then? Where's Sam? Sam saved your life. Which side of the line do you put him on?*

She didn't know. And she didn't want to think about it anymore. Claire sat under the pounding hard rain of the hot water and let it all go for a while, until the water started to run cool and she remembered that Eve probably wanted to shower, too. *Crap.* She jumped up, turned off the taps, and dried off, realised she hadn't brought more clothes in with her, and wrapped in the towel for the fast trip to her room.

When she opened the bathroom door, Michael was standing right outside. He looked up, saw she wasn't dressed, and looked briefly conflicted.

He solved it by turning his back. 'Go get some clothes on,' he said. 'Then I need to talk to you.'

'What time is it?' she asked. He didn't answer, and she felt something sick take hold in her stomach. 'Michael? *What time is it?*'

'Just get dressed,' he said. 'And come downstairs.'

She raced to her room, dropped the towel, and grabbed her little travel clock.

It was *four a.m.* Dawn was just a couple of hours away. 'No,' she whispered. 'No…' She'd been asleep for *hours*.

No time to waste, then. Claire put on underwear, jeans, and a T-shirt, grabbed her shoes and socks, and hurried to the stairs.

She stopped on the first step down when she heard Amelie's voice. *Amelie? In the house? Why?* Sam, she kind of expected – not that Michael liked any vampires, but hey, he was family, right? And besides, Sam seemed OK. And sure enough, she caught sight of Sam's copper-coloured hair when she eased down another step; he was standing in the far corner, near the kitchen, with his arms folded.

Amelie and Michael were in the centre of the room.

'Hey!' Eve's voice, coming from behind her,

made her jump. Claire turned and saw Eve standing there in a thick black bathrobe, clothes in her arms. 'I'm taking my shower. Tell them I'll be there soon, OK?'

Eve looked tired, her make-up sweated or smeared away. Claire felt guilty about using all the hot water. 'OK,' she said, and edged another step down towards the living room. Eve's footsteps creaked behind her, and the bathroom door closed. The water went on.

Claire heard Amelie say, '...can't take it back. Do you understand? Once you make this choice, it is done. There can be no returning.'

That didn't sound good. No, that didn't sound good at all. Claire still felt shaky and sick, as if she'd drunk half a gallon of that red punch at the party, and she didn't feel in any shape to face Amelie again. Only so much scary she could deal with in one day. Maybe she'd just wait for Eve...

'I understand,' Michael said. 'But there isn't a lot of choice anymore. I can't live like this, trapped in this house. I need to *leave*. I can't help Shane if I'm stuck here.'

'You may not be able to help Shane at all,' Amelie said coolly. 'I would not base such a choice on the love of one friend. It may turn out badly for you both.'

'Life is risk, right? So I have to risk it.'

She shook her head. 'Samuel, please speak to him. Explain.'

Sam stirred from where he stood in the corner, but he didn't come closer. 'She's right, kid. You don't know what you're getting into. You think you do, but...you don't. You've got a good thing here: you're alive; you're safe; you have friends who care about you. Family. Stay where you are.'

Michael let out a hollow laugh that sounded a little crazy. '*Stay where I am?* Jesus Christ, what choice do I have? This house is twenty-five hundred square feet of tomb. I'm not alive. I'm *buried* alive.'

Sam shook his head and bent his head, avoiding Michael's stare.

Amelie stepped closer to him. 'Michael. Please think what you are asking. It is not only difficult for you; it is difficult for *me*. If I give you your freedom from this house, it comes at a terrible price. There will be great pain, and the loss of things that neither you nor I can fully name. What you are will change, and change forever. You would live and die at my command, do you understand? And you would never be even the half human you are now, never again.' She shook her head slowly. 'I believe you will regret this, and regret is like cancer to us. It rots our will to live.'

'Yeah? What do you think it's like, being trapped here when people need me?' Michael asked. His fists were clenched, his face tense and flushed. 'I've watched my girlfriend nearly get killed five feet away from me, and I couldn't do anything because she was outside the house. Now it's Shane, and he's all alone out there. It couldn't be worse than this, Amelie. Trust me. If you're not going to save Shane, then you have to do this for me. Please.'

He was asking Amelie for...what? Something she could do that would set him free? Claire eased down another step, and saw Sam's eyes shift and lock on her. She expected him to say something, but he just gave her a very small shake of his head. Warning her.

She retreated back to the top of the stairs, hesitating. Maybe she should get Eve... No, the shower was still running. She should wait. Michael wouldn't do anything stupid...would he?

While she was hesitating, she heard Amelie say something that she couldn't quite understand, except for one word.

'Vampire.'

And she heard Michael say, 'Yes.'

'No!' Claire jumped up and pelted down the steps, fast as she could, but before she could get to the bottom Sam was standing there, looking up at her. Blocking her path. She looked over the railing at Michael and Amelie, and saw Michael watching her.

He looked scared, but he gave her a smile – broken, like the one Shane had put on for her in the cage. Trying to show it didn't matter.

'It's OK, Claire,' he said. 'I know what I'm

doing. This is the way it has to be.'

'No, it doesn't!' She edged down another step, clinging to the rail with both hands. She felt hot and disoriented again, but she figured if she was going to fall, at least Sam was there to cushion her. 'Michael, *please*. Don't do this!'

'Oliver tried to make me a vampire. He made me into—' Michael made a disgusted gesture at himself. 'I'm half-alive, Claire, and there's no going back. I can only go forward.'

She couldn't say anything to that, because he was right. Right at every point. He couldn't go back to being just a regular guy; he couldn't live with being stuck here, helpless. Maybe he could have, if Shane hadn't been taken, but now...

'Michael, please.' Her eyes were filling up with tears. 'I don't want you to change.'

'Everybody changes.'

'Not as you will,' Amelie said. She was standing there like the Snow Queen, all perfect and white and smooth, nothing really human about her at all. 'You will not be the man she knows, Michael. Or the one Eve loves. Will you risk that, too?'

Michael took in a deep breath and turned back towards her. 'Yes,' he said. 'I will.'

Amelie stood in silence for a moment, then nodded. 'Sam,' she said. 'Take the child away. This wants no witnesses.'

'I'm not leaving!' Claire said.

Yeah, good plan. Sam walked up three steps, scooped her into his arms, and carried her upstairs. Claire tried to grab for the railing, but her fingers slipped away. 'Michael! Michael, *no*! Don't do this!'

Sam carried her to her room and dumped her on the bed, and before she could struggle up to a sitting position he was already outside, closing the door.

Later, thinking back on it, Claire couldn't say if she heard the scream or felt it; either way, it seemed to vibrate through the bones and boards of the Glass House, through her head, and she moaned and clapped her hands over her ears. That didn't stop it. The scream just went on and on, shrill and painful as a steam whistle, and Claire felt something...pull at her, like she was made of cloth, and a gigantic, malicious kid was yanking at her loose threads.

And then it just...stopped.

She slid off the bed, ran to the door, and opened it. Sam was nowhere to be seen. Eve was rushing out of the bathroom, clutching her bathrobe around her dripping body, her black hair plastered wet against her face. 'What's happening?' she yelled. 'Michael? Where's Michael?'

The two girls exchanged a desperate look, and then ran for the stairs.

⋈ ⋈ ⋈

Amelie was sitting in an armchair, the one Michael usually used; she looked drawn and tired, and her head was bent. Sam was crouched next to her, holding her hand, and he rose to his feet when Eve and Claire arrived breathlessly at the bottom of the stairs.

'She's resting,' he said. 'It takes a lot to do what she did. A lot of strength, and a lot of will. Leave her alone. Let her recover.'

'Where's Michael?' Eve demanded. Her voice was shaking. 'What did you do to Michael, you bastard?'

'Easy, child. Sam had nothing to do with it. I set him free,' Amelie said. She raised her head and let it rest against the back of the chair, eyes closed. 'So much pain in him. I thought he could be happy here, but I see I was wrong. One such as Michael can never stay caged for long.'

'What do you mean, you set him free?' Eve was stammering now, her face ashen without any Goth cosmetics to help. '*You killed him?*'

'Yes,' Amelie said. 'I killed him. *Sam!*'

Claire couldn't see why she snapped the other vampire's name until Sam turned in a blur, and met another blur coming at them from across the room. That turned into a struggle, two bodies moving too fast for Claire's eyes to follow until it ended and one was flat on his back on the floor.

That was Michael on his back...but not the

Michael she knew. Not the one she'd seen five minutes before, talking to Amelie, making this choice. This Michael was *terrifying*. Sam was having trouble holding him; Michael was struggling, trying to throw him off, and he was *snarling*, oh God, and his skin – his skin was the pale colour of marble and ashes...

'Help me up,' Amelie said quietly. Claire looked at her, stunned. Amelie was holding out a queenly hand, clearly expecting to be obeyed. Claire gave her help up to her feet, just because she'd always been taught to be polite, and braced the vampire, as she seemed about to lose her balance. Amelie found her balance and gave her a weary, thin smile. She let go of Claire's arm, and walked slowly – painfully – to where Sam was fighting to keep Michael down.

Claire looked at Eve. Eve was backed into the corner, her hands in fists covering her mouth. Her eyes were huge.

Claire put her arm around her.

Amelie put one white hand on Michael's forehead, and he instantly stopped struggling. Stopped moving at all, staring straight up at the ceiling with fierce, strange eyes. 'Peace,' Amelie whispered. 'Peace, my poor child. The pain will pass; the hunger will pass. This will help.' She reached into a pocket of her dress and took out a very small, very thin silver knife – no bigger than a fingernail – and sliced a gash across her palm.

She didn't bleed like a normal person; the blood seeped out, thicker than normal, and darker. Amelie put it to Michael's lips, pressed it, and closed her eyes.

Eve screamed beneath the cover of her hands, then turned blindly and hid her face against Claire. Claire wrapped her in a tight, shaking hug.

When Amelie withdrew her hand, the gash was closed, and there was no blood on Michael's lips. He closed his eyes, swallowing, gasping. After a few long seconds, Amelie nodded to Sam, who let go and stepped back, and Michael slowly rolled over on his side and met Claire's horrified stare.

His *eyes*. They were the same colour, and...not the same at all. Michael licked his pale lips, and she saw the bright white flicker of snake fangs in his mouth.

She shuddered.

'Behold,' Amelie said softly, 'the youngest of our kind. From this day on, Michael Glass, you are one of the eternal of the Great City, and all will be yours. Rise. Take your place among your people.'

'Yeah,' Sam said. 'Welcome to hell.'

Michael got to his feet. Neither of them helped him up.

'That's it?' Michael asked. His voice sounded strange – deep in his throat, deeper than Claire remembered. It gave her a little shiver at the base of her spine. 'It's done?'

'Yes,' Amelie said. 'It's done.'

Michael walked towards the door. He had to stop and brace himself against the wall on the way, but he looked stronger every second. Stronger than Claire felt comfortable with, in fact.

'Michael,' Amelie said. 'Vampires can be killed, and many know the ways. If you grow careless, you will die, no matter how many laws Morganville holds to protect us from our enemies.' Amelie glanced at the two girls, standing together in the corner. 'Vampires cannot live among humans. It is too difficult, too tempting. You understand? They must leave your house. You must have time to learn what you are.'

Michael looked at Eve and Claire – more at Claire than Eve, as if he couldn't stand to really face her yet. He looked more like himself now, more in control. Except for the pale skin, he might nearly have been normal.

'No,' he said. 'This is their home, and it's my home, and it's Shane's home. We're a family. I'm not giving that up.'

'Do you know why I stopped you?' Amelie said. 'Why I ordered Sam to stop you? Because your instincts cannot be trusted, Michael, not at this point. You cannot care, because your feelings for them will hurt them. Do you understand? Were you not moving towards these two girls with the intention of feeding on them?'

His eyes went wide and, suddenly, very dark. 'No.'

'Think.'

'*No.*'

'You were,' Sam said quietly, from behind him. 'I know, Michael. I was there once. And there was no one to stop me.'

Michael didn't try to deny it again; he looked at Eve, right at her, with such terrible dawning pain that it hurt to see it.

'It won't happen again.' Eve hadn't said a word since all this had started, so it was a little shocking to hear her say that, so calmly. So...*normally*. 'I know Michael. He wouldn't have done this if he was going to hurt any of us. He'd die first.'

'He did die,' Amelie said. 'The human part of him is gone. What is left is mine.' She said it with a little regret, which didn't surprise Claire much; she'd seen it in Amelie's infinitely weary eyes as she'd helped her up.

'Come, Michael. You need food. I will show you where to go.'

'Wait a minute,' he said. 'Please.' And he stepped away from her, and held out his hand to Eve.

Amelie drew breath to tell him something – probably *no* – but she didn't speak. Sam didn't, either, but he turned and walked away, aimlessly circling the room. Claire reluctantly let go of Eve, and Eve walked directly to Michael, no hesitation at all.

He took both of her hands in his.

'I'm sorry. There wasn't any other way.' Michael swallowed, his eyes fixed on Eve's. 'I've been feeling it, more and more. Like this...pressure inside. It's not just that I needed to do this to help Shane. I just...needed it to stay sane. And I'm sorry. You're going to hate me.'

'Why?' Eve asked. It was half bravado, it had to be, but she sounded certain. 'Because you're vamped? Please. I loved you when you were only halfway here at all. As long as you're with me, I can deal, Michael. For you, I can deal.'

He kissed her, and Claire blinked and looked away. There was a lot of hunger in that kiss, and desperation, and it was way too personal.

Eve wasn't the first one to pull away, either.

When he stepped back from her, he was the old Michael after all, never mind the paler skin and the odd shine to his eyes. That smile...he was *Michael*, and everything was going to be OK.

He wiped away Eve's silent tears with his thumbs, kissed her again, very lightly, and said, 'I'll be back. Amelie's right, I need to—' He hesitated, glanced at Amelie, and then back down at Eve. 'I need to feed. I guess I need to get used to saying that.' His smile looked a little dimmer this time. 'I'm going to miss dinners.'

'You won't,' Sam said. 'You can still eat solid foods if you want. I do.'

For some reason, that seemed really important. It was something they could hold on to.

'I'll make dinner tonight,' Claire said. 'To celebrate getting Shane home.'

'It's a deal.' Michael let go of Eve and stepped back. 'I'm ready.'

'Then come outside,' Amelie said. 'Come back to the world.'

Michael might have become a vampire, but watching him stand outside in the night air, breathing in his freedom... Claire thought that was as human as it could get.

CHAPTER ELEVEN

Eve changed into what Claire thought of as 'Goth camo'...black pants, a black silk shirt with red skulls embroidered at the collar, and a black vest with loads of pockets that could hold things. Things like stakes and crosses, as it turned out. 'Just in case,' Eve said, catching Claire's look. 'What?'

'Nothing,' she sighed. 'Just don't use them on Michael.'

Eve stopped for a second, stricken, and then nodded. She was still getting her head around it, Claire knew. Well, Claire was doing the same thing. She kept expecting to hear Michael's guitar downstairs; she kept wondering about what time it was. Not dawn yet – she checked the Internet and found out that they still had time, but if Michael didn't come back soon...

The front door opened and closed. Eve snatched a stake from her pocket, wide-eyed, and Claire motioned to her to stay where she was, then sneaked carefully to the corner.

She nearly ran into Michael, who was moving way more quietly than she was used to. He looked nearly as surprised as she did. Behind him was Sam, but there was no sign of Amelie.

'You OK?' she asked. Michael nodded. He looked...better, in some strange sort of way. At peace. 'Not going to...?' She mimed fangs in her neck. He smiled.

'No way, kid.' He ruffled her hair lightly. 'There's a deal on the table for Shane.'

'A deal?' Eve sounded tense as she came around into view, and Claire didn't blame her. Deals hadn't gone especially well for them so far.

'If we get Monica back safely, Shane goes free. The Morrells still have influence in this town, even with the vamps.' Of which Michael was one now, but he didn't seem to be lumping himself in quite yet. 'Oliver was willing to trade. Or maybe not willing – convinced.'

'Shane for Monica? Sweet!' Eve realised she was holding a stake in her hand, blushed, and put it away. Neither Sam nor Michael seemed all that bothered. 'Ah, sorry. Nothing personal...so it's you two and us against the world, or what?'

'No,' Sam said, and looked at Michael. 'It's the three of you. I can't go with you.'

'What? But...you—'

'I'm sorry.' Sam honestly sounded like he meant it. 'Amelie's orders. Vampires stay neutral – Michael's the only exception because of his agreement with Amelie. I can't help you.'

'But—'

'I can't,' he repeated, with emphasis, and sighed. 'You'll get some help from the human community – that's all I can tell you. Good luck.' He started to walk away, towards the door, then turned back. 'Thank you, Claire. Eve.'

'What for?'

Sam's smile was suddenly luminous, and it looked just like Michael's. 'You brought me to Amelie. And she talked to me. That counts.'

There was a story behind that, Claire was sure, full of heartbreak and longing; she could see it, for a second, written all over his face. Amelie? He loved *Amelie*? That was kind of like loving the *Mona Lisa* – the painting, not the person. Presuming Amelie even had enough emotion in her to feel something for Sam these days.

Maybe once she had. Wow.

Sam nodded to Michael, equal to equal, and he left, closing the door behind him.

'Hey,' Eve said. 'Did he have an invitation? To get into the house?'

'He didn't need one,' Michael said. 'The house adjusted itself once I...changed. Now humans need an invitation. Except for you, since you live here.'

'OK, that's stupid.'

'It's Protection,' Michael said. 'You know how it works.'

Claire didn't, but she was fascinated. Not the time, though. 'Um, he said the town was sending help...?'

'Richard Morrell,' Michael said. 'Monica's cop brother. And he's bringing Hess and Lowe with him.'

'That's it?' Claire squeaked. Because there were a lot of bikers. Like, a *lot*. Not to mention Shane's dad, who frankly scared her worse than most of the vampires just because he didn't seem to have any rules.

Funny, the vampires seemed to be all about rules. Who knew?

'I'm going to want you both to stay here,' Michael said.

'No,' Eve said flatly. Claire echoed it.

'Seriously, you need to stay. This is going to get dangerous.'

'Dangerous? Dude, they *killed kids*. On campus!' Eve shot back. 'We were *there*! Don't you get it? We're not safe here, and maybe we can help you. At the very least, we can grab Monica and hustle her skanky ass back to her dad while all you brave, strong menfolk hold off the bad guys. Right?'

'Not Claire, then.'

'Claire,' Claire said, 'decides for herself. In case you forgot.'

'Claire *doesn't* decide when it's something like this, because Claire is sixteen and Michael doesn't want to be explaining her tragic accidental death to her parents. So, no.'

'What're you going to do?' Eve asked, and cocked her head to one side. 'Lock her in her room?'

He looked from one of them to the other, his frown deepening. 'Oh, crap. What is this, Girl Solidarity?'

'Bet your ass,' Eve said. 'Somebody's got to keep you in line.' Her smile faded, because that was true now, not just a funny idea. Michael cleared his throat.

'Did you hear that?'

'What?'

'A car. Brakes. Outside.'

'Great,' Eve said. 'Vampire hearing, too. I'm never going to be able to keep a secret around here. Bad enough when you were a ghost...' She was doing a good job of looking like she wasn't freaked-out, but Claire thought she was. So did Michael, apparently, because he reached out and touched her cheek – just one small gesture, but it said a lot.

'Stay here,' he said.

He should have known they wouldn't – not completely, anyway. Claire and Eve followed him partway down the hall, enough to watch him unlock the front door and swing it open.

Richard Morrell stood on the doorstep in his police uniform. Next to him were Detectives Hess and Lowe, both looking even more exhausted than normal.

'Michael,' Richard said, and nodded to him.

He tried to move across the threshold, and was stopped cold. Hess and Lowe exchanged a curious look and tried to come across, as well. Nothing.

'Come in,' Michael said, and stepped back. This time, all three men could enter.

Richard was looking at Michael closely. 'You're kidding,' he said. 'You've got to be kidding. All this time, and she picks *you?*'

Hess and Lowe exchanged looks, a second behind the curve, and both appeared startled.

'Yeah,' Michael said. 'What about it?'

Richard smiled, all teeth. 'Nothing, man. Congratulations, and all that. You're going to be the talk of the town. Get used to it.'

Michael shut the door behind them. 'Whatever. How much time do we have to get to Shane?'

'Not much,' Hess said. 'And the thing is, we don't have anyplace to start. No leads.'

'Well, we've got one. We know the van went through the Underground,' Richard said. 'We've got an eyewitness. Right?' He looked straight at

Claire, who nodded. 'We pulled all the surveillance tapes, and we tracked the van in and out of the Underground half a dozen times, but it finally disappeared. Problem is, one white van looks a lot like other white vans, especially on NightSight surveillance cameras.'

'We know that Shane's dad had maps of Morganville. Shane provided them. You're sure he didn't say *anything* about where his father might be making his base of operations?' Hess asked. 'Any of you?'

'He never said anything,' Claire said. 'Not to me. Michael?' Michael shook his head. 'God, I can't believe *nobody* knows where these guys are! They have to be somewhere!'

'Actually, two people probably know exactly where they are,' Richard said. 'Shane, and the biker, Des. One of them, maybe both, has to know the places Frank was using.'

'And nobody's asked them?' Eve questioned, and then her expression turned blank with horror. 'Oh *God*. Somebody *has*.'

'It's not so bad as that,' Lowe offered. 'I was there observing. They're all right.'

'That doesn't mean they'll stay that way,' Michael said. 'Especially now. Or was that the plan, Richard? Get the two neutral cops here with you so your guys could beat the information out of Shane?'

Richard smiled slowly. 'You know, that's not a bad idea, but no. I honestly thought you guys would have a place for us to start looking. We can go with that plan B if you come up empty, though. I never liked that kid anyway.'

Michael's eyes were narrowing, and Claire felt the whole barely reasonable alliance starting to come apart.

'Wait!' she said. 'Um, I think I have something. Maybe.'

'Maybe?' Richard turned to her. 'Better be good. It's your boyfriend on the line, and if anything happens to my sister, I swear I'll torch him myself.'

Claire looked at Michael, then Eve. 'I saw him,' she said. 'Shane's dad. He was in Common Grounds.'

'He was *what*?'

'In Common Grounds. It was the same day I met Sam for the first time. I wondered what he was doing there, but—'

Richard interrupted her, grabbing the neck of her T-shirt and hauling her forward. 'Who was he talking to? Who?' He shook her.

'Hey!' She smacked at his hand, and to her surprise, he let go. 'He was talking to Oliver.'

Silence. They all stared at her, and then Hess put a hand to his forehead. Lowe said, 'Whoa, whoa, whoa, hang on a second. Why would the Fearless Vampire Killer be talking to Oliver? He knows, right? Who Oliver is? What Oliver is?'

Claire nodded. 'Shane must have told him. He knows.'

'And Oliver knows who Frank Collins is,' Hess said. 'He'd know him on sight. So we've got two mortal enemies sitting down together, and we don't know why. When was it, Claire?'

'Right before Brandon was killed.'

Another silence, and this one was deep. Lowe and Hess were staring at each other. Richard was frowning. After a long moment, Lowe said slowly, 'Anybody want to take a bet?'

'Spit it out, Detective,' Richard said. 'If you know something, say so.'

'I'm not saying I know. I'm saying I've got a hundred dollars that says Oliver knew all about Frank Collins rolling back into town, and he used Frank to get rid of a troublemaking child-molesting bastard who'd outlived his usefulness.'

Claire asked, 'Why didn't he just kill him, if he wanted him dead?'

'Vampires do not kill each other. They just don't. So this way, he and Frank both get what they want. Oliver gets Morganville in chaos, Amelie losing control and I heard about the attack on her downtown. Maybe Oliver was hoping they'd take her out, leave him in charge. Brandon was probably a small price to pay.' He paused for thought. 'I'm guessing here, but I'll bet Oliver made Frank a whole lot of promises he never intended to keep. Brandon was a sign of good faith, to get Frank to commit. And holding on to Shane was insurance. No way would Oliver have let Frank keep on killing, though. Chaos is one thing. A bloodbath is another.'

'How does this help?' Michael asked. 'We still don't know where they are.'

Hess reached in his pocket and pulled out a folding pocket map – a Morganville map. It was marked in grids, colour-coded: yellow for the university, pale red for the human enclaves, blue for the vampires. The centre of town, Founder's Square, was black. 'Here,' he said, and walked to the dining room table. Michael moved his guitar case out of the way, and Hess spread the map out. 'Travis, you know who owns what near the square, right?'

'Yeah.' Lowe leant forward, fished some reading glasses out of his coat pocket, and looked closer. 'OK, these are warehouses here. Vallery Kosomov owns some of them. Most of these belong to Josefina Lowell.'

'Anything owned by Oliver down there?'

'Why down there?' Lowe asked.

'You want to answer that one, Officer Morrell?' Hess asked. Richard edged in to consider the map, and marked out something with his finger.

'Underground runs right through here,' he said.

'This is the only area of the Underground where we *didn't* see the van come and go.'

'Which tells you what?' Hess asked.

'*Crap.* They were faking the video. Showing us where they weren't, sending us all over town. And hiding where they were.' Richard looked up at Hess, then Lowe. 'Oliver's warehouses are off of Bond Street. It's mostly storage.'

'Gentlemen, we have exactly' – Hess consulted his watch – 'fifty-two minutes. Let's get moving.'

They all moved to the door, and it was going fine until Richard Morrell glanced at Claire and Eve, put his arm up like a barricade, and said, 'Oh, I don't think so, kids.'

'We've got a right to—'

'Yeah, I'm getting all choked up about your rights, Eve. You stay here.'

'Michael's going!' Claire said, and winced, because she sounded like a disappointed little kid instead of the responsible, trustworthy adult she'd intended.

Richard rolled his eyes nearly as well as Eve. 'You sound like my sister,' he said. 'That's really not attractive. And it's not going to work. Michael can take care of himself on a whole bunch of levels you can't, kid, so you. Stay. Here.'

And Hess and Lowe backed him up.

Michael just looked vaguely sorry to be in the middle of it, but relieved all the same that they weren't going. It was Michael who took Eve's car keys from the tray on the hall table, where she always left them. 'Just in case,' he said, and dropped them, in his pocket. 'Not that I don't trust you or anything, just that I know you never listen to me.'

He slammed the door on Eve's frustrated cry.

And that, Claire thought, was that.

'I can't believe they left us,' Claire said numbly, staring at the door. Eve kicked it hard enough to leave a black mark on the wood and stalked away, into the living room. She stood at the window until the police cruiser pulled away from the curb and glided off into the night. Then she turned and looked at Claire.

She was smiling.

'What?' Claire asked, confused, as Eve grinned wider. 'Are we happy about getting left behind?'

'Yes, we're happy. Because now I know where they're going,' Eve said, and reached in her pocket. She pulled out a second key ring and shook it with a merry, metallic jingle. 'And I've got a spare set of keys. Let's go save their asses.'

It was a good thing the Morganville police force was otherwise occupied, because Claire thought that Eve probably broke every traffic law that was on the books. Twice. She couldn't bring herself to open her eyes very often – just peeks every other block or so – but it seemed like they were going very, very fast, and taking corners at speeds that would have given a driver's-ed instructor a heart attack. Not much traffic, at least, in this predawn darkness. That was something, Claire supposed. She clung to the stiff aftermarket shoulder belt as Eve screeched the big black Cadillac through a hairpin right-hand turn, then another, and into one of the storm-drain tunnels.

'Oh God,' Claire whispered. If she'd been in danger of motion sickness before, it was ten times worse in the tunnel. She squeezed her eyes tight shut and tried to breathe. Between the dark, the panic, and the closed-in spaces, it wasn't exactly her best rescue attempt ever.

'Almost there,' Eve said, but Claire thought she said it to herself. Eve wasn't calm, either. That was...not comforting. 'Left turn up ahead...'

'That's not a turn!' Claire yelped, and braced herself against the dashboard as Eve slammed on the brakes and the big car shimmied and sprayed shallow water as it skidded. 'That's a dead end!'

'Nope, that's a turn,' Eve panted, fought the wheel, and somehow – Claire had no idea how – got the car to make the impossible corner with only a little bang and scrape up against the concrete wall. 'Ouch. That's gonna leave a mark.' And she laughed, high and wild, and hit the gas again. 'Hold on, Claire Bear! Next stop, Crazytown!'

Claire thought they were already there, actually.

She lost track of the nauseatingly twisty course they were following. In fact, she started to think that Eve didn't know where she was going at all, and was just making random turns hoping to find an exit, when suddenly the tunnel ended, and the car hit an upslope, and they rocketed out into the open darkness again.

'Bond Street,' Eve said. 'Home of upscale vampire shopping, fine restaurants, and...oh shit.'

She hit the brakes and brought them to a fast, complete stop that tossed Claire painfully against the restraints. Not that Claire noticed all that much, because like Eve, she was pretty much horror-struck by what she was seeing ahead.

'Tell me that's not the place,' she said.

Because if it was, the place was on fire.

Richard Morrell's police cruiser was parked at the wrought-iron gates, its doors hanging open. The guys had bailed out fast. Eve moved the Caddy closer, then shut off the engine, and the two girls looked in dawning horror at the flames shooting out from the windows and roof of the big stone building.

'Where's the fire department?' Claire asked. 'Where are the cops?'

'I don't know, but we can't count on help. Not tonight.' Eve opened the door on her side and stepped out. 'Do you see them? Anywhere?'

'No!' Claire flinched as glass exploded from one of the upper windows. 'Do you?'

'We have to go in!'

'*Go in?*' Claire was about to point out how crazy that was, but then she saw someone inside the gates, lying very still. 'Eve!' She ran to the gate and rattled it, but it was locked tight.

'Up!' Eve yelled, and scrambled up on the wrought iron. Claire followed. It was slippery and sharp, and cut her hands, but somehow she made it to the top, then dangled from the crossbar and let herself fall on the other side. She hit hard, and rolled clumsily back to her feet. Eve, who'd come down a lot more gracefully, was already moving towards the guy lying on the ground...

...who was one of Frank's guys. Dead. Eve looked up at Claire wordlessly and showed her the blood on her hand, shaking her head. 'He was shot,' she said. 'Oh, God. They're inside, Claire. *Michael's inside!*'

Only he wasn't, because between one blink and the next, as Eve tried to rush into the open smoke-filled door, Michael plunged out of it, and he grabbed her and hauled her back. 'No!' he yelled. 'What the hell are you doing here?'

'Michael!' Eve turned and threw herself into his arms. 'Where's Monica?'

'In there.' Michael looked terrible – smoke-stained and red-eyed, with little burnt patches in his shirt. 'The others went in to get her. I…I had to come out.'

Vampires could be killed by fire. Claire remembered that from the list she'd made shortly after moving to Morganville. She couldn't believe he'd risked his just barely begun life to get as far as he'd gone.

'Damn right you can't!' Eve yelled. 'If you go and get yourself killed for *Monica Morrell*, I'll never forgive you!'

'It wouldn't be for Monica,' he said. 'You know that.'

They stared at the flames, waiting. Seconds ticked by, and there was no sign of anyone: no Monica, and no cops, either. The horizon was getting lighter in the east, Claire realised, going from dark blue to twilight.

Dawn was coming, and they were almost out of time to get Monica to Founder's Square, if they could get her at all.

If she was still alive.

'Sun's coming!' Michael shouted over the roar of the fire.

Claire didn't ask how he knew. He'd known when he was a ghost; she figured it was probably the same time sense as a vampire's. Made sense. It would be a survival trait, to know when to get under cover. 'You need to get out of here!' she yelled back. A thick, black billow of smoke belched out of the doorway and made her double over, coughing. They all retreated. 'Michael, you have to go! Now!'

'No!'

'At least get in the police car!' Eve pointed to it, on the other side of the fence. 'Tinted windows! We'll wait here, I swear!'

'I'm not leaving you!'

The sun crested the far horizon in a tiny sliver of gold, and where it touched him, Michael's pale skin started to sizzle and smoke. He hissed in pain and slapped at it. A pale, licking flame took hold on his hand.

Claire and Eve screamed, and Eve tackled him into the shadows. That helped, but not much; he was still burning, just more slowly. Michael groaned and looked like he was trying not to scream.

'Claire!' Eve tossed her the car keys. 'Ram the gate! Get it open! Do it!'

'But...your car!'

'It's just a freakin' *car*! Come on, move it! We'll never get him over the fence!'

Claire scrambled back over the slick, warm iron of the fence, slicing her hands in two or three more places, and barely felt the impact when she fell this time. She was up and running for the Caddy –

– and then she changed course, threw herself into the driver's seat of the police car, and started it with the keys hanging from the ignition.

This had to be some kind of crime, right? But in an emergency…

She backed it up almost to the end of the block, put the car in drive, and pressed the gas pedal to the floor.

She screamed and managed to hang on to the wheel somehow as the gate rushed up at her; there was a bone-jarring *crunch*, and she slammed on the brakes. The gates flew open, bent and mangled, and the police car gave a roar and died, sputtering. Claire got out and opened the back door as Eve rushed Michael towards her; Michael dived in, and Claire slammed the door behind him. Eve was right – the windows were heavily tinted, probably to protect vampire cops from the sun. He'd be OK in there.

Claire hoped.

'What about the others?' she yelled at Eve, who shook her head. They both turned to look at the warehouse, which was fully on fire now, shooting flames twenty or thirty feet into the morning sky. 'Oh God. Oh *God*! We have to do something!'

Just then, two figures staggered out of the side door, bathed in black smoke, and collapsed to the pavement. Eve and Claire dashed to them. For a second, Claire didn't even know who they were, so blackened were they by smoke, and then she recognised Joe Hess under the grime.

The other one was Travis Lowe. They were both

coughing and retching up black stuff.

'Get up!' Eve ordered, and grabbed Hess's arm to drag him away from the building. 'Come on, get up!'

He did, weaving badly, and Claire managed to get Lowe to do the same. They made it about halfway to the police car, and then Lowe sat down in the open parking lot, coughing his lungs out, gasping. Claire crouched down next to him, wishing she could do something, wishing the damn fire department would come, wishing...

'We're too late,' Eve said. She was watching the sun climb over the horizon. 'It's dawn. We're too late.'

Hess gasped, 'No. Not yet. Richard...had Monica—'

'What? Where?' Claire spun to look at him. Hess was nearly as badly off as his partner, but he was able to form words, at least. 'They're still alive?'

'Should have been right behind us,' Lowe wheezed.

Claire didn't think about it. If she'd given herself time, she would have talked herself out of it, but her brain was on hold and all that was left was instinct. It wasn't just that there was still hope to save Shane; it was that she couldn't leave anybody to die like that.

She just couldn't.

She heard Eve yelling her name, but she didn't stop, couldn't stop; she kept running until she was in the smoke, and then she dropped to her knees and crawled into the hot, suffocating darkness. She flailed with her hands, trying to find something, anything, and kept her eyes tight shut. She could barely breathe, even close to the ground, and every breath she did manage to take was tainted and toxic, more harm than good.

OK, this was a really bad idea.

She didn't dare crawl too far; in the chaos and darkness, she'd never find her way out again. Something fell near her with a huge crash, and fire roared overhead. Claire went flat on the floor and curled into a ball, then – when she wasn't roasted or crushed – forced herself to keep moving. *One minute. One minute and then straight back out.*

She wasn't sure she could survive a minute in here.

Her searching fingers brushed cloth. Claire opened her eyes and was instantly sorry, because the smoke burnt and stung, and she couldn't see a thing anyway. But she had her hand on cloth, and yes, that was a leg, a pant leg...

And that was a hand that turned and gripped hers. An unrecognizable voice rasped, 'Get Monica out!'

A new burst of fire lit up the darkness, and she saw Richard Morrell lying there, curled around his sister. Protecting her. Monica looked up, and there was sheer terror in her face. She reached out blindly. Claire took her hands and pulled her back the way she'd come in, straight back. She felt the draft of air coming in the door, and that helped guide her. 'Grab your brother!' she yelled. Monica took Richard's hand, and Claire hauled with all her strength, dragging them both.

She didn't make it.

She wasn't sure how it happened exactly... One minute she was pulling; the next she was down, and she couldn't breathe, couldn't stop coughing. *Oh no. No no no.* But she couldn't get up, couldn't force her body to move.

Shane...

Somebody grabbed her by the ankles and yanked, hard. Claire had just enough presence of mind left to hold on to Monica's wrist.

'Shit!' Eve was groaning, coughing, and all of a sudden Claire was outside lying in the sun, watching black smoke billow into the air. 'Claire! Breathe, dammit!'

It wasn't so much breathing as hacking up a lung, but at least air was moving in and out. She heard someone else coughing next to her, and raised her head to see Monica on her hands and knees, spitting out black phlegm.

And now Eve was dragging Richard Morrell out by his feet.

Eve collapsed next to them, coughing, too, and somewhere on the distant edges of the fire's roar, as if somebody had flipped a switch, Claire heard sirens. Oh, *now* they were coming. Perfect. Someone's tax dollars at work, even if it wasn't hers...

Claire rolled painfully to her feet. There were burnt patches in her clothes, and she smelt burnt hair, too. She was going to hurt later, but for now, she was just glad to be alive.

'Get Monica,' she wheezed at Eve, and grabbed one of Monica's arms. Eve grabbed the other, and they half dragged her across the parking lot to the shattered gate. Hess and Lowe were leaning up against the police car. Lowe, incredibly, was smoking a cigarette, but he dropped it and managed to get to his feet to stumble over to where Richard was lying, and help him up.

'Michael!' Eve rapped on the window of the police car. Claire blinked her watering eyes; she could just barely see his shadow through the tinted glass. 'Move over!' Eve opened the back door carefully, making sure he was out of the direct sun, and loaded Monica into the back seat, then got in with them. Monica made a groan of protest. 'Oh, shut up already and be grateful.'

Claire went around to the front seat, got in, and asked blankly, 'Who's driving?'

Richard Morrell slid in behind the wheel. 'Joe

and Travis will stay here,' he said. 'I'll bring you back for your car. Everybody, hold on.'

As Richard backed the car out and then accelerated towards Founder's Square, lights and sirens going, Monica managed to get her first coherent words out between coughs.

'Claire...bitch!' Her voice sounded raw and hoarse. 'You...think this...makes us...friends?'

'God, no,' Claire said. 'But I think you kinda owe me.'

Monica just glared.

'I'll call it even if Shane walks away.'

Monica coughed again. 'You wish.'

CHAPTER TWELVE

Founder's Square was insane. Richard had to stop the car almost a block away, just outside of a cordon of police cars with flashing lights. Claire got out and had another coughing fit, bad enough that Eve patted her nervously on the back and did the talking for her to the grim-faced uniformed policewoman standing guard at the barricade. 'We need to see Mayor Morrell,' she said.

'Mayor's busy,' the policewoman said. 'You'll have to wait.'

'But—'

Monica got out of the back seat, and the cop's eyes widened. 'Miss Morrell?' Well, Claire admitted, the smoke-stained scarecrow with frizzed hair didn't look much like the usual Monica. She secretly hoped somebody would take pictures. And put them on the Internet.

When Richard got out, as well, the policewoman

gulped. 'Jesus. Sorry, sir. Hang on, I'll get someone here.' The policewoman got on her radio and passed on information; while they waited, she passed out bottled water from her squad car. Claire took two bottles and ducked back into the patrol car's back seat, where Michael was sitting, eyes shut tight. He stirred and looked at her when she called his name. He didn't look good – paper pale, burnt in places, and apparently sick, too. She handed him the water. 'I don't know if it'll help, but...?'

Michael nodded and gulped some down. Claire cracked her own bottle and swallowed, nearly moaning in ecstasy. Nothing had ever tasted so good in Claire's entire life as that lukewarm, flat water washing away the smoke from her throat.

'I thought—' Michael licked his lips and let his head flop back against the seat. 'I thought I'd be stronger. I've seen other vampires in the daytime.'

'Older ones,' Claire said. 'I think it must take time. Amelie can even walk around in the daylight, but she's really old. You just have to be patient, Michael.'

'Patient?' He closed his eyes. 'Claire. Today's the first day I've been outside of my house for nearly a year, my best friend's still under a death sentence, and you're telling me to be *patient*?'

It did sound stupid, when he put it that way. She drank her water silently, wiping sweat from her forehead and then grimacing at the sooty mess.

It's going to be all right, she told herself. *We'll get Shane. We'll all go home. It'll be fine.*

Which even now she knew wasn't very likely, but she had to have something to hold on to.

It was only about a five-minute wait, and the mayor came himself, trailed by an anxious entourage and two uniformed paramedics, who swooped in on Monica and Richard, ignoring Claire and Eve. 'Hey, we're fine, thanks,' Eve said sarcastically. 'Flesh wounds. Look, we kept our part of the bargain. We want Shane. Right now.'

The mayor, hugging his soot-stained daughter, barely even glanced their way. 'You're too late,' he said.

Claire's knees went out from under her. It came to her in a blinding rush – the fire, the smoke, the terror. *Shane.* Oh no, no, it couldn't be...

The mayor must have realised what she was thinking, and what Eve was thinking, too, from the expressions on their faces, because he looked momentarily annoyed.

'No, not that,' he said. 'Richard said you were en route. I said I'd wait. I don't break my word.'

'Much,' Eve muttered, and covered it with a fake cough. 'OK, then why are we too late?'

'He's already gone,' the mayor said. 'His father staged an attack just before dawn, when our attention was on the warehouse fire. Broke Shane and the other one out of the cages, killed five of my men. They were heading out of town, but we've got them cornered this time. It'll all be over soon.'

'But...Shane!' Claire looked at him pleadingly. 'We kept our part of the bargain – please, can't you just let him go?'

Mayor Morrell frowned at her. 'Our agreement was that I'd let him go if you brought my daughter back. Well, he's free. If he gets himself killed trying to save his no-good father, that's no business of mine,' the mayor said. He put his arm around Monica and Richard. 'Come on, kids. You can tell me what happened.'

'*I'll* tell you what happened,' Eve said angrily. 'We saved both of their lives. You can thank us for that anytime, by the way.'

From the glare he threw Eve, the mayor really didn't find that funny. 'If you hadn't put them in danger in the first place, none of this would have happened,' he said. 'Consider yourselves lucky that I don't toss you in jail for aiding and abetting a vampire hunter. Now, if you want my advice, go home.' He kissed his daughter's filthy hair. 'Come on, princess.'

'Dad,' Richard said. 'She's right. They did save our lives.'

The mayor looked more than just annoyed now, at this minor rebellion in the family ranks. 'Son, I know that you may feel some gratitude towards these girls, but—'

'Just tell us where Shane is,' Claire said. 'Please. That's all we want.'

The two Morrell men exchanged long looks, and then Richard said, 'You know the old hospital? The one on Grand Street?'

Eve nodded. 'Our Lady? I thought they tore that thing down.'

'Scheduled for demolition at the end of the week,' Richard said. 'I'll take you there.'

Claire almost cried; she was so relieved. Not that the problem was solved – it wasn't – but at least they had another step to take.

'Richard,' the mayor said. 'You don't owe them anything.'

'I do, though.' Richard looked from Eve, to Claire. 'And I won't forget it.'

Eve grinned. 'Awww. Don't worry, Officer. We won't let you.'

There were vampires out in the daytime. Claire figured that was unusual, but she realised just how unusual when Richard Morrell, slowing the police car to a crawl, whistled. 'Oliver's called out the troops,' he said. 'Not good for your friend. Or his father.'

The streets around the massive bulk of the old hospital were lined with cars…big cars, dark-tinted windows. Lots of police cars, too, but it was those other autos that looked…menacing.

As did the people standing in shadows, surrounding the building. Some wore heavy coats and hats, even in the oppressive heat. There had to be at least a hundred gathered, and a lot of them were vampires.

And right in the centre, standing right at the edge of the border of sunlight and shadow, stood Oliver. He was wearing a long black leather coat, and a leather broad-brimmed hat, and his hands were cased in gloves.

'Oh, man. I don't think you guys are going to do any good here,' Richard said. Oliver's head turned towards them, and he stepped out into the sunlight. The vampire approached, moving at a slow, leisurely pace. 'Maybe I ought to take you on home.'

In less time than it took to tell Richard no, Oliver had crossed the open space and jerked open the back door of the police cruiser. 'Maybe you should join us instead,' Oliver said, and bared his teeth in a smile. 'Ah, Michael. Out of the house at last, I see. Felicitations on your birthday. I would suggest, for your own safety, that you stay strictly in the shadows this morning. Not that you'll have the strength to do anything else.'

And he grabbed Claire, who was sitting nearest the door, by the throat.

Claire heard Michael and Eve yelling, and felt Eve trying to hold on to her, but there was no way

Eve could match Oliver's strength. He simply pulled Claire out of the car like a rag doll, his fingers wrapped cruelly tight around her throat, and dragged her out into the street.

'Shane! Shane Collins!' he shouted. 'I have something for you! I want you to watch this very carefully!'

Claire grabbed at his hand with both of her own, trying to pry his grip free, but it was no good. He knew just how tightly to hold on without *quite* crushing her throat or cutting off her breathing. She fought back another panicked bout of coughing, and tried to think of something, anything, to do.

'I'm going to kill this girl,' Oliver continued, 'unless she swears herself to me and my service, in front of all of these witnesses. Shane, you can save her by making the same deal. You have two minutes to consider your decision.'

'Why?' Claire whispered. It came out as a mouse squeak, barely audible. Oliver, who was staring at the decaying facade of the old hospital, with its weather-stained weeping angels and moulding baroque stonework, turned his attention briefly to her. The morning was warm and cloudless, the sun a hot brass penny in a bright blue sky. It seemed wrong for a vampire to be out here.

He wasn't even sweating.

'Why what, Claire? It's an imprecise question.

You have a better mind than that.'

She fought for breath, helplessly clawing at his fingers. 'Why...kill Brandon?'

He lost his smile, and his eyes turned wary. 'Clever,' he said. 'Cleverness may not be good for you after all. The question you should be asking is, why do I want your service?'

'All right,' she wheezed. 'Why?'

'Because Amelie has some use for you,' he said. 'And I am not accustomed to giving Amelie what she wants. It has nothing to do with you, and everything to do with history. But, sadly, I'm making it your problem. Cheer up; if your boyfriend swears on your behalf, I'll keep him alive. Let you see him from time to time. Star-crossed lovers are so entertaining.'

Amelie didn't seem to have much of a use for her, Claire reflected, but she didn't argue about it. Couldn't, in fact. Couldn't do much of anything but stand on tiptoe, gag for each breath, and hope that somehow, she'd figure a way out of this stupid situation that she'd gotten herself into. Again.

'One minute!' Oliver called. There was movement inside of the building, flickers at the windows. 'Well. It appears we have a domestic disturbance.'

What he meant was, Shane's dad was kicking the crap out of him. Claire struggled to see what was going on, but Oliver's grip was too tight. She could see only from the corner of her eye, and what she could see wasn't good. Shane was in the doorway of the hospital, trying to get free, but someone dragged him back.

'Thirty seconds!' Oliver announced. 'Well, this is coming down to the wire. I'm a bit surprised, Claire. The boy really is fighting for the chance to save you. You should be very impressed.'

'You should take your hands off of her, Oliver,' said a voice from behind them, accompanied by the unmistakable sound of a shotgun being pumped. 'Seriously. I'm not in a good mood, I'm tired, and I just want to go home.'

'Richard,' Oliver said, and turned to regard him. 'You look like hell, my friend. Don't you think you should go be with your family, instead of worrying about these…outcasts?'

Richard stepped forward and put the shotgun under Oliver's chin. 'Yeah, I should. But I owe them. I said—'

Oliver backhanded him. Richard went flying and rolled to a limp stop on the pavement, the shotgun clattering to the ground.

'I heard you the first time,' Oliver said mildly. 'My, you do make friends in strange places, Claire. I suppose you'll have to tell me all about that later.' He raised his voice. 'Time's up! Claire Danvers, do you swear your life, your blood, and your service to me, now and for your lifetime, that I may command you in all things? Do say yes, my dear, because if you don't, I'll simply close my hand. It's a very messy way to go. Takes minutes for you to choke to death, and Shane gets to watch the whole thing.'

Claire couldn't believe she'd ever thought Oliver was kind, or reasonable, or *human*. She stared at his cold, cold eyes, and saw a thin, blood-coloured trickle of sweat run down his face under the hat.

She was no longer standing on tiptoe, she realised. Her feet were flat on the ground.

He's getting weaker!

Not that it would do her any good.

'Wait.' Shane's voice. Claire breathed in a shallow gasp and saw him limping across the open ground from the hospital building towards her. His face was bloody, and there was something wrong with his ankle, but he wasn't stopping. 'You want a servant? How about me?'

'Ah. The hero appears.' Oliver turned towards him, and as he did, Claire got a better look at Shane. She saw the fear in his eyes, and her heart just broke for him. He'd been through so much; he didn't deserve this, too. Not this. 'I thought you might say that. What if I take you both, then? I'm a generous, fair boss. Ask Eve.'

'Don't believe anything he says. He's working with your dad,' Claire wheezed. 'He's been working with him the whole time. He arranged for Brandon to be killed. Shane—'

'I know all that,' Shane said. 'Politics, right, Oliver? Mind games, you and Amelie. We're just pawns to you. *Well, she's not a pawn.* Let her go.'

'All right, my young knight,' Oliver said, and smiled. 'If you insist.'

He was going to kill her, he really was...

Shane had something in his hand, and he threw it right in Oliver's eyes.

It looked like water, but it must have burnt like acid. Oliver let go of Claire and screamed, stumbling backward, tearing the hat from his head and bending over, clawing at his face...

Shane grabbed Claire's hand, and pulled her with him in a limping run.

Straight into the old hospital building.

With a roar, the cops, the vampires, and their servants came rushing across the open sunlit parking lot. Some of the vampires went down, hammered by the hot sun, but not all of them. Not nearly all of them.

Shane pushed Claire through the doorway and yelled, 'Now!'

A huge, heavy wooden desk dropped down on its side, blocking the doorway with a crash, and then another one dropped on top of it from the balcony above.

Shane, breathing hard, grabbed Claire and

pulled her into a hug. 'You OK?' he asked. 'No fang marks or anything?'

'I'm fine,' she gasped. 'Oh, *God*, Shane!'

'So this charcoal look, that's just fashion. You're OK.'

She clung to him tightly. 'There was a fire.'

'No kidding. Dad makes one hell of a diversion.' Shane swallowed and pushed her back. 'Did you get Monica out of there? Dad told me – well, he meant to leave her in there.' She nodded. Shane's eyes glittered with relief. 'I tried to stop this, Claire. He won't listen to me.'

'He never did. Didn't you know that?'

He shrugged, and looked around. 'Funny, I keep thinking he will. Where's Eve? In the police car?'

With Michael, she almost said, and realised it probably wasn't the best moment to announce that Shane's best friend was now a full-fledged vampire. Shane was just barely warming up to the whole ghost issue. 'Yeah. In the police car.' She took a corner of his shirt and lifted it to wipe at the blood on his face.

'Ouch.'

'Where's your dad?'

'They've been moving out,' he said. 'He tried to get me to go. I said I'd damn well go when I had you back. So... I guess now would be a good time.'

There was a clatter of metal off to the side, and Claire's world gradually expanded past the miracle of seeing Shane again to take in the room where she stood. It was a big lobby, floored in scarred, ugly green plastic tile. What little furniture remained in the room was mostly bolted down, like the reception desk; the walls were black and furry with thick streaks of mould, and lights hung at odd angles overhead, clearly ready to fall at the slightest jolt. There was a creaky-looking second floor overlooking the lobby, and around it dented filing cabinets blocked the windows.

It smelt like dead things – worse, it *felt* that way, like terrible things had been done here over the years. Claire was reminded of the Glass House, and the energy stored inside of it...What kind of energy was stored here? And what had it come from? She shuddered even thinking about it.

'They're coming!' someone called from up above, and Shane raised a hand in acknowledgment. 'Time to get the hell out, man!'

'Coming.' He grabbed Claire's hand. 'Come on. We have a way out.'

'We do?'

'Morgue tunnels.'

'What?'

'Trust me.'

'I do, but...*morgue tunnels*?'

'Yeah,' Shane said. 'They were sealed off in the mid-fifties, but we opened up one end. It's not on the maps. Nobody's watching it.'

'Then who's in here with you?'

'Couple of Dad's guys,' Shane said.

'That's it?' She was horrified. 'You know there are about a hundred angry people outside, right? And they have guns?'

Behind them, the battering at the doors strengthened. The desks blocking access grated across the floor, one torturous inch at a time. She could see daylight spilling inside.

'We'd better move,' Shane said. 'Come on.'

Claire let him tow her along, and looked back over her shoulder to see the desks shuddering under the impact of bodies. They slid across the tile with another groan, and one of them cracked in half, drawers spilling out in a noisy clatter.

Shane waved to a big guy in black leather as they passed, and the three of them ran down the second-floor hallway. It was dark, filthy, and scary, but not as scary as the sounds coming from the lobby behind them. Shane had a flashlight, and he switched it on to pick out obstacles in the way – fallen IV stands, an abandoned, dust-covered wheelchair, a gurney tipped over on its side. 'Faster,' she gasped, because she heard a final crash from the lobby.

They were inside.

Claire didn't think more than half the vampires had made it successfully across the sun-drenched parking lot, but those who'd been strong enough were inside now, and it was nice and dark for them. No contest.

Shane knew where he was going. He turned right at a corner, then left, yanked up a fire exit door, and pushed Claire inside. 'Up!' he said. 'Two flights, then go left!'

There were things on the stairs; Claire couldn't see them very well, even in the glow of Shane's flashlight, but they smelt dead, sickly rotten. She tried not to breathe, avoided the sticky puddles of dried – whatever that was, she couldn't think of it as blood – and kept running up the steps. First landing, then another set of stairs, these clear except for some broken bottles she vaulted over.

She yanked the fire door two flights up, and nearly dislocated her shoulder.

It was blocked.

'Shane!'

He pushed her out of the way, grabbed the handle, and pulled. 'Shit!' He kicked it furiously, looked blank for a second, then turned to the next flight of stairs. 'One more! Go!'

The fifth-floor door was open, and Claire darted through it into the dark.

Her foot caught on something, and she toppled foward, hit the floor, and rolled. Shane's flashlight bounced a ball of light towards her, lighting up scarred linoleum tile, stacks of leaning boxes...

...and a skeleton. Claire yelped and scrambled

back from it, then realised that it was one of those medical teaching skeletons, scattered out on the floor from where she'd tripped over it.

Shane grabbed her by the arm, hauled her up, and pulled her along. Claire looked over her shoulder. She couldn't see the biker guy, the one who'd been following them. Where had he—

She heard a scream.

Oh.

Shane hurried her down the long hall, then turned left and pulled Claire after him. There was another set of fire stairs. He opened the door, and they raced down one flight.

This exit was open. Shane pulled her out into another long, dark hallway and moved fast, counting doorways under his breath.

He stopped in front of number thirteen.

'Inside,' he said, and kicked it open. Metal gave with a shriek, and the door flew back to slam against tile. Something broke with a clatter like dropped plates.

Claire felt a chill take hold, because she had walked into what looked like a morgue. Stainless steel trays, stainless steel lockers on the wall, some gaping open to reveal sliding trays.

Yes, she was pretty sure it was the morgue. And pretty sure it was going to feature prominently in her nightmares from now on, provided she ever got to sleep again.

'This way,' Shane said, and pulled open what looked like a laundry chute. 'Claire.'

'Oh, hell, *no*!' Because if she hated tight spaces, there couldn't be anything much worse than this. She had no idea how long it was, but it was small, it was dark, and had he said something about *morgue tunnels*? Was this a body chute? Maybe there was a corpse still stuck in it! Oh God...

There were noises coming from outside the mob, coming fast.

'Sorry, no time,' Shane said, and picked her up and dumped her into the chute feet-first.

She tried not to scream. She thought she might have actually succeeded as she slid helplessly through the dark down a cold, metal tunnel meant only for the dead.

CHAPTER THIRTEEN

She landed hard, on stone, in the dark, and suppressed a burning need to whimper. A hand closed on her arm and helped her up. She heard a thumping clatter behind her, and got out of the way just in time as Shane – she thought it was Shane, anyway – tumbled out of the chute after her.

And the lights came on.

Well, not *lights* exactly...one light, and it was a flashlight.

And Shane's dad was holding it.

He took one fast, cold look at his son, then one at Claire, and said, 'Where's Des?'

Shane looked shocked. 'Dad – you were supposed to go! That was the whole point!'

'Where the hell is Des?'

'He's gone!' Shane shouted. 'Dammit, Dad—'

Frank Collins looked blackly furious, face twisting, and he swung the flashlight away from them. Claire blinked spots away, and saw that he was aiming it at two of his guys standing in the dark. 'Right,' he said. 'Let's do this.'

'Do what?' Shane demanded, getting to his feet. He winced as he put his weight on his wounded ankle. 'Dad, what the hell is going on? You said you were leaving!'

'Didn't kill enough vampires to leave,' Frank Collins said. 'But I'm about to even the score.'

The two guys he had trained his light on were crouched next to a makeshift circuit board built out of what looked like old computer parts. It was hooked up to a car battery. One of the two guys held two wires by the insulated parts, but the tips were bare copper, freshly stripped.

Things fell together.

Shane's dad had used him, again. Used him as bait, letting him think he was being the hero, distracting the vampires to give his dad time to escape.

Used him to get a large number of vampires in one place. But they weren't just vampires; there were people there, too. Cops, and wannabe vampires. And people who were just there because they owed Oliver.

It was cold-blooded murder.

Richard had said it. *Demolition this week*. The explosives were already in place.

'They're going to blow the building!' Claire

screamed, and lunged. She couldn't fight the bikers, but she didn't need to.

All she had to do was yank at the wires under the circuit board.

They gave with a blue white *pop*, and she was lucky not to be fried. One of the bikers reached her then, grabbed her, and threw her back, looking at the mess and shaking his head. 'Got a problem!' he yelled. 'She trashed the board! Gonna take time to rewire!'

Frank's face went scarlet with fury, and he ran towards her, fist in the air. 'You stupid little—'

Shane caught his fist in an open palm and held it there. 'Don't,' he said. 'Enough, Dad. No more.'

Frank tried to hit him. Shane ducked. He caught the second blow in an open palm again.

The third one, he blocked, and punched back. Just once.

Frank went down, flat on his ass, something like fear in his face.

'Enough,' Shane said. Claire had never seen him look taller, or more frightening. 'You've still got time to run, Dad. You'd better do it while you can. They'll figure out where we are soon, and you know what? I'm not dying for you. Not anymore.'

Frank's mouth opened, then closed. He wiped blood from his mouth, staring at Shane, as he got to his feet.

'I thought you understood,' he said. 'I thought you *wanted*—'

'You know what I want, Dad?' Shane asked. 'I want my life back. I want my girlfriend. And I want you to leave and never come back.'

Frank's eyes went flat, like a shark's. 'Your mother's turning over in her grave, watching you betray your own kind. Your own *father*. Siding with the parasites that infest this sick town.'

Shane didn't answer him. The two of them stared at each other in tense, angry silence for a few seconds, and then Claire heard metal clattering from up above. She tugged on Shane's arm urgently. 'I think they found the chute,' she said. 'Shane—'

Shane's dad said, 'I should have left you in the damn cage to fry, you ungrateful little bastard. You're no son of mine.'

'Hallelujah,' Shane said softly. 'Free at last.'

His dad turned off the flashlight, and Claire heard running footsteps in the dark.

Shane grabbed Claire's sweating hand, and they ran the opposite direction, with Shane breathlessly counting steps, until there was a golden glow of light at the end of the tunnel.

Shane wanted to run, but escape was impossible. Unless they made it out of Morganville, and even then, Claire understood – finally – that the vampires wouldn't let them leave. Not with what they'd done, or nearly done.

She needed to make it right.

Claire worked it out in her head before she said anything to him; Shane was talking in a breathless monologue, spinning a plan to steal a car, head out of town, maybe out of state.

Claire kept quiet until she saw the cherry red and blue flashers of a Morganville police cruiser coming down the darkened street, and then she let go of Shane's hand and said, 'Trust me.'

'What?'

'Just trust me.'

She stepped out in front of the police car, which came to a fast, controlled stop. A floodlight blinded her, and she stood still for it. She sensed Shane retreating, and said, sharply, 'Shane, no! Stay where you are!'

'What the hell are you doing?'

'Surrendering,' she said, and put her hands in the air. 'Come on. You, too.'

She didn't think he would, for a long terrifying second, and then he stepped out into the street with her, put his hands up, and laced his fingers behind his head. The police cruiser's doors popped open, and Shane dropped to his knees. Claire blinked at him, then followed suit.

She was on the ground in seconds, pinned by someone's hot, hard hand, and she heard a male voice say, 'Heller here. We've got Danvers and the Collins kid. They're alive.'

She didn't hear the reply, but she was too busy

wondering if she'd made an awful mistake as cold steel handcuffs clicked shut around her wrists. The policeman hauled her upright by her elbow, and she winced at the pull on her sore muscles. Next to her, Shane was getting the same treatment. He wasn't resisting. He looked...tense.

'It's OK,' she told him. 'Trust me.'

His eyes were wild, but he nodded.

Better be right, she thought, and swallowed hard as they were shoved inside the back of the police car.

The police didn't talk to her or Shane at all. The ride was short, and silent, and when the cruiser pulled into the parking garage at City Hall, there was a welcoming committee standing there waiting. Claire almost cried at the sight of Michael and Eve – smoke-stained but standing side by side, holding hands. They looked worried. Next to them was Richard Morrell, with a bandage on his head.

And Mayor Morrell. She couldn't read his expression at all – annoyed, but she thought that was usual for him. Claire caught a glimpse of red hair, and saw Sam leaning against a pillar up on the dock. Apart from Michael, he was the only vampire present. At least, the only one she could see.

The cruiser's doors were opened, and Claire slid out. The mayor looked her over, then Shane. His eyes narrowed.

'My sources say somebody set up a spark board down under the hospital,' he said. 'Connected up the wires and got ready to blow the building. Looks like somebody trashed it before anything happened.'

Shane said, 'Claire pulled the wires. My dad was going to blow it and kill everybody inside.'

The Morrells, father and son, exchanged a look. Even Sam raised his head, though he stayed where he was, arms folded, looking relaxed and neutral. 'And where's your dad?' Richard asked. 'Shane, you don't owe him. You know that.'

'Yeah,' Shane said. 'I know. He's gone. I wish I could tell you he wouldn't be back, but—' He shrugged. 'Let Claire go, man. She saved people. She didn't hurt anybody.'

Mayor Morrell nodded at the cop standing behind Claire. She felt her handcuffs jiggle, then loosen, and gratefully folded her arms across her chest.

'What about Shane?' she asked.

'The vampires caught two of Frank's men. They admitted that Frank murdered Brandon. Shane's in the clear,' Richard said.

Shane blinked at him. 'What?'

'Go home,' Richard said, and the cop unlocked Shane's handcuffs, as well. 'Sam's taken care of getting word out to the vampires. They don't like you much, so watch your step, but you're not guilty of any crimes. Not major ones.'

'Great!' Eve said, and grabbed Claire's hand, then Shane's. 'We're outta here.'

Eve's Cadillac was parked a few spaces away. The back and side windows had been blacked out, Claire realised, and there was a fresh smell of paint in the air, and two cans of spray enamel lying on the ground. She got in the front seat, and Michael slid into the back seat. Shane hesitated, looking in at him, then climbed in and slammed the door.

Eve started the car. 'Shane?'

'Yeah?'

'I'm freaking *killing* you when we get home.'

'Good,' Shane said. 'Because right now, death seems like a better idea than talking about any of this.'

The town was strangely quiet – fires out, mobs dispersed, nothing to see here, move along. But Claire didn't really think it was over. Not at all. She leant against the window on the ride home, exhausted and unhappy. There was an ominous silence coming from the back seat, a feeling like thunderclouds rolling in and ready to break. Eve rambled on nervously about Shane's dad, and where he might have gone; nobody responded. *I hope he leaves*, Claire thought. *I hope he gets away*. Not because he shouldn't pay – he should – but because if he did, all it meant for Shane was more grief. Losing the last member of his already destroyed family. Better if his dad just... disappeared.

'Have you told Shane?' Eve asked. Claire sat up, blinking and yawning, as Eve pulled the Caddy to a halt in front of their house.

'About what?'

Eve pointed at Michael. 'You know.'

Claire turned to look at him. Shane was staring straight ahead, his face like stone. 'Let me guess,' he said. 'You came up with some magical fairy who granted you your freedom, and now you can come and go whenever you want,' he said. 'Tell me that's it, Michael. Because I've been thinking about why you're sitting in this car the whole way, and I can't really come up with any other answer that won't make me vomit.'

'Shane—' Michael said, and then shook his head. 'Yeah. My fairy godmother came and granted me a wish. Let's just get past this.'

'Get past it?' Shane said. 'How exactly do I do that? Fuck off.'

He got out of the car and stalked up the walkway. Eve grabbed a huge black umbrella and hurried around to Michael's side of the car; she opened it like a valet, and he stepped out, grabbed the umbrella, and ran after Shane. Even with the thin shade, his skin began to smoke lightly as it cooked.

Michael made it to the shade of the porch, he

dropped the umbrella, and Shane turned and punched him.

Hard.

Michael rode the punch, caught the second one in his open palm, stepped in, and hugged him.

'Get off me!' Shane yelled, and shoved him back. '*Damn!* Get off!'

'I wasn't going to bite you, idiot,' Michael said wearily. 'Jesus. I'm just glad you're alive.'

'Wish I could say the same, but since you're *not*—' Shane slammed open the door and vanished inside, leaving Michael leaning against the wall.

Claire and Eve came slowly up the walk.

'I'll—' Claire swallowed hard. 'I'll talk to him. I'm sorry. He's just a little... It's been a long day, you know? He'll be OK.'

Michael nodded. Eve put an arm around him and helped him into the house.

Shane was nowhere to be seen when Claire entered the living room, but she heard his door slam upstairs. Damn, he was fast when he wanted to be. And bitter.

Who said *girls* were moody? She eyed the couch – it was the first comfortable spot to lie down – with weary longing. Maybe she should just let Shane get through it alone. Not like he wasn't used to dealing with trauma.

Then again...just because he could do it alone

didn't mean he ought to have to.

There was something odd about the room, and for a long second, Claire couldn't put her finger on it. Then it dawned on her.

The room smelt like flowers. Roses, to be exact.

Claire frowned, turned, and saw a huge bunch of red roses lying on the side table. There was an envelope next to it with her name on it in old-fashioned copper-plate handwriting.

She tore it open and unfolded the papers inside.

Dear Claire,

My informal Protection is no longer sufficient for you and your friends, and I think you know that now. More drastic steps must be taken, and soon, or your friends will pay the price. Oliver will not allow today's events to go unanswered. You have been brave, but extremely foolish in your enemies.

Consider my proposal carefully.

I shall not offer it again.

There wasn't a signature, but Claire didn't have any doubt who had written it. Amelie. The letter was watermarked with her seal.

The other papers in the stack looked legal. She read them, frowning, trying to understand what they meant, and some of the language leapt out at her.

I, Claire Elizabeth Danvers, swear my life, my blood, and my service to the Founder, now and for my lifetime, that the Founder may command me in all things.

It was the same thing Oliver had said, back at the hospital, when he'd been trying to make her…

…make her his slave.

Claire dropped the paper like it had caught on fire. No, she couldn't do that. She couldn't.

Or your friends will pay the price.

Claire swallowed, stuffed the contract back into the envelope, and shoved it in her pocket just as Eve came around the corner and said, 'Roses! Jeez, who died?'

'Nobody,' Claire said hoarsely. 'They're for you. From Michael.'

Michael looked surprised, but his back was to Eve, and if he had any sense at all, he'd play along.

Claire went upstairs to take a shower.

Being clean made it better. Not a whole lot better, but some. She sat for a while, staring at the white envelope with her name on it, wishing she could talk to Shane about it, or Eve, or Michael, but not daring to do any of that because this was *her choice.* Not theirs. And she knew what they'd say, anyway.

Not enough no in the world, that's what they'd say.

It was after dark when Shane finally knocked on her door. She opened it and stood there looking at him. Just looking, because somehow she didn't think she'd ever see enough of him. He looked tired, and rumpled, and sleep creased.

And he was so beautiful she felt her heart break into a million little sharp-edged pieces.

He shifted uncertainly. 'Can I come in? Or do you just want me to—?' He pointed back down the hall. She stepped back and let him inside, then shut the door behind him. 'I freaked about Michael.'

'Yeah, you think?'

'Why didn't you tell me?'

'Well, it didn't exactly seem like the right time,' she said tiredly, and sat down on the bed, back to the headboard. 'Come on, Shane. We were running for our lives.'

He granted that argument with a shrug. 'How did this happen?'

'You mean, who? Amelie. She was here, and Michael asked.' Claire looked at him for a long second before she added the coup de grace. 'He asked because he wanted to be able to leave the house.'

Shane looked stricken. He lowered himself down on the corner of the bed, staring at her with those wounded, vulnerable eyes. The ones that made her heart break all over again. 'No,' he said. 'Not because of me. Tell me it wasn't—'

'He said it wasn't. Not, you know, completely, anyway. He had to do this, Shane. He couldn't live like this, not for ever.'

Shane looked away. 'Christ. I mean, he knows how I feel about vampires. Now I'm living with one. Now I'm *best friends* with one. That's not good.'

'Doesn't have to be bad, either,' she said. 'Shane, don't be angry, OK? He did what he thought he had to do.'

'Don't we all?' He flopped back on the bed, hands under his head. Staring up at the ceiling. 'Long day.'

'Yeah.'

'So,' he said. 'You got plans for tonight? Because suddenly I'm free.'

He made her laugh, even though she thought she didn't have any of that left. Shane rolled up on one elbow, and the gentleness in the way he smiled at her made her breath catch in her throat.

He reached out and tugged at her hair, smiling. 'You're all wild today,' he said. 'Hero.'

'Me? No way.'

'Yeah, you. You saved lives, Claire. Granted, some people I'd just as soon see gone, but...still. I think you even saved my dad. If he'd blown up that building, killed all those people...he couldn't have walked away from it. I couldn't have let him.' They just looked at each other, and Claire felt tension coiling up between them, pulling them closer. She saw him leaning towards her, drawn by the same thing. He reached out and traced one hand slowly along her bare foot. 'So. What's the plan, hero? Want to watch a movie?'

She felt odd. Crazy and strange and full of uncertainty. 'No.'

'Kill some video zombies?'

'No.'

'If we get down to canasta, I'm jumping... off...the...what are you doing?'

She stretched out across the bed on her side, facing him. 'Nothing. What do you want to do?'

'Oh, let's not go there.'

'Why not?'

'Don't you have school tomorrow?'

She kissed him. It wasn't an innocent kiss – anything but. She felt like those roses downstairs, dark and red and full of passion, and it was new to her, so new, but she couldn't stop the feeling that she had to do this, *now*, because she'd almost lost him, and—

Shane leant his forehead against hers and broke the kiss with a gasp, like a drowning man. 'Hang on,' he said. 'Slow down. I'm not going anywhere. You know that, right? You don't have to put out to keep me here. Well, as long as you eventually—'

'Shut up.'

He did, mainly by pressing his lips back to hers. A slower kiss this time, warm and then hot. She thought she'd never get enough of the *taste* of him; it just jolted through her like raw current and lit her up inside. Lit her up in ways she knew weren't good, or at least weren't completely legal.

'Want to play baseball?' she asked. Shane's eyes opened, and he stopped stroking her hair.

'What?'

'First base,' she said. 'You're already there.'

'I'm not running the bases.'

'Well, you could at least steal second.'

'Jeez, Claire. I used to distract myself with sports stats at times like these, but now you've gone and ruined it.' Another damp, hot kiss, and his hands trailed down her neck, feather-light. Over her shoulders, brushing skin her thin jersey nightshirt left bare. Down...

'Dammit.' He rolled over on his back, breathing hard, staring at the ceiling again.

'What?' she asked. 'Shane?'

'You could have died,' he said. 'You're sixteen, Claire.'

'Nearly seventeen.' She moved up against his side, cuddling close.

'Yeah, that makes it all better. Look—'

'You want to wait?'

'Yeah,' he said. 'Well, obviously, not my first

choice, but I'm all about second thoughts right now. But the thing is…I don't want to leave you.' His arm was around her, and there was nothing in the world to her but the warmth of his body against her, and his whisper, and the utterly vulnerable need in his eyes. 'But it's not going to be easy for me to say no. So help me out here.'

Her heart was pounding. 'You want to stay?'

'Yes. I—' He opened his mouth, then closed it, then tried again. 'I need to stay. I need you.'

She kissed him, very gently. 'Then stay.'

'OK, but so far as baseball goes, second base is as far as I go.'

'You're sure about that?'

'I swear.'

And somehow, he kept his word, no matter how hard she tried to convince him.

Shane was still asleep, curled in a heap among the pillows, snoring lightly. She'd gotten his shirt off at some point, and Claire lay in the soft glow of the rising sun, watching the light gleaming on the strong muscles of his back. She wanted to touch him…but she didn't want him to wake up. He needed to sleep, and she had something she had to do.

Something he wasn't going to like.

Claire eased out of bed, moving very carefully, and found her blue jeans crumpled on the floor. The envelope was still in the back pocket. She opened it and slipped out the stiff, formal paper, unfolded it, and read the note again.

She put the contract on the desk, looked at Shane, and thought about the risk of losing him. Of Eve and Michael, too.

I, Claire Elizabeth Danvers, swear my life, my blood, and my service...

Shane had said she was a hero, but she didn't feel like one. She felt like a scared teenager with a whole lot to lose. *I can't watch him get hurt,* she thought. *Not if there's anything I can do to stop it. Michael – Eve – I can't take the risk.*

How bad could it be?

Claire opened the drawer and found a pen.

Read on for a peek at Eve Rosser's diary...

And don't miss Midnight Alley, *the third book
in the Morganville Vampires series, available from
Allison & Busby.*

From the diary of Eve Rosser

How do you write about thinking you were going
to die? Because I don't know. I don't know how I
feel or why I feel it. All I know is that I'm scared,
and I feel naked all the time, and I just want to
crawl into bed and stay there for a long, long time.
Shane's dad – God, I thought *my* parents were
worthy of being hit by a train, but Shane's dad
needs to be nuked from orbit. Shane says he's still in
Morganville, but at least he and his wrecking crew
are out of our house, and Shane looks more or less
intact. His dad's an ass, did I mention? *Ass.*

Michael's back. I don't want to think about that,
because I saw him die. I saw them drag him out,
and even though I didn't see what they did to him
after, I know they did things to his body before they
dumped him in a hole in the ground. I can't ask him
about what that was like, what he remembers. I
don't want to know.

Claire's...well, Claire. Little fragile Claire, she still seems to just bounce on. I don't know how she does it. I'm writing this before I fall asleep, and she's down snuggling with Shane on the couch, and those two seem to really be hitting it off. I probably should sit her down and tell her the facts of life about Shane, though. I mean, she's *sixteen*. Going on forty, sure, but...*sixteen*!

Of course, I thought I was badass at sixteen, too. Wait, I was badass at sixteen. Oh yeah.

I'm in love with a dead guy. Does that make me weird? I mean, weirder than usual? Seriously.

Although according to the *Cosmo* Boyfriend Quiz, Michael scores pretty high, with extra points for being a musician, being sensitive and artistic, and having great hands. Besides, he's like an eight on a ten-point scale, with one being a creepy serial killer and ten being Johnny Depp.

And if he wasn't dead? *Score.* But he is. Dead, I mean. Half the time, anyway, and I'm starting to see some limitations. He'll never take me out to dinner. He'll never squire me to the club and make all the other girls salivate, which is part of the fun. He'll never...well, there are a lot of things he'll never do, and one of them is walk out the doors of this house. Or even be around during the daytime, if I need him.

No matter how many positives there are, that's got to knock him down on technical fouls.

Of course, he does get extra points for wearing those totally sweet Joe Boxer underwear. (I wish I could say that I knew that because I'd gotten his belt unbuckled, but no. Laundry. Sigh.)

In conclusion: me, weird for loving a dead guy. But dead guy: totally hot.

I'm still confused.

Like there wasn't enough trauma in my life right now, my little brother Jason is following me. I wasn't sure about it at first... I thought maybe I'd imagined it.

You know how you see something out of the corner of your eye, but when you look straight on, nothing? Well, that's Jason. Vanishes like smoke. Like Michael at sunrise. Pick your favourite cliché.

Except today I thought I saw him, I turned my head and there he was. Big as life, twice as scary. Not physically big, I mean; Jason's a weed, but he's feral as hell and he never backs away. Even before his girlfriends started ending up dead, the local thugs avoided fights with him. I can't imagine a couple of years of jail taught him anything but how to be even scarier.

Even at the distance of twenty feet or so, he was plenty terrifying. Not that he was doing anything scare-inducing; he was just standing there. Smiling. It was on campus at TPU, middle of the day, tons of people around, and I still felt violated.

I wondered what he was going to do; I mean, it would be typically creeptastic Jason behaviour to just stand there and smile and then leave, but he stuck his hands in the pockets of his black hoodie, and walked slowly towards me. He is a little shorter than me and a lot thinner – heroin chic, my bro. He's still Gothing up, dying his brown hair into black spikes, and he had on more eye-liner than I did. He was wearing some faded, distressed jeans, clunky black boots, and a loose black shirt. Nothing special about the look, exactly, but what he did with it was…unsettling. I wanted him to stop coming towards me, but I wasn't willing to back up, and I'd feel pretty stupid screaming for help when Jason wasn't doing anything. He didn't even have a weapon that I could see. Not that he ever needed one.

He stopped just about four inches too close.

'So,' Jason said. 'Long time no see, Eve.'

I didn't answer. I just watched him to see what he'd do. God knew he was capable of anything. Anything at all.

'Just wanted you to know that I'm out,' he said, and shrugged. 'I know you'll probably want to throw a party and shit, but resist.'

'What do you want?' I wanted to sound tough. I think I probably just sounded scared.

'Went by to see the folks. I figured I'd find you there, but Mom said you moved out.' Jason had the same eyes I did. It was like looking into a mirror. A crazy, deeply disturbed, sexually twisted mirror.

'Moved? I didn't move. They threw me out.'

He didn't seem surprised. 'Didn't give it up to Brandon, I guess.'

'No.' I felt bad, having this conversation. I'd sworn that I'd never talk to Jason again, and yet...talking. Chatting, even. Not good. 'What do you want?'

'World peace.' He gave me that strange little smile again. 'Who'd you sign with?'

'Nobody.'

'Gutsy. Stupid, but gutsy.' Jason just wouldn't stop smiling. It was getting on my last nerve. Any second now, I was going to snap, scream, and run like a little girl. 'Guess who was there to meet me when I walked out of the hole under the jail where they stuck me?'

I didn't want to know. I didn't. But somehow he made me ask anyway. 'Who?' *Please don't say Brandon.*

'Brandon,' Jason said. He didn't blink. 'Wanted to get all old-times-sake on my ass. I never really thanked you for all that you did to help me out with that little problem, did I?'

'Jason—' I couldn't help it. I took a step back, just a little one, but enough. And he laughed. It didn't sound right, but that just made it match everything else about him.

'Oh, relax. I'm not going to do it here,' he said, and the laughter disappeared. What was left was quiet and dark and a whole lot worse. 'I know where you live, sis. I know where you work. I know who your friends are. And you know Morganville isn't big enough to hide from me, don't you?'

I didn't say anything. I wasn't sure I could force words out past the invisible noose choking me. Jason looked me over good, up and down, and that smile came back again. Scary, soft, and somehow just *wrong*.

'You look good,' he said. 'You got a guy, Eve? One of those two jerks you share the house with, maybe? You always did like the blond one. I remember. Read all your Trapper Keeper doodles about how hot he was. *Ooooh, Michael!*'

He was just trying to get to me, and I couldn't afford to let him. At least I could be sure that he wouldn't be able to hurt Michael, and Shane could generally take care of himself.

Jason raised his eyebrows, shrugged again, and pulled the hood up on his black fleece jacket. He walked away a couple of steps, then turned and looked back at me. 'Put in a good word for me with your other roomie. Claire, right? Cute. Just my size.'

I felt like someone had just dumped a giant bucket of slime down my back. All my resolutions about not letting Jason get to me went out the window. 'She's a *kid*, Jase. Stay away. I'm warning you.'

He wiggled all ten fingers at me and grinned. 'Booga booga. Watch me shake.'

And then he just walked away, and in five steps he was behind a hedge, and when I ran after, I couldn't spot him. Too many people walking around, hurrying to classes, playing Frisbee, hanging out. Until you get a good, close look at him, Jason fits right in.

I guess I'd better talk to Shane about doubling up on Claire's protection duties. He's already taking it way too seriously, but maybe...yeah.

Probably ought to go talk to him right now.

They've got Shane and it's my fault.

I told him. I told him about me, about Brandon, and most of all, about Jason. So he promised he'd watch out for Claire, right? But he wasn't going to do the sensible thing, like actually *stay* with her. No, he was going to *follow Jason*.

And he followed Jason right to Brandon, and I guess he saw Brandon get bagged by his father. So, being Shane, does he gallop off and get the cavalry? *No.* Boy rides his white horse straight into enemy camp and thinks he can talk assholes out of being assholes. Worse, he does it for *Brandon.*

I think they probably made him watch. Oh God.

And it's my fault.

So now the vamps have got Shane in a cage at Founder's Square and they're going to kill him, and Michael locked me in my room, the *bastard*, when I tried to get out and save him. Like I'm some *kid* like Claire! Like I'm an idiot! Oh, no, but did he lock up Claire? Of course not! He sent Claire out on some mission or other, and he's going to get *her* killed too. God, I *hate him*! I am *so* killing him later. Doesn't matter anyway – he comes back. But I'll kill him so he feels it. I've got stakes and everything.

OK, I might have overreacted when I wanted to cowboy up and go out and kill vampires, but still, *locking me in my room?* Who does he think he is? I am so totally not sleeping with him, ever. I don't care what a hottie he is.

We've got to do something for Shane. His dad won't do squat, and nobody else will, either. It's just us now. By 'us' I mean me and Claire, because Michael's no damn use.

Did I mention I'm going to kill him?

God, that was my fault. Again. I nearly got Claire raped, and for what? I didn't have to take her with me to the Dead Girls' Dance. I knew it wasn't safe. I just was too punk-ass chicken to go myself, without some kind of wingman. Claire had no idea how many vampires there were at the frat house, but I did – dozens. They like campus events like this. Maybe they do have a sense of humour, who knows, but I wasn't surprised to find out that Sam would be there.

I thought, in and out, grab Sam, get him to help…I didn't count on the crowd or the fact that Claire might be in danger from somebody other than fanged night stalkers. So when she disappeared, I was looking in the wrong places, asking the vamps…and it was just sheer luck that I heard her yell my name over the music when I banged on that door.

Without Sam's help, things would have gone way worse. Way, way worse. I can't believe I nearly let that happen to her.

There was something going on with the vamps meeting at the frat house – what, I don't know, but whatever it was, it made it easy for Shane's dad to target the place for his Shock and Awe Retribution Tour. Killed a few kids in the process, but that's life to Mr Collins. God, I hate that man. I can't believe he's half of Shane's DNA.

I hope Claire's OK. We got her upstairs and into bed; she wasn't making any sense by then, and she was clearly going out. I know she's going to be angry that I didn't wake her up, but she has to sleep through this.

I'm going to nap, too. Been a long day, and we've still got to save Shane.

❧ ❧ ❧

Shane's OK.

Michael's not.

I didn't mean for it to be this way. Not this way. Maybe I pushed him into it; maybe...maybe it wasn't me at all. But I was a total bitch to him when he was feeling his worst, wasn't I? I didn't know he'd do *this*.

I guess it's a good thing...maybe. Michael was trapped before, and now he isn't. Now he can get out of the house, do whatever he wants. Go wherever he wants. Not only that, he's one of the ruling class – one of the vamps. So...does that make him more dead? Less dead? Dear *Cosmo* Boyfriend Quiz: What kind of points does your boyfriend get for getting burnt by daylight, craving blood, and never tanning? Not that he isn't still completely hot, and I can tell, even though I can see the difference in his eyes, that he's trying. He's trying to be the Michael he was.

He's trying to be with me.

I hate vampires. I *hate* them.

How can I be in love with one? How is that *right*!

I'm trying not to let him know how much that bothers me.

So there's this paper, *The Fang Report*, put out by a guy who calls himself Captain Obvious. It's cheap and smart-ass and it makes me laugh until I want to pee, but today's edition: not so funny.

Because it has a picture of Michael, and it outs him as the newest vamp in town. Shane's dad may not be around, but if he still is, or even if he stirred up would-be vampire slayers in Morganville, Michael's now an easy target. And because he was one of *us*, one of the regular folks, he's going to be hated. Especially by wannabe Renfields like Monica and her crew, who will believe they should have been next up on the immortality wait list.

Oh, and the news got better. At the bottom of the second page there was something else, something worse: they've found a second body dumped in town. Another girl about my age – I knew her from school, a little. She isn't a vamp victim, wasn't drained of blood. Raped, strangled, and stabbed. Second one in a few days.

And conveniently enough, Jason called this afternoon. Michael answered the phone and handed it to me – didn't recognise Jason's voice, and obviously Jason didn't self-incriminate. I knew him the second he said my name. I didn't answer. Michael hadn't gone far, and I guess he sensed something or my body language gave it away, because he came to me and put his hands on my shoulders. I leant back against him, pulled in a quick breath, and said to Jason, 'What do you want?'

'You keep asking me that.' Jason sounded amused, and stoned. 'Just want to connect with my family. No crime in that, right? So how'd you sleep, sis? No bad dreams or anything?'

'Leave me alone, Jason.' I hung up. I didn't slam the phone down, just put it back in the cradle, and then I turned and Michael was right there.

'Nothing's going to happen,' he said, and kissed my forehead. 'We'll be OK.'

I'm in love, and I want to be happy, but there's this part of me right now that wonders if Michael really knows what he's talking about.

Because it's Morganville, and *OK* isn't really in our vocabulary.